A VAMPIRE'S CHOICE

DEATHLESS NIGHT SERIES #6

L.E. WILSON

NOTE FROM THE AUTHOR

This book was previously released as "Blood Choice" with a different cover.

ALSO BY L.E. WILSON

Deathless Night Series (The Vampires)

A Vampire Bewitched

A Vampire's Vengeance

A Vampire Possessed

A Vampire Betrayed

A Vampire's Submission

A Vampire's Choice

The Kincaid Werewolves (The Werewolves)

Lone Wolf's Claim

A Wolf's Honor

The Alpha's Redemption

A Wolf's Promise

A Wolf's Treasure (coming 2020)

The Alpha's Surrender (coming 2020)

The Sergones Coven (Dragon Shifters & Vampires)

Fire of the Dreki

Blood of the Master

Copyright © 2017 by Everblood Publishing, LLC

All rights reserved. No part of this publication may be reproduced, distributed, or transmitted in any form or by any means, including photocopying, recording, or other electronic or mechanical methods, without the prior written permission of the publisher, except in the case of brief quotations embodied in critical reviews and certain other noncommercial uses permitted by copyright law. For permission requests, email the publisher, addressed "Attention: Permissions Coordinator," at the address below.

All characters and events in this book are fictitious. Any resemblance to actual persons – living or dead – is purely coincidental.

le@lewilsonauthor.com

ISBN: 978-1-945499-45-6

Print Edition

Publication Date: October 27, 2017

Editing: Jinxie Gervasio @ jinxiesworld.com

Cover Design by Coffee and Characters

PROLOGUE

THE MOUNTAINS OF WESTERN CANADA - CURRENT DAY

Shea's thick-soled boots made no sound as she ran through the wet underbrush with the light-footedness of a wraith. She dodged the towering hemlock trees with little thought or effort, ignoring the icy drops of water dripping from the branches after the afternoon's rain. Her steady breathing left a trail of clouds floating behind her, barely discernible in the shadowy moonlight.

The smell of blood lured her from ahead.

The stench of death pushed her from behind.

A huff of warm breath touched the back of her neck, and the tiny hairs all over her body stood at attention as a shiver of revulsion skated across her skin. Her fangs shot down, preparing for a fight.

She forced herself to run harder.

Pumping her arms and pushing off her toes, she increased her speed, as impossible as it seemed.

Just a little farther. She just had to make it a little bit farther.

He was waiting.

CHAPTER 1

LONDON, ENGLAND - 1826

"What are you doing, sister?"

The woman froze, one hand stretched too close to the fire. After a slight pause, she pulled her arm in and straightened. Turning only her head, a string of golden ringlets fell over a bare shoulder to cascade down a thin back. Green eyes, much like Shea's own, narrowed in on her face. "What do you want, Shea?"

Remembering her place, Shea dropped into a quick curtsy, her brow furrowed with confusion. "I am only concerned that you were about to hurt yourself." Her older sister had been holding her hand directly over the open flames in the fireplace, with no concern for the pain or what she was doing to her skin. Even now, Shea could smell the nauseating stench of burning flesh and could see the burned edges of her sister's sleeve. If she hadn't spoken, her gown would have caught fire.

"Why would I do that, Shea? I am about to marry the man of my dreams and live in this beautiful home." She swung her arm in a wide circle, taking in the entire sitting room and the rich furnishings that filled it. "You should be grateful that I took you out of that hovel of a home father raised us in and brought you with me, not sneaking around spying on me."

Shea let her arms fall to her sides and she straightened her back in indignation. She took a step forward before again remembering their agreement and retreating to a proper distance. "I am very grateful, Elise, you know that. However, that doesn't mean that I'm going to allow you to set yourself on fire." Anxiety and concern swiftly spun into annoyance. "And I wasn't spying for the gods' sake, I was only passing by the doorway on my way to fetch the tea and biscuits, and saw what you were doing."

"Watch what you say!" Elise's haughty demeanor was completely unlike her, even if she *were* about to become a great lady. "Do not speak of your gods here, or we will both be burned alive."

A thread of unease wound its way around Shea's heart. This wasn't the first time in the last few days her sister had spoken as if they didn't have the same upbringing, and the same history, despite their current positions in society. "*My* gods? Are they not *your* gods anymore?"

Elise turned away with a swish of her full skirts, stretching her hands back out to the fire, with no reaction of pain to the red, scalded skin on her left palm. "Of course they are. We just shouldn't speak of them. There's a reason our bloodline has been 'lost' in the family records."

Her tone was dismissive, yet Shea hovered, afraid to

leave her sister. The door opened, and she was relieved to see Matthew, Elise's fiancé, enter the room. He gave Shea a polite smile when she curtsied to him, before moving past her to take his place at her sister's side. "There you are." Raising her hand to his lips, he placed a chaste kiss on the back. With a frown, he turned it over and gasped. "Elise! What have you done to your hand?"

Elise smiled politely up at him. "I was only trying to chase away the chill, and I got a little too close to the flame. I can't seem to get warm enough today."

"Mrs. Richards will know what to use to ease the pain for you." He turned to Shea. "Please go fetch the cook."

But Elise shook her head. "Do not interrupt her in her daily duties. She's very busy getting everything ready for the wedding. And besides, I'm fine. Truly."

He smiled down at her, an adoring expression on his face. "Yes. The wedding." Matthew immediately turned back to Shea. "Would you please fetch us some tea?"

Shea dropped into a curtsy. "Right away, sir." Still in the submissive pose, she asked, "Is there anything else *you* require, my lady?"

"No, Shea. That will be all. Thank you."

Leaving her in the capable hands of her future husband, Shea murmured the correct response and left them to their wedding talk. Her fingers twisted together in her apron as she rushed to the kitchen to get the tea and cakes.

Elise was acting strangely. So strangely, in fact, that Shea was becoming convinced that woman was not her sister at all.

Then who is she, if not my sister?

Shea didn't know, but that was not the person she had grown up with. Not the person whose friendship she valued more than anything else in the entire world. The thing in that room, though it resembled her sister in appearance, made Shea's skin crawl and the blood freeze in her veins.

There. She'd finally admitted it. If only to herself.

The closeness she and her sister shared was the reason Shea was here with Elise, in her new home, with her future family.

Her sister had met Matthew by chance at the market, and sparks had flown at first glance. He'd asked to call on her, and though she'd tried to refuse him, telling Shea he was too much the dandy for her, he hadn't given up until she'd agreed. The fact that she came from a lower social status, and was actually barely above living on the streets, made no difference to him. Matthew was the fourth son in a long line of sons up for the title of earl, and therefore, was given free reign to live his life as he wished for the most part, especially when he really wanted something. And he had really wanted Elise.

Within a month, he had proposed the union of marriage, and her sister had accepted, on the condition that Shea could come with her. Matthew had agreed, and had even been gracious enough to hire her into his household as her sister's lady's maid. She would make her own money, and would be included in everything they did.

Well, maybe not everything. Shea blushed at the thought. But when they traveled, Shea would go also. And when they had children, Shea would take over as nanny.

And if, by some chance, Shea met someone, Matthew had offered to give her a small dowry to take to her new husband. It was a perfect situation for both of them. Their father could barely support himself and her mother, never mind his two daughters. But he had done his best by them, and besides, material comforts were not important. What was important was that they stay warm and fed—and alive.

For Shea and her sister came from a very special bloodline. A secret bloodline. One that was only known by certain members of the holy community, and one that needed to survive for the good of the world.

Or so she'd been told since she was three.

Shea retrieved the tea tray and took it back to the sitting room. As she approached the closed door, she heard Matthew's voice, raised to a high pitch.

"What do you mean, Elise? Are you changing your mind?"

"Matthew, please don't shout."

"Don't shout? Don't shout? My bride-to-be is telling me she has changed her mind the day before our wedding, and you're telling me not to shout?"

Shea stopped outside the door and set the tray down quietly on the stand. Leaning in closer, she pressed her ear to the wooden door.

There was a rustle of clothing, and then her sister's voice. "You're being dramatic. I'm not cancelling our nuptials, I only want a little more time—"

"Time for what, Elise? What exactly do you need time for?"

"You wouldn't understand."

"You're correct. I don't understand. I don't understand any of this. Not at all." A pause. "I thought you loved me."

"Matthew, please." There was a grunt. More rustling of clothing. And then her sister's voice again. Only it wasn't her sister's voice. Not at all.

"Get off me." Followed by the sharp sound of skin striking skin, and then absolute silence.

Shea straightened up, her heart pounding as she heard footsteps coming toward the door. Leaving the tea tray on the stand where she had set it, she picked up her skirts and hurried away.

She rounded the corner to the dining area just as the door to the sitting room was flung open. Peeking around the doorjamb, she watched as her sister—or something that looked like her sister—marched in the opposite direction and headed upstairs to her rooms.

A few seconds later, Matthew stumbled out into the hallway. Their eyes met, the bewilderment in his matching her own feelings, and for a moment, Shea thought he was going to come talk to her. But he walked past, striding down the hall and out the front door.

Shea ran outside after him. "Matthew! Please wait!" She realized belatedly that she had called him by his first name, but it wasn't important. Not right now.

He stopped and turned to her, waiting for her to catch up.

She dropped into a curtsy. "If I may speak to you a moment?"

"Of course you may, Shea. Please stand up, and tell me; what the bloody *hell* is going on with your sister?"

Clasping her hands in front of her, Shea glanced up at

her future brother-in-law. "I apologize for listening. I brought the tea and heard raised voices—"

He waved a hand in dismissal. "It's fine, Shea."

She closed her eyes, praying he wouldn't think she was crazy. She supposed there was no way to say it other than to just come right out with it. "I have reason to believe that woman is not my sister."

"I'm sorry?"

Opening her eyes, she lifted her chin. "That isn't my sister, Matthew. That isn't the woman you proposed to."

Thick dark eyebrows rose nearly to his hairline. "Then who, pray tell, is it?"

She could tell he was frustrated, but also that he wasn't taking her seriously. "I don't know. I don't know who it is. I only know it's not Elise. But please don't kick us out just yet. I promise I will get to the bottom of this."

His handsome features softened. "I'm not going to kick you out, Shea. I just want to know what's wrong with my bride-to-be."

He didn't understand what she was trying to say. He thought her sister was having her woman's flow or something. The fight drained out of her as she realized it was very likely that he would call the men with the white coats to take her away in their carriage if she kept on. With a polite smile, she promised him she would talk to her.

Matthew gave her a grateful nod, and continued to the stables. A few minutes later, she saw him astride his new black stallion. He gave her a wave as he kicked the horse into a trot, and then a gallop, as they headed off toward the meadow on the other side of the fence.

Once he was gone, Shea hurried to the stables and

requested a carriage. She needed to talk to her father. He would know what to do. If she didn't tarry and got straight to the point, she would be back in time to help Elise get ready for dinner.

Funny how fate can wreck even the most meticulous of planning.

CHAPTER 2

TWO WEEKS EARLIER - CURRENT DAY

"What are you doing here?" Shea whispered. A light breeze lifted the loose tendrils of her hair, and raised chill bumps across her sensitized skin. Or maybe it was the way the dark warlock's topaz eyes stared all the way through to the deepest secrets of her soul.

His scent drifted to her on the light breeze. It filled her nostrils, making her upper lip twitch, exposing her fangs before she could stop herself. The taste of his scent made her mouth water and the back of her throat burn with thirst. She ached to pierce the firm skin stretched tight over the strong pulse in his throat until she could taste the dark essence of him. Her blood pounded, keeping beat along with the music coming from inside the renovated building that was now a popular gay club in Seattle's infamous Capital Hill neighborhood. It was 70's night, and the place was filling up fast. Soon people would start spilling out to the outdoor patio, but for right now, it was just the two of them.

And Cruthú, of course. His raven.

"Hello, Shea." Jesse's low timbre stroked her like a lover's caress. He looked different somehow, and after a moment, she realized it was his clothing. Instead of the usual black, a burgundy cashmere clung to his muscled torso. Her hand twitched toward it, to feel the soft material stretched across the hard muscle of the arm beneath. But she pulled it back, even though he was nowhere near touching range. His long, lean legs were covered in tailored charcoal slacks, and expensive shoes had replaced the black, heavy-treaded boots she was used to seeing on him. His dark hair was different, too—a bit longer—the wavy ends falling just past his collar.

He sprawled casually in his chair as she took in his changed appearance, one large hand resting on the small table in front of him, fingers wrapped around a sweating bottle of local beer. It was still full.

A trickle of fear slid down her spine as she watched him trace designs in the condensation with the tip of one finger without taking his eyes from her face. It had only been a few weeks since he'd released her from his mountain prison, but it was obvious he'd been following her. No one could have told him she came to this club, even if he'd had the nerve to ask them. No one else knew. Shea glanced around, ensuring herself they were completely alone, at least for the moment. "What are you doing here?" she repeated, louder this time.

His fingers stilled on the bottle, but despite his calm demeanor, she knew he was aware of her proximity. Very aware. Yet, while her pulse paused and stuttered as if it tried to relay everything she felt in Morse code, she could hear his beating strong and steady beneath the orchestral sounds of disco.

"Won't you sit down?" He nodded at the chair across from him.

Shea hesitated. A quick glance around ensured her they were still the only ones on the patio. She swallowed nervously. He'd never hurt her in any way while she'd been with him, but she still didn't trust him.

One side of Jesse's mouth quirked up in a sardonic mask of a smile. "I mean you no harm, Shea. I just want to talk."

Pulling the chair out from the table, she angled it so her back was to the half wall surrounding the patio and she was facing the door that led inside to the dance floor. As soon as she sat down, the raven hopped along the wall to stand near her and squawked in greeting, picking up a strand of Shea's long hair and running it through her beak. She reached back and stroked the silky feathers of the bird's cheek. "Hey, Cruthú."

"She missed you." He paused, allowing Shea to absorb the heavier meaning implied with those words before he continued, "I wanted to come and check on you after our phone call. I was concerned. I'm glad to see you are safe and well."

Shea didn't know how to respond. "There was no need for you to do that."

"Of course there was. I had no idea you were in possession of one of the boxes the demons are after, or I would have checked on you sooner."

Shea didn't know how he hadn't known. He seemed to know everything.

Jesse lowered his eyes to the untouched bottle of beer. He spun the bottle with his fingertips, until it balanced on a tilt. Removing his fingers, it continued to spin for a few seconds by itself.

Shea watched the bottle spin, fascinated, until he grabbed it and stopped the momentum.

When he lifted his gaze again, the intensity within made them glow bright as the sun. "I missed you, as well." Clearing his throat, he glanced away and went on before she could respond to that surprising statement. "What happened to the box?"

It took her a moment to answer him, unsure if he was friend or foe at this point. "It's gone."

His eyes flashed back to her face. One eyebrow lifted. "Gone?"

She nodded, not seeing the harm in telling him what happened in either scenario. "The demons got their hands on Dante's mate and threatened her life. He gave up the box to save her." Jesse knew vampires, and therefore, she knew he was well-aware of the weakness they had for their mates. She wasn't giving any secrets away.

The warlock cocked his head and stared at her. "They didn't kill her."

"No. They tried, but Dante and Laney both survived."

"Good." His face was grim. "But the demons got the box anyway."

"Yes." Her tone was bleak. During their phone call a few days earlier, Jesse had warned her of the consequences if this were to occur.

"If they've found the others, the last clue will lead them to their original blood. It will allow them to reanimate to their true forms." He gazed past her shoulder, his forehead creasing. "They will destroy this world, you know."

Shea stopped petting the raven and dropped her hand back into her lap. She waited until his attention once again focused on her. It took a few seconds, and she knew he was seeing a future they could not allow to occur. A future of hell on earth. "Luukas plans to find it before they do."

"The blood?"

"Yes."

He didn't appear reassured. "And how will he do that? When I last spoke with you, you didn't even know what it was you had until I told you. Does he have any idea where the blood is hidden?"

With a sigh, Shea shook her head. She didn't bother arguing the point that he could have saved this all from happening if he had just told her about it from the beginning. "No. But finding it first is our only hope."

"He won't be able to stop them now, Shea. I can't stop them. No one can."

"But you released them—" She slammed her mouth shut with an audible click before she could say anymore. She wanted to ask him why. Why he had done such a thing. What did he hope to gain from it?

However, she didn't really need to ask. She knew. He'd helped free them because he was evil, like Leeha. Like the demons.

"Releasing them was easier than sending them back will be. They wanted to be free. They don't want to go back. It would take more blood and magic than I alone possess to do so."

The implications of his words began to truly sink in. Fear loosened her bowels and clenched at her heart. "There has to be a way to send them back to hell...to chain them to the altar again. It was done once before, it can be done again." For if what he said was true, they were all well and truly fucked—humans, animals, and supernatural creatures alike.

"The first time it was done by a full coven of witches using a lost form of dark magic. Keira is powerful in her own right, but even if I wanted to help, it wouldn't be enough with only the two of us."

"What if there were six of you?"

He cocked his head at her. "Six?"

"There are five Moss witches residing with us now. Keira and her sister, Emma, Grace, Ryan, and Laney. Some of them knew of their heritage, some didn't. Keira is working with them, strengthening their magic and their control. Laney is a Protector." She stuttered to a halt before she said too much. "With your help—"

"No, Shea. I'm sorry."

She would think he was upset about being unable to help her, but for the stubborn set of his jaw.

Shea sat back in her chair and averted her eyes from the enticing male. There was more going on here than he was telling her.

The silence stretched between them. It would have been deafening if not for the music and the small sounds the raven made as she tried to get Shea to stroke her again. A human couple wandered out into the area, the males heading to the opposite side of the patio to make out in the corner.

Shea ran her hand down Cruthú's soft feathers one last time, then stood. "I should go."

Jesse stood also, reaching for her hand across the small tabletop.

She tensed, pulling it out of his reach with a quiet hiss, flashing her fangs at the male. "Don't touch me."

Pain darkened his golden eyes, but he pulled his hand back and held his clenched fist at his side. That tiny glimpse into his soul was gone so fast, Shea wondered if she had imagined it. "I'm sorry. I only wanted to try to convince you to stay a bit longer."

"I can't, Jesse. I have to go." *Away from you.* His masculine scent permeated her nose, causing the thirst to burn with an intensity that tilted the world around her. She needed to feed, and as much as she wanted to, she couldn't drink from him. Instinct told her such intimacy would be devastating for her, and not just because of the physical pain it would cause. "I need to go," she repeated.

"Let me come with you—"

"No!" She wanted to tell him that she preferred to be alone, wanted to tell him that out of all the males she knew, his company was the one she wanted least, but she couldn't force herself to form the words. It would be a lie, and she couldn't bring herself to lie to him. Not with the way he was looking at her, seeing right through to her soul. She lowered her voice. "No. You can't. If the others saw you here, they would kill you."

His expression hardened. "They could try."

He wasn't being cocky. It was the truth. She'd heard

about the battle between Jesse and Luukas. Even with Keira's magic thrown in to help, Luukas was convinced Jesse had only been toying with them. They'd survived for one reason: because Jesse had left the scene and allowed them to leave.

"I need to go. Goodbye, Cruthú." She paused, the next words catching in her throat for reasons she didn't want to define. "Goodbye, Jesse."

Turning away before he could say anything else, she made her way through the burgeoning crowd inside the dark club. A few males bumped into her accidentally as she edged around the dance floor, but Shea's hisses of pain were drowned out by the thumping beat of the music.

Once safely outside again, she waved to the bouncer and strolled down the street with a casual swagger until she reached the corner, so as not to raise suspicion. But as Cruthú circled the sky above her, she felt anything but calm.

An icy chill slithered down her spine.

The raven's eyes weren't the only ones watching her.

CHAPTER 3

Jesse watched Shea until she was out of sight. The female was a strange combination of street thug and elegance, and he knew she would be just at home in a brawl as in a ballroom.

It utterly intrigued him.

But he'd been a fool to come here and face her, hoping for…what? That she would tell him she missed him, too? Run into his arms and allow him to hold her as he so longed to do? Her aversion to touching him hadn't changed.

He narrowed his eyes as he watched her go out of her way to avoid walking into a group of males heading toward the club just before she'd turned the corner.

Jesse glanced up at Cruthú, reassuring himself that she knew what was asked of her, and turned to walk in the opposite direction. As he strolled past aged apartment buildings, small shops, and couples heading out for the night, his mind spun with all he had learned that night.

Shea had jerked away every time someone had accidentally brushed against her as she'd made her way through the throng of writhing bodies on the dance floor. Her sounds of pain had not gone unnoticed by him, though no one else would have heard, but he'd assumed it was the blood lust he'd sensed that made her grumpy. She was thirsty, which he would assume was the reason she was here.

But, perhaps he was wrong. Was it possible her aversion to being touched wasn't caused only by her repulsion to him? He'd witnessed her fear when she'd been his guest up north, and his gut had told him there was more going on with her than met the eye. And it appeared his instincts had been right. She'd even told him straight out he could not touch her. But it appeared she wasn't afraid of *him*, merely of his touch. And anyone else's, it seemed.

A vampire who required blood to survive, yet was repulsed by touch. And the mystery thickened....

Then something else occurred to him, and his heart nearly dropped right out of his chest. If he would never be able to touch her, he would never feel if her skin was as soft as it looked, or feel the touch of her small hands exploring him in return.

It was a sobering vision of the future. One that he would have to do something about. Immediately.

He didn't follow her. There was no need. He knew exactly where she lived, and the raven would keep an eye on her. His friend would let him know if Shea went off course or got herself into any trouble she couldn't handle on her own.

After their phone call a few days before, when she had

called to ask him about the box, Jesse had done little but pace the confines of his room, waiting for the phone to ring again so he could hear her voice on the other end and know that she was safe. Their short time away from each other had been torture for him. He found he could barely eat. And at night, when he would lie in the bed she had slept in, the scent of her would surround him until he could think of little else but burying himself inside her. And when he would finally fall asleep, her whiskey voice would whisper to him in his dreams.

Unable to sit and do nothing any longer, Jesse had gathered a few things and come to Seattle. It was time to go on a little trip, and he thought perhaps he could convince the vampire, convince *Shea*, to come with him.

Cruthú, his only friend, had eagerly voiced her opinion about the trip from her perch near his bed as she'd watched him pack, and had made herself at home in his truck as soon as he'd opened the door. She'd ridden on the passenger seat the entire way, only getting out to stretch her wings when he'd stopped for gas. Jesse was happy she'd decided to come with him. He didn't like leaving her.

Or perhaps it was only that if the bird ever left him, he would be utterly alone.

As he strolled down the rain-slickened street, he breathed in the salty sea air and thought about what Shea had just told him. He needed to find out where the demons had taken the box, and whether they were still in the area. Shea did not seem inclined to share anything more than what she had already told him, and if he tried to approach Luukas or any of the other vampires, he doubted they would give him the chance to defend himself before they went for his head, let alone the time to speak to them. Of course, there was no way he could justify what he had done to the Master Vampire, or his part in releasing the demons from their place in hell. And he wouldn't bother to try. He had his reasons for doing what he did.

It was true, what he had told Shea about sending them back. He, alone, would not be able to do it. He needed a spell to do that. A spell that was lost around the same time his father had shown up again. But the demons didn't know that, and he planned on using that threat to get them to do what he wanted them to do—the reason he'd helped Leeha bring them back.

CHAPTER 4

Shea locked her apartment door behind her and leaned against it with a shaky exhale. She thought she'd be able to breath again once she was safely inside.

She'd been wrong.

Bending at the waist, she untied her boots and kicked them off, leaving them lined up neatly on the mat by the door. Her skin felt hot and tight, and she plucked at the front of her silk top before finally just pulling it up and off. Wearing only her jeans and bra, she made her way through her small apartment to the little galley kitchen and grabbed a water out of the fridge.

Jesse's sudden appearance had shaken her more than she wanted to admit. So much so, her stomach felt like Cruthú was fluttering around inside of it. So, after about an hour of prowling the streets of Seattle, she'd given up on finding a female to feed on and had just come straight home. It was a pure stroke of luck that she hadn't run into any of the guys on her way upstairs. One look at her flushed face and protruding fangs and they would've known something was up. And like the pain in the asses they were, they would've pestered her about it until she wanted to scream—because they were nosy, and because they worried like the brothers she'd never known she'd wanted, but was very grateful to have.

But even if they had caught her on her way in, she knew she wouldn't have told them what was really causing her discomfort. She had no intention of telling them about Jesse showing up at the club, or that she had spoken to him. For reasons even Shea herself couldn't fully comprehend, she felt protective of the dark warlock. She just hoped this act of kindness didn't come back to bite her in the ass anytime soon.

She'd just changed into a pair of loose pajama pants and a white cotton tank when there was a knock on the door. Pausing with one hand in her sock drawer, Shea closed her eyes. Her hands began to shake. Quietly closing the drawer, she placed them over her stomach. Butterflies were slamming around in there again, and she was glad she hadn't fed.

It was *him*. She didn't know how she knew it, she just did.

His scent came to her as soon as she left her bedroom; woodsy and masculine with a touch of something dark and wicked. It called to her like a warrior's song. His blood would taste sinful and forbidden, she knew, and her fangs shot down into her mouth even as her womb clenched with longing of a completely different kind. Closing her eyes, she battled the urge to fling open the door just so she could lay her eyes on his face.

"Shea, I know you're there." His low voice came through the heavy wood. "Open the door." It wasn't a request.

She should definitely *not* open the door. As a matter of fact, she should leave him out there for the others to find. But before the thought had even completely formed, she found her hand on the lock, then on the latch, and she swung the door open wide.

He was even more alluring than just a few hours ago. Impossible, but true. Cruthú sat quietly on his shoulder, her talons making deep impressions in the soft cashmere of his dark, blood-red sweater, yet he didn't appear to be in any pain. His eyes immediately dropped to her mouth, then down to her nipples, easily seen protruding beneath the thin material of her tank top. They hardened even more beneath the weight of his stare, and his lips parted on a harsh exhale.

She crossed her arms to cover herself, and to keep herself from yanking off her shirt and baring her breasts to his hungry gaze. "Please go away," she whispered. Though if she were to be honest with herself, she didn't really mean it. She'd done nothing but think of him since he'd let her go.

He ignored her, and continued his perusal all the way down to her bare toes, peeking out from the hem of her pants, and then slowly back up to her face. "I can't," he said simply. "Let me in, Shea."

His golden eyes locked with hers, bright and intense, and after a slight hesitation she stepped back out of the way so he could enter. He came inside, but kept his distance, much to her relief, and continued past her into her small apartment. Shea closed and locked the door behind him, taking a few moments to gather her composure before joining him in the other room. It didn't do much good.

She found him in the kitchen, rummaging through her fridge. He helped himself to a bottle of water and took it to the kitchen island, seating himself on a stool. Cruthú hopped down and went to investigate the pages of a magazine lying near the sink.

He looked like he belonged there.

"You shouldn't be here," she told him. "If the others caught you—"

"They won't."

"Your scent is everywhere. They will know you were here. Luukas will recognize it."

He gave a small shrug, completely unconcerned. "Possibly."

"What am I supposed to tell him?"

"Whatever you'd like."

Why was he making this so hard for her? Shea closed her eyes. "Jesse, please. Just go." *I couldn't stand it if anything happened to you.*

He was silent for a long time, then suddenly his mouth quirked up in a semblance of a smile. "Worried about me, Shea?"

She shook her head. *Yes.* "No. I'm worried about *me* when they find out I allowed you into my apartment." The lie was bitter on her tongue. She was terrified for him. Luukas was healing from his ordeal well with Keira's help, though lately he seemed to be backsliding. But he would rip Jesse apart if he found out he was here, and he had five witches and four other vampires to help him.

The fact that she didn't include herself in that group didn't escape her, but it wasn't something she was willing to examine too closely at the moment.

Tipping the bottle up to his mouth, Jesse never took his eyes from hers as he drank, his Adam's apple sliding up and down with each big swallow. When he had quenched his thirst, he set it on the counter and leaned back in his stool. "I came to invite you on an adventure."

She crossed her arms over her chest again when his golden stare fell and lingered. Shea didn't want to feed into the idea of going anywhere with him, but to distract him—and herself—from the way he stared at her breasts, she asked, "An adventure?"

"Yes."

"Why in the world would you think that I would want to go anywhere with you?" It was a reasonable question. But the answer, when it came, completely floored her.

"I think you know."

"No, I don't."

"Shall I spell it out, then?"

"Please."

"Fine." He leaned forward in his chair, pinning her to the spot with the heat glowing from his eyes. And though he never raised his voice, each word cut into her like a knife, whittling away her defenses until there was nothing left but a wall as thin as paper between them. "Because I sensed you in that altar room before I even knew you were there. Because ever since I first laid eyes on you, I've needed you near me. Because I long to touch your skin and hear your voice—all the time. Because I crave the feel of your hands on me with everything inside me. Because I nearly come when I imagine you feeding from me—and I imagine that quite often." He paused. "Because I've never felt such a loss as the day you walked away from me."

The paper ripped, leaving a jagged hole. "Stop." She threw up her hands, halting any more words he'd been about to say.

"Why?"

"Because you're talking crazy." But the thing was, he wasn't. Everything he said...she had felt those things, too.

"Is it crazy, Shea?"

His chest rose and fell rapidly beneath his sweater, the show of emotion unusual for him. Shea had never heard so much as a flutter of his pulse to give away what he was feeling before. But she heard it now. Loud and clear.

"I've missed you," he told her simply.

The world tilted around her again. The way he looked at her, the longing in his voice, the scent of his desire for her, his words...but she couldn't be with him. "Jesse, no—"

"Come with me, Shea. Be with me. Even if just for a little while."

Despite the slight thread of fear that still tangled its way around her gut, the urge to touch him was so strong she took a step forward and started to reach across the island before she caught herself. Curling her hands into fists at her sides, she shook her head. "I can't. We can't."

"Why not?"

She laughed, the sound ugly and raw in her own ears. "Why not?" She practically spat the words at him. "Because you kept me a prisoner for weeks. Because you tried to kill Luukas! Right after you drove him so completely mad, he believed he had killed Keira—his mate! And you did it with nothing but the power of your sick mind. Because you helped that she-bitch unleash the hounds from hell, and you don't seem to have the slightest remorse about any of it!"

He was irritatingly calm after her outburst. "You know nothing of my remorse, or lack thereof. I have my own reasons for everything I do, Shea."

She crossed her arms and leaned back against the counter. "Oh, yeah? What would those reasons be? What possible excuse could you have for any of those things?"

His eyes darkened, narrowed in challenge. "Yes, I kept you prisoner in my room. To *protect* you. It was the only way I could be assured that Leeha wouldn't get her hands on you. The spell that kept you a prisoner in my room kept *her* out. Although she couldn't possess you without me, she was spiteful and temperamental, and not ever to be trusted. And yes, I fought with Luukas. *Fought* with him. I was ordered to kill him, and his witch. Did you know that? But I didn't." Jesse took another drink from his water. Staring at the counter in front of him, he said quietly, "I only had to make it look good, before I allowed them to escape." He sighed heavily, like the weight of the world was on his shoulders, and finished off the bottle.

Shea continued to give him the same stony stare, but she wasn't feeling quite so self-righteous anymore. "Okay, fine. But what about the rest of it? That doesn't excuse the fact that you played a very large part in Leeha's insane plan to populate the earth with actual demons from hell."

"I have my reasons for that, also."

She waited, honestly curious as to what possible reason he could have for doing such a horrendous thing.

Getting up from the counter, he began to pace. "It's a long story. Too long to get into right now."

"I have the time." She wasn't very successful at hiding the snide tone of her voice, but she wasn't about to let him get out of this one without hearing his reasoning behind it.

Jesse suddenly veered from his path and came to stand before her, so close she could feel the heat from his body. His heart pounded in her ears. "Come with me, and I will tell you all of it."

A deal. He was offering her a deal. The scent of his skin—and his blood—engulfed her, making her muscles tense, her fangs ache, and her throat burn. More than that, she could feel the power of his will and the answer he wanted to hear from her. His golden gaze bore into hers. Shea did everything she could to keep him out of her mind, to no avail. Her head began to pound from fighting him. Sliding out from between him and the counter, she paced over to the floor-to-ceiling window that made up her outer living room wall, breaking the connection. Turning her back to the view, she shook her head. "No, Jesse. I can't."

He took a deep breath, running a hand through his dark hair much like Nikulas did when he was feeling anxious. Then he stilled. His eyes narrowed in challenge. "Not even if it meant you would be helping me hunt down the demon's blood before they could find it themselves?"

Shea eyed him with suspicion. "What did you just say?"

He sauntered toward her, all lean muscle and masculine confidence beneath his expensive clothes. Stopping just out of reach, he said, "We can stop the demons, Shea. You and me. We could bring the blood back to Luukas and let him do with it what he will."

She searched his features, wanting to trust what he was saying, but knowing she'd be an absolute idiot to do so. "Why would you do that? I thought you wanted them here. Why would you help me after everything you've done to achieve that?"

"Because more than anything else, I want to be with you."

Shea froze, his frank admission throwing her off again. He was telling the truth this time, she had no doubt. For a brief moment, the butterflies returned as she stared up at his handsome face, and she dared to hope.

But then reality came crashing down upon her, and she gave him a sad smile. Her heart deflated in her chest; aching for a future with this dangerous male she hadn't admitted to herself that she wanted, until this very moment when she realized she could never, ever, have it. "That's impossible, Jesse. We can't be together."

"We can, Shea. Leeha is dead. And I can"—he rolled his eyes on a loud, suffering sigh—"come to a mutual understanding with Luukas. We'll work it all out."

"No." She shook her head. "We can't."

He raised a hand to touch her face. "Shea—"

She stepped back. "No! Don't touch me. You *can't* touch me, Jesse."

CHAPTER 5

Jesse dropped his hand, but didn't back away. He cocked his head to the side so he could see the reflection of the overhead light on her face. Shea's pulse was beating rapidly and her forehead had a sheen of sweat covering it. He finally understood why she was so frightened of him. But he would never do anything to physically harm her. "I swear to you, I would not touch you unless you wanted me to."

But she just gave him a sad, nervous smile. "No. You don't understand. You can't touch me. Not ever. You would hurt me, Jesse."

He recoiled from her words. "Shea, I would never harm you."

"Yes, you would. It would be unintentional, but it would happen." She took a deep breath, hugging herself, like she was trying to make herself smaller. "Something happened to me when Luukas disappeared. I didn't know it until the day Nik told us his brother was missing. He was so upset, and as I was about to leave, I reached out to hug him. As soon as I touched him, something... happened. I nearly ended up on the floor."

"What exactly are you saying?"

She paused a moment. "I'm saying I can't touch you. I literally can't. And you can't touch me. If I even so much as brush up against a male, I feel like"—she glanced around, like the words she was looking for were written on the walls—"I'm being electrocuted or something."

Jesse studied her, taking in every small movement of her eyes. Every breath. She wasn't lying. It suddenly all began clicking into place. He'd heard her hiss in pain when the others had brought her into the altar room that first time. Although he hadn't realized what the sound was at first, it had traveled up the corridor to him, distressing him and hurrying his steps. And the way she'd recoiled from him in his room when he'd only been trying to console her. And the way she'd tried to avoid the dancers at the club, hissing in pain when they accidentally bumped into her. His earlier pondering had been correct.

It was Keira's curse. Leeha had bragged about it to him in one of her more talkative moments. "But, how do you feed?"

"Females don't affect me, only males. I can...touch females." She wouldn't look at him.

Jesse studied her guilty expression. "You do other things with the women as well, other than feed. Sexual things." It wasn't a question, or an accusation. Just an observation. His blood heated at the thought of her with another woman, but not in the way he would expect. The thought of her with someone else, anyone else, had him grinding his teeth together and clenching his fists at his sides. He'd never felt such possessiveness with anyone else. Yet, in the weeks he'd had her in his home, he'd come to think of this female as his own.

She lifted her chin and straightened her spine. "Sometimes." The word was said defiantly, despite the spots of color decorating her cheeks. Her discomfort with the conversation told him all he needed to know, even if he hadn't just plucked it from her mind.

"Have you been with anyone since you left me?" He didn't know why he asked. He really didn't want to know.

She stared at him a moment. "Not like that. No."

Jesse swallowed his ire. He knew what it was like to feel alone. He'd spent most of his life that way. "That's not something to be ashamed of, Shea. Everyone needs to be touched, to be held and loved. It's human nature, and vampire also, I would imagine. It doesn't matter what gender you are with." However, he intended to see to it that she would be touching no one else from this moment forward.

Shea crossed her arms and tilted her head in a way that he was coming to recognize as her telltale defensive gesture. "Yeah, well. Tell that to my father. He's probably rolling over in his grave as we speak."

"Your father was old-fashioned, then."

The snorting sound she made was definitely not ladylike. "You have no idea."

"And yet, he has such a heathen for a daughter."

An adorable crease appeared between her brows as she scowled, until she realized he was teasing her. The lines relaxed, to be replaced by a forlorn expression. "He actually never knew of the thing I became."

Jesse approached her slowly. Distracted by her memories, she held her ground this time, and warmth filled him that she trusted him to get so close, whether she realized it or not. Very carefully, he picked up a tendril of her dark hair from where it lay over the front of her shoulder. It was just as fine and silky as he'd always imagined. No wonder his raven was so enthralled with it. Catching and holding her gaze, he lifted the strand to his nose. "You are not a 'thing', Shea. I don't ever want to hear you calling yourself that." Her hair smelled wonderful. "What is that smell?"

"Pantene." The sarcasm was back. Turning her head so her hair slipped out of his fingers, she put distance between them, taking on a casual mien as she walked past him to stand by the cold fireplace.

But she didn't fool him. He could hear her heart pounding and see the flush of her skin. And he could sense the battle she was fighting with herself in her mind. She was not as unaffected by his nearness as she tried to appear. "Come with me, Shea."

She shook her head, but when she looked at him, her green eyes were bright with longing and unshed tears. "Why? It would only be torture for us both."

Her words gave him hope. "To be so close and yet so far away?"

"Yes." The word tore from her on a hiss.

Ah. Finally. Some honesty. "I have quite a few tricks up my sleeve, Shea. Perhaps I could figure out a way to alleviate your pain."

Hope flashed across her lovely features, but it was gone before he could appreciate it, to be replaced by a cynical smile. "And what if you can't?"

"I still want to spend time with you," he told her sincerely.

Throwing her arms out to the side, she looked to the heavens. "Why? Why the hell would you want to be with a female you couldn't touch?"

"Because I care for you."

"You barely know me."

"Then give me the chance to do so."

"Jesse—"

He stormed over to her, stopping close enough that her spine stiffened, and she looked up at him with a hiss of warning and a flash of her fangs. Gods, she was beautiful when she was vamped out. It made him instantly hard. "Give me a few days of your time, Shea. That's all I ask. Give me a damn chance to try to help you."

Indecision battled in her thoughts.

He pressed his advantage. "Come with me. Let's save the world. Together. And maybe we can save you in the process." He waited with bated breath as she fought with her decision. Gently, Jesse pressed harder into her mind, amazed at the speed of her vampire brain as she thought of and discarded every side to her arguments.

Finally, she relaxed. Her decision had been made.

"Okay."

Backing off slightly, he smiled. "Okay." Her decision, he knew, had little to do with him, and a lot to do with helping Luukas and the other Hunters. At least, that's what she chose to believe.

She rubbed her forehead with the fingers of one hand, as though her head hurt. "I just need to pack a bag."

He glanced out the window. If they hurried, they would have just enough time to make it back to his home for the day. "I'll wait." There was no way in hell he was letting her out of his sight until he had her safely away from here.

Then, and only then, would he tell her the truth.

CHAPTER 6

Shea finished packing a small duffle with a few changes of clothes and other necessities. She'd changed back into a pair of jeans along with a black, long-sleeved, cotton shirt. Her boots and rain-resistant pullover would complete the ensemble. Picking up the bag, she glanced around her room to make sure she hadn't forgotten anything.

What the hell am I doing?

She'd gone round and round with that question ever since she'd agreed to this insane trip. And it all kept coming back to one thing:

What if he can help me?

But even if he couldn't, there was an even better reason to do this.

What if we can find the blood before the demons do?

Those three thoughts had been fighting for dominance ever since she'd agreed to go with the dark warlock. She was taking a huge chance, but she couldn't deny she felt something for him, something so strong she was willing to put her life in his hands. Something that made her willing to disobey Luukas, her maker. And, maybe, just maybe, if they were successful in their endeavor, the Master Vampire wouldn't lop off Jesse's head when they returned.

Or hers.

She wasn't fooled by what Jesse had told her. He wouldn't give up what he'd been working toward that easily, just to be alone with her. He had no intention of helping her stop the demons. However, if she went with him, maybe she could put a wrench in his plans. Perhaps she could even talk him over to their side.

Hopefully, Luukas wouldn't find out what she was up to and call her back before she could accomplish what she was setting out to do. If he did, she would have to obey. It was the nature of the relationship between a Master Vampire and his children, though Luukas rarely implemented it. Now she just had to think up something to tell the rest of the Hunters: a good reason for her to be going off on her own without telling them about Jesse.

"Tell them you need some time away." Jesse's voice came from behind her. "Tell them that watching all of them running around with their mates is upsetting to you as the only one still alone, and how you probably will never find someone of your own...etc. etc. Act the part of the emotional female and those boys will be more than happy to give you a little space."

Shea turned to find him leaning casually against the

doorframe of her bedroom. A chill slithered down her spine. "So, you can not only influence minds, but read them?"

He lifted a shoulder in response. "Are you ready?"

"I just need to stop up at Luukas's apartment and tell him I'm leaving for a while."

"Cruthú and I will wait for you in the parking garage. Second floor down. And, Shea?"

She finished tying her boot, stood, and looked over at him, her mind on what she was going to say.

"Don't keep us waiting long. Or I will come to Luukas's door and retrieve you myself."

She didn't doubt for a second he would do just that. "I'll be there in a few minutes."

Giving her a nod, he headed for the front door, only pausing a moment for the raven to come back to her perch on his shoulder. She clicked her beak at Shea as they left.

As soon as they were gone, Shea dropped her bag and sank down onto the couch. Putting her head in her shaking hands, she seriously wondered if there wasn't a thread of truth in what Jesse had offered up as her excuse. Was she running away from all the happy couples around her? Is that why she was so eager to grasp at the first male that wanted her?

She scowled at her own thoughts. That wasn't the reason, and she knew it. She wasn't quite *that* pathetic. There was a real connection between her and Jesse. She'd felt it back at the fortress where he'd saved her life, and it had only grown stronger while they'd been apart.

If she were to be completely honest with herself, and

with him, she would admit she'd missed him, too. That she looked for him everywhere she went. That every morning when she came home, she ignored the pang of disappointment that hit her when she opened her door to find her apartment dark and empty. And that a small thrill had shot through her when she'd looked across the patio at the club to find him sitting there, watching her. And it had nothing to do with fear.

Plus, if there was any chance at all that he could fix what was broken within her, she needed to take it. Her personal life aside, she was no good as one of Luukas's Hunters if she couldn't even fight in hand to hand combat with a male who was threatening her maker.

Feeling determined, if not completely better, about her decision, she soon found herself knocking on Luukas's door. The Master Vampire himself answered it. He looked tired and distracted. She didn't want to feel good about his suffering, but she hoped it would work to her advantage.

"Shea." He took in the clothes and the bag at her feet. "Where are you going?"

She forced herself to look directly at him as the lie slipped easily from her tongue, a little too easily. "I thought I'd do a little research on my own. See what I could find out about the demons loitering about."

"I've already got people watching them. They're heading back to China, it seems. At least the main group."

Guilt wracked her, but Shea pushed it aside. "Yes, I know. But I thought I would try another path, and go north to Leeha's fortress to see if I could find any other clues. Maybe find any stragglers and see if I can learn anything." She looked down at her hands, then back up at the male that had done so much for her. "And honestly, Luukas, I just need a little time to myself. Being around you all is starting to wear on me. I can't even sleep in my own apartment without hearing Christian and his own private, exotic dancer next door." The disgust in her tone wasn't only for Luukas's benefit. "Even Dante has someone now." She didn't expound on what she was saying. Luukas was very intelligent. He would figure it out. To go into more detail would look suspicious.

His grey eyes softened with concern. "Perhaps there is someone out there for you, Shea. I'm sure fate wouldn't be so cruel as to leave you alone for the rest of your eternal life."

She gave him a sad smile. "Perhaps."

He rubbed his unshaven jaw. "Alright. I guess it won't hurt to see what you can find out. Go on and do what you need to do. But you are to report in to me every other night, and keep your cell on you so that I know your location at all times. No exceptions. If you need help, no matter how insignificant, send an alert. You know how. I'll be here until Nik and Aiden call in and we get a plan of action together. At that time, I will need you to return, whether you've discovered anything or not."

"I understand." Bending down to pick up her bag, she paused before she left. "And Luukas, thank you." She wanted to say more, but again held back, hoping it would be enough when he found out the truth.

He gave her a nod, and shut the door.

Jesse was waiting for her right where he said he would be. She found him leaning against a dark SUV not far from the elevator, feeding Cruthú bites of something from his pocket. The bird greeted her between nibbles, and when Jesse spotted her, his golden eyes lit with triumph.

"Don't get too cocky about all of this," she told him as she opened the back door and threw her bag in. "This isn't a 'yes.'"

"But it's definitely a 'maybe,'" he countered.

Shea closed the door and turned to face him. Reaching out to Cruthú, she stroked her feathers, careful not to accidentally touch him. "I don't know what I'm doing here," she whispered. She wouldn't look at him. She was afraid to. Afraid at what she would see reflected in his eyes.

"It will be okay, Shea."

She could only nod.

"We need to go now. Emma and Grace are coming." The bell sounded above the elevator doors, signaling that they were about to open.

"Oh, shit." Shea flashed around the vehicle and got in the passenger's side just as the doors slid open, revealing the two witches. They looked worried, not their usual happy selves. But then again, their mates were far from home, following demons around while trying not to attract their notice. Not an easy feat for several reasons.

Sliding down in the seat, Shea glared at Jesse as he got in the driver's side—just as casual as could be—and told Cruthú to go sit by her. The bird hopped over onto her lap and fluffed her feathers before settling down for the ride. "I'm glad you find this so amusing."

He laughed outright, and even waved at the witches as

he backed out of the space a little faster than was necessary, cutting off their path.

Shea's stomach flipped as she listened to the masculine sound of his laughter. It brought her joy to hear it, and she realized that this was the first time she had. "I've never heard you laugh before." The words came out before she realized that she was going to say them.

Jesse immediately sobered, and she wished she had kept her mouth shut. Glancing over at her, he brought the car to a full stop at the intersection. "I guess I don't normally have much of a reason to do so." He concentrated on the red light, and said no more about it. It turned green, and he stomped down on the gas.

Cautiously, Shea sat up. They were heading toward I-5. "So, where are we going?"

"I need to go back to the mountain and get some things before we leave."

"I thought the interior of the mountain had completely caved in after your fight with Luukas."

"It did. But my rooms managed to be spared, and I still live there."

"That's good, because that's where I told Luukas I was going and he's tracking my phone."

Jesse shot her a look, one side of his mouth lifted in a curious smile. "Of course he is."

She studied his strong profile, wanting to ask him about his promise to help her with her affliction. But she was too afraid her suspicions were right, and he'd only told her that to get her to come with him. After opening and closing her mouth a few times, she turned to stare out the window with a sigh.

"Let's take care of our demon problem first, as we are short on time. And then I promise you, Shea, we will find out what it is that's affecting you, and I *will* find out what it feels like to have you burning with passion beneath me."

A shot of liquid heat flared within her and Shea cleared her throat to cover the way her breath caught. His words affected her more than she would like to admit. She couldn't even scold him for being in her head and invading her privacy.

She needed to change the subject. "Do you know where the demons are headed?"

"Yes. China, I believe. The clues will direct them to the exact location. The monks hid the blood there generations ago, and they are the only ones who would know where it is." He paused. "My plan is to go straight to the source, and beat the demons at their own game."

"That explains why Waano took Aiden there. Though he didn't do anything to stop them." A thought occurred to her. "What if they won't tell us?"

"They will. They'll have no choice."

She stared out the window as the city lights faded into the distance. They would make good time. There wasn't much traffic this time of night. "Is that how we're going to get across the border into Canada? By you doing some of your evil witchy coercion?"

His hands tightened on the steering wheel. "You think I am evil."

Again, he willed the answer out of her mouth. "Yes." Then she turned to glare at him. "Stop doing that."

"Doing what?"

"Making me say things."

"I'm not making you say anything, Shea. It is what you believe."

"But you're forcing me to say it."

"Perhaps," he finally admitted a tense minute later. "I just need to hear the truth from you."

"I wouldn't lie to you, Jesse. I don't really believe in lying. Lies only come back to haunt you later."

He gave her a sideways glance. "You lied to Luukas."

"I had to. He would never have allowed me to come with you." Besides, it hadn't all been lies. She rubbed her forehead again. "Please don't mess with my head anymore."

With a sigh, he glanced over at her, longer this time as he studied her profile. "All right," he finally agreed. "If you promise to only ever tell me the truth. Always."

She turned her head and caught his eyes, holding his gaze steady with hers. "I promise I will never lie to you. Now, please watch the road."

After a short nod, he did as she asked, turning on some music for the ride when she angled her body away from him to stare out the window. The song was beautiful—an instrumental with an eerie violin lead. But Shea couldn't relax, as much as she tried.

They spent the rest of the three-hour ride in uncomfortable silence, other than the music. Shea tried to concentrate on the task at hand, but she couldn't focus with him sitting so close. His scent filled the interior, tantalizing her senses, until she thought she would go mad before they ever arrived. She even lowered the window, but it didn't help; she could *feel* him beside her, sense him there, as if his blood was already merged with hers, flowing inside her veins. It made her restless, and if Cruthú hadn't been fast asleep in her lap, she would've been squirming around on the seat like a bitch in heat. It was downright embarrassing.

Jesse, on the other hand, appeared completely unaffected by her proximity, despite his passionate words back at her apartment.

Shea was beginning to believe she was a complete idiot to agree to this.

They arrived at the border, and just as he'd promised, they sailed through customs without a hitch and arrived at the fortress shortly thereafter. The majestic, snow-capped mountain was little more than a pile of rubble now, thanks to the battle that had taken place there between him and Luukas. As Jesse went off the dirt track to circumvent the base of the remainder of the mountain, Shea leaned forward, looking out the windshield.

"You did this on purpose," she said softly as she took in the destruction. "*You* destroyed Leeha's fortress. It was your plan all along. That's why your rooms survived the battle."

He didn't respond at first. Pulling the vehicle into a sheltered spot within the thick undergrowth of the pine and cottonwood trees near the back entrance, he threw it into park and shut off the engine. They sat there, neither of them making a move to get out, as the air between them charged with emotion.

"Why?" she whispered.

Removing his hands from the steering wheel, Jesse let them fall into his lap. When he finally looked at her, his eyes were like twin orbs of molten gold in the darkness.

"It was time." He kept his voice down, as though he didn't want to disturb the peacefulness. "Leeha had done enough. She was unstable. She needed to be stopped."

As Shea sat wondering what this could mean, if anything, Cruthú woke from her nap and fluffed her feathers, then gave a good shake. Settling down again, she made no move to get off Shea's lap.

"She likes you." There was a hint of wonder in his voice, but not surprise.

"Stop trying to change the subject." But she gave the silly bird a scratch beneath the feathers on the back of her head. When she looked back up at Jesse, he was watching her, his expression intense. "What?"

He dropped his eyes, and put his arm out for the raven to hop onto. Shea's lap felt cold without her there.

"I promise I will tell you why I did it, Shea. I will tell you everything. But not right now."

"Why not right now? I'd like to know."

"And you will. But I want you to know me a little better first, before you judge me." He paused, and she saw his throat working as he swallowed. "I don't want to fuck this up between us," he finally admitted. Then he opened the door and got out, holding his arm up for the raven. Cruthú took flight, stretching her wings before they went inside. Grabbing Shea's bag from the backseat, Jesse said, "It will be day soon, we'll stay here so you can get some sleep, and leave at sundown."

Then he closed the doors and walked away a few paces before he waited for her to join him.

Shea stared at his back. He was standing stiff as a rod, his face tilted to the sky as he watched the raven soar above the towering pines. She wished she could read his mind as easily as he did hers. A raindrop hit the windshield, followed quickly by a few more. Taking a reinforcing breath, she got out of the SUV and went to join the dark warlock in his lair.

CHAPTER 7

Christian sat at the counter and watched as Ryan unpacked the groceries he'd just brought upstairs for her. She was filling out, and no longer looked too thin for her large eyes. And she smiled a lot more since she'd settled into his home with him. But something was bothering her tonight. "What is it, *she'ashil?* What's wrong?"

She closed the pantry door and smiled at him. "Nothing, really. I'm just trying to figure out what I'm supposed to do."

"Do?" He could think of many things he'd like her to do right now, and they all involved a lot less clothing.

"Yeah. They're trying to tell me something, but I can't figure out what it is."

Ah, her spirit helpers. At least that's what his Navajo mother would've called them. His father would have called her psycho.

Christian called her *"she'ashil"*—sweetheart.

He studied her closely. Sometimes the spirits would

become too excited at her being able to hear them and they would overwhelm her, all screaming at her at once, but she was working to get them to understand that she couldn't figure out what they wanted of her when they did that.

Still, at times, they forgot. In the past, the only thing that would save her sanity was to shoot herself full of heroin. That was, until she'd met him. Now she didn't need the opiates to drown out the voices when a little vampire blood did the trick. And it was a lot better for her health. "Is it too much?" In a way, Christian hoped she would say yes, for then he would have an excuse to give her his blood. His fangs and his cock ached just thinking about it.

She turned to put some broccoli in the fridge, and as always, Christian couldn't take his eyes from her bright hair flowing down her back...all the colors of a summer sunset.

"No, they're not screaming at me, at least. Just forgetting to not talk over each other." She faced him and frowned. "Something about a spell."

Christian came around to her side of the island and leaned back against the counter across from her. "A spell?"

She nodded, listening hard. But then shook her head. "I can't make it out. Something about a spell...hidden...it's coming...and they want me to have it." She sighed and shrugged. "I don't know."

There was a knock on the door right before it opened. Christian shot over to the entryway, fangs bared, but caught the scent of their guest right before she poked her head inside.

"Hey, Christian. Sorry. I didn't know you were still here. I told Ryan I'd let her borrow this." Grace came walking in with a book in her hands, smiling brightly.

He sensed no fear at all from her, despite what had to be his menacing appearance. She really was the perfect mate for Aiden. "Hey, Grace," he told her as she patted him on the arm on her way past him.

Returning to the counter, he watched the two witches greet each other with a hug. His heart warmed toward their visitor, and all the witches actually. They'd accepted Ryan into their fold like she'd always been there, even if his female still strayed on the side of caution around them.

There was only one female who hadn't taken to her, and he had no idea why. It's not like he and Shea were ever anything more than friends.

"Here you go, sweet cheeks," Grace said. "The history of the Moss witches! Or at least as much of it as we could piece together so far. Maybe you can add whatever you can remember to it." She dropped the large book onto the counter.

As she swung it up and around, an old piece of parchment paper slid out and fluttered to the floor. Grace bent down to get it, and nearly knocked heads with Ryan as she went down.

Christian leaped over the counter as Ryan slapped her hands over her ears and fell to her knees. Her eyes squeezed shut and tears streamed down her cheeks. He grabbed her wrists and forced her to look up at him as Grace knelt by his side with the paper in her hand.

"Ryan! *She'ashil*! Tell them to shut up. Just tell them to

shut up." He repeated himself over and over as her eyes went from his mouth to the paper and back.

"What's happening?" Grace asked.

He forgot that Grace had never seen them get this bad before. "It's the voices. They're trying to tell her something, but they get too fucking enthusiastic about it sometimes." Christian tried again to get Ryan's attention. "Just *tell* them."

Squeezing her eyes shut again, Ryan did as Christian told her and screamed at the voices. "I can't help you if... one at a time...shut up! Just shut the hell up!" A few seconds later, she opened her eyes and slowly lowered her hands away from her ears. She held them at the ready, though, just in case.

"What is it, Ryan?" Grace asked. "What were they saying?"

She took Christian's hand and squeezed, but her eyes were on the parchment. "What is that?"

Grace looked down at the paper. "It's an old spell my parents left for me. I found it after they died, but I have no idea what it is."

"Can I see it?" Ryan held out her free hand and Grace gave her the spell.

Christian watched as she studied the scrawls on the page. He wanted to wipe the tears from her cheeks, but she was concentrating so hard on the ragged piece of paper, he didn't want to interrupt.

When she looked up at him, her turquoise blue eyes were filled with fright.

"What is it?" he asked.

Ryan's eyes never left his. "This isn't just a spell. This is *the* spell."

"What do you mean?"

"*The* spell for what?" Grace asked at the same time.

Ryan looked back and forth between them. "It's the spell that will send the demons back to hell. For good."

"How do you know this, Ryan?" Grace asked her.

"The spirits told her," Christian answered for her.

"But can you read it?" Grace asked. "Or can they?"

Ryan nodded, and her frightened eyes went back to Christian. He knew exactly why she was scared. As the only one who could read the spell, it would be up to her to perform it.

It would be up to his female to send the demons back to hell.

Grace jumped to her feet. "I have to tell Keira!" She whipped out her cell phone. "I have to tell Aiden!" Putting it to her ear, she listened while it rang. While she waited for someone to answer, she asked Ryan, "Will this get that fucker out of Aiden?"

Christian helped Ryan stand up. "If it doesn't, I'll rip it out of him myself. If Nik doesn't figure out a way to do it first."

But his heart thumped in fear at the thought of Ryan facing those things, even as his body hardened and his fangs shot down instinctively to protect her.

CHAPTER 8

Jesse set Shea's bag down near the end of his bed, then lit the kerosene lamp on the small, round table. It was the only furniture he had, other than the chest of drawers that held his few items of clothing, and Cruthú's perch. It was all he needed. Having too much "stuff" only created clutter, both physically and spiritually. When he turned, he found his vampire standing just outside the doorway, looking around his room with an unreadable expression on her face.

However, he didn't need to read her expression, or her mind, to know what she was thinking. "I won't spell you inside this time, Shea. There's no need. We're the only ones anywhere near this mountain. You're free to leave whenever you wish. Although I hope you'll stay. At least for awhile."

That seemed to surprise her. "They're all gone? Even Leeha's mutants?"

She was referring to the gray-skinned vampire

hybrids, Leeha's first attempts at creating bodies for the demons to possess. Human bodies were much too weak to handle the possession for more than a few hours. So, she had created a vampire, who in turn created more vampires, only to discover that they didn't last long, either. Once the demons took over the juvenile vampires, the bodies began to morph and rot at a rapid pace, turning into something that resembled creatures in old horror films—only a hell of a lot more terrifying.

Eventually, Leeha had tried using an older vampire, one created by Luukas. The bodies turned by the powerful Master Vampire had worked the best, although even those would not last forever. Once the demons were in residence, the bodies would die. Some just did it faster than others.

It had angered Leeha to no end that her creation was so much weaker than Luukas's. And Jesse had to admit that at times, he'd had a hard time containing his enjoyment of that fact.

"Jesse?"

With a start, he realized he'd never answered Shea's question. "The gray ones are all gone. The bodies couldn't handle the possession for very long and they died."

"Where did they go, after the bodies died?"

"Off to possess others, I would imagine." But he was quick to add, "Don't worry, I'll get them under control. Making sure they can't re-animate their true forms is much more important right now. The power they have now is nothing compared to what they'll be able to do as their true selves." The lies were sour on his tongue. He didn't like deceiving her like this, but he knew she wouldn't have come with him if she knew the truth.

Although her green eyes were still wary, she nodded in agreement. But he saw her mind working, and soon, she came to the realization he'd been hoping to avoid discussing.

"Do all of the host bodies die? Once they're possessed?"

He only paused a moment. He wouldn't lie to her about this. "Eventually, yes." He knew well where she was going with her questions.

"So, Aiden—" Her eyes silently begged him to tell her what she wanted to hear.

He hated causing her pain. "Yes. He will die, too. Eventually."

She opened her mouth to speak, closed it, and swallowed hard a few times before forcing the word out from between clenched teeth. "When?"

He shrugged. "It's hard to say. It seems to depend on the age of the vampire and how they were created. Even their own will to survive. There are many factors."

She nodded, and he could practically hear the gears of her supernatural mind turning in rapid succession. It was tempting to jump in there to witness it for himself, but he resisted the urge, knowing she didn't like it. "Aiden is older than the vampires that followed Leeha here, the ones she changed. And he's a survivor. So, we still have time to save him."

"Perhaps." It wasn't what she wanted to hear, but he refused to fill her full of false hope. She would only hate him more for it in the end.

Joining her at the door, he ran his eyes over her delicate features. "Please, Shea. Come in. I swear to you, you can leave here whenever you would like."

With a last nervous glance over her shoulder at the dark passageway, she stepped inside. Her eyes went immediately to the bed. "Where am I going to sleep?"

Ah, so that's what all the hesitancy was all about. "You can have the bed, of course."

"Where are you going to sleep?"

His body reacted immediately to the husky tone of her voice and the way she hid her eyes from him as she asked the question. She wanted him, as much as he wanted her. It was both a relief and a torment to know.

And now he had her completely alone. "Shea. Look at me."

He may have said that a bit more harshly than he'd intended to, for those tilted eyes of hers immediately snapped up to his in surprise. Softening his tone, he told her what he'd been fantasizing about the entire ride there. "I want to see you."

"I'm right here." Tiny lines of confusion appeared between her brows.

He wished he could smooth them away with his thumb. "I want to see all of you," he clarified.

He knew the moment she got his meaning. She flashed her fangs with a hiss of warning. "Jesse, no. That's a bad idea."

But he didn't stop. "I've imagined what you would look like naked in my bed since the moment I first saw you, Shea. Your breasts, the curve of your hips, and your long, beautiful legs…your sex. I want to see you."

"Jesse—"

The last syllable of his name ended in a low growl that was meant to warn him, but failed miserably. The only thing her reaction succeeded in doing was to make him impossibly hard. Jesse had the sudden urge to yank the collar of his shirt away from his throat and expose his artery for her to take. He wanted to feel her fangs sink into him, feeding on his blood as he plunged into her tight body. He wanted to run his hands over every curve, taste the salt of her sweet skin—

But he couldn't do that. It would cause her pain. However, there were other ways to be intimate. "I want to watch you come for me."

Her lips parted on a swift intake of breath, and the tip of her tongue shot out to wet her bottom lip.

It was becoming difficult to get enough air in his lungs. "I won't touch you, I swear. I just—" He paused, trying to think of a way to convey to her all he was feeling with words alone. "I want to be closer to you. Let me be closer to you."

Then he waited to see how she would respond to his brash words.

Shea stood perfectly still near the end of the bed, lips parted in a semi-snarl, fangs exposed, her chest rising and falling rapidly with her quick breaths. The air was thick with tension between them. Her nipples were hard, straining toward him through the soft fabric of her clothes. Her hands were clenched into tight fists at her sides. Her feet were slightly apart, legs braced, knees locked.

And her eyes—those beautiful, bright, sea-green eyes—were zeroed in on him with a hunger that was far more than sexual. It was the intense stare of a wild animal stalking its prey.

And he was that prey.

Gods, that look almost made him come in his pants. He'd never been on this end of the cycle of life. He was always the one in control. But Jesse would happily hand over that power to the stunning, intelligent, vivacious, dangerous creature in front of him. "Shea..." His voice was gruff with need. He took a halting step toward her, about to fall to his knees and beg if need be.

Her voice cut through the tension. "I want to see you, too."

He gave her a swift nod.

"Lower the light, please."

Jesse reached out with his mind and turned down the flame until the room was lit with only a soft glow. Cruthú chattered at him from her perch. He stroked her feathers and murmured to her without taking his eyes from his vampire, and the raven tucked her beak under her wing, settling down for the day.

Shea sat on the bed and started to unlace her boots. Pulling out one of the wooden chairs from the table, he turned it to face her and sat down, rubbing his palms on his thighs. He hadn't felt this anxious since...well, he never had.

Once her boots were off and lined up neatly beside the bed, she raised her head, but didn't stand. She was nervous. He could feel it. But he didn't say anything else, afraid the sound of his voice would pull them out of the moment, and she would stop what was happening before they even got started.

When her eyes skittered around the room, looking anywhere but at him, he knew he would have to take the initiative, so he kicked off his shoes and stood to remove his sweater.

It got the effect he wanted. Her nervous gaze shot back over to him, and when she saw what he was doing, she stood also, following his lead with shaky movements.

Pulling the luxurious knit over his head, he dropped it carelessly to the floor. Shea's eyes ran over his bare chest and stomach. The heat of her gaze branded him like fire, and it was pure torture to imagine what it would feel like to have her touch him. He heard her pulse kick up as she pulled off her shirt, laying it neatly on the bed. The tops of her breasts spilled from the confines of a red, low-cut bra, threatening to break free with every breath she took. She hesitated, uncertain.

"Take off your jeans," he ordered in a husky tone. Jesse didn't want to rush, but he was uncomfortably hard, and they'd barely gotten started. He sat down again to remove his socks, never taking his eyes from her while he dropped them to the side and stood. His hands dropped to his own waistband, but he made no move to undo the fastening and ease his own discomfort. Not yet. She wasn't seeing anymore until he did. "Do it, Shea."

As if in a trance, she undid the fastening and slid her hands inside. Slowly, she pushed the material from her rounded hips, revealing nothing but a slip of red lace covering her sex. She bent over as she pushed them down to her ankles and lifted each foot to pull them off.

Jesse let out a sound of frustration when her hair swung forward, covering the sight of her breasts. But then she straightened and stood proudly before him in nothing but her red bra and panties, and he discovered his imagination had been severely, horribly, lacking. He'd pictured this moment many, many times over the past weeks, but nothing had prepared him for the reality of his vampire nearly nude and hungry for him.

Her face and chest flushed with color as he ran his eyes from her full breasts, down her smooth stomach, over the curve of her hips and shapely legs, to her bare toes, and all the way back again. He savored this moment, taking his time. She had a beauty mark next to her navel, shaped like quarter moon, and the crimson color of the underwear she'd chosen was striking on her, with her ivory skin and dark hair. It almost made him hesitant to say what he was about to say. Almost, but not quite.

"Now, take off the rest."

The corners of her mouth curved up in a nervous, yet teasing, smile. "You first, warlock."

With narrowed eyes, he complied, pushing his slacks down his legs and kicking them off to join his sweater. He debated staying in his boxer briefs for his own self-control, but decided against it when he took in her reaction to what she was seeing so far. Hooking his thumbs beneath the waistband, he lifted it up and over the swollen mass of his manhood, and then slid them down his hips and legs. His sex hung thick and heavy, drops of pre-come glistening on the tip.

Shea stared with unabashed curiosity, her tongue flicking out to lick her lips again, like she was imagining tasting him. She even took a step forward, before stopping again with a growl of frustration.

"Shea."

She tore her eyes away to look up at him.

"The rest. Take it off."

Instead of obeying him right away, she closed her eyes tight for a moment. When she opened them again, they were shiny with unshed tears. "I want to touch you," she whispered, flashing her fangs on a hiss as her eyes dropped back down his body. "Jesse, I want to touch you more than anything."

Blood surged, swelling his cock even as her impatience and sorrow washed over him. He pushed those feelings away. He would worry about that later. Right now, he wanted to please her. "I want you to touch me, too, love." He said nothing else, knowing there was no point. But he would make this as good as he could for her. "Now do as I told you, and take off the rest." His tone would brook no more argument. "I'm going to make you come, Shea, without ever touching you. I'm going to make you come so hard you won't even realize that it's not me doing it."

Reaching behind her, Shea unclasped her bra and shrugged the straps off her shoulders. Her breasts spilled from the cups, full and round, with large, rose-colored areolas and firm nipples. She set it on her pile of clothes and faced him again.

Perfect. She was fucking perfect.

After a moment of indecision, she slid off her underwear, and as Jesse stood staring at this stunning female before him, he was overcome with the urge to make her his own in every way possible. And never allow her to leave him again.

Grabbing the chair from behind him without taking

his eyes from her, he carried it across the room and swung it around in front of him, setting it down as close to the bed as he dared. "Get on the bed, love."

Shea sat down, scooting back until she was leaning up against the wall.

"No, lay down."

She did as he requested, and he took a seat on the chair. For a moment, he just looked at the amazing sight laid out before him.

Gods, what to do with her first? Jesse had to admit, this was a new situation for him. He kept his voice low. "I want you to imagine my hands touching you, my lips and tongue on your skin. But I don't want you to do anything until I tell you to do it. Can you handle that?"

"Yes." She fisted the blanket on either side of her and rubbed her thighs together eagerly.

Jesse leaned back in the chair and took himself in his hand. A low moan escaped before he could stop himself.

Shea tensed, watching him closely.

"Touch your breasts. Show me how you like to be touched."

She immediately did as he said, the flesh spilling from her small hands as she manipulated her breasts, squeezing them and then running her palms lightly over the nipples. They puckered to her touch, and she pinched them between her fingers as her hips moved restlessly on the bed.

"No. Don't close your eyes. Look at me. Look at what you're doing to me."

Her eyes darkened until they were nearly black as she watched him run his hand up and down his shaft, squeezing the base as he swelled even larger, the head glistening with his desire.

Shea moaned, biting her bottom lip, her fangs drawing drops of blood that she tasted with her tongue. Her back arched as one hand left her breast to ease toward her sex, but she stopped short and looked at him uncertainly.

Jesse watched every move, becoming more determined with every passing second that one day soon, it would be his hands and his mouth making her squirm. "Shea, I want you to spread your legs. I want to look at you. I want to see your desire for me."

Slowly, she let her knees fall apart.

Jesse leaned to the side to see. "Wider."

She slid her legs open wider, exposing herself completely for his viewing pleasure. Her sex was smooth and plump under the "V" of dark curls protecting it. Jesse leaned closer and started reaching for her before he caught himself and pulled his hand back. He wrapped it around his sex again. "Use your hands and open yourself more for me."

"Jesse—"

"Show me." He knew she would lose her nerve if he let her, so he didn't plan on letting her. If he had to threaten her into a fucking orgasm, he would.

Hesitant at first, she ran both hands down her stomach, then did as he told her, sliding her fingers through the curls and opening herself wider.

Jesse moaned, tightening his fist around the base of his cock again in an effort for control. He wanted to bury his nose in those curls, and run his tongue through the glistening folds of satiny skin she'd revealed. She was already so wet for him—he wanted to taste her desire. He could see her swollen clitoris, pulsing with her blood flow.

Moving around to the end of the bed, he braced his weight on his palms and leaned down until his face was as close to her as he dared. Inhaling the unique scent of her sex, he closed his eyes. "I want to taste you, Shea. So badly."

She moaned, her hips rising off the bed in offering. "Jesse, please."

Pushing himself away from her, he kneeled at the end between her legs, careful not to touch her skin. "Touch your breast. Only one. Leave your other hand where it is."

She followed his order, her back arching as she massaged the firm mound.

"Pinch your nipple between your fingers. Imagine it's my mouth on you, warm and wet, and my tongue flicking it." He pumped his fist up and down his length.

Rolling her nipple between her fingers, Shea bared her fangs as she watched him pleasure himself.

"Lift your hips, and put one finger inside yourself." She did, sliding it in and out as her other hand continued to play with her nipple.

Jesse cupped his balls with his free hand as he watched her, but slowed his other hand, afraid he would spend himself before she did. "Keep playing with your nipple, and move your fingers to your clit."

Her eyes rolled back in her head and her back arched when she touched the little bundle of nerves. Jesse reached out to her, wrapping her in his aura. He felt her lust for him, and shared his with her. When her eyes opened again, they were hot and bright. She moved her fingers, her fangs bared as she played with herself, her breath coming in short pants.

Gods, she was beautiful. "I want to fuck you so badly, Shea. I want to feel your wet heat tight around my sex." His balls tightened as he watched her work herself up. He fought for control. "I can't hold back much longer. Come for me, love. I want you to come for me."

She cried out. It was a frustrated sound. "I can't."

"Yes, you can. I want to see you come, Shea."

"This isn't enough. Jesse, I want more."

Jesse knew what she needed. And he knew how to give it to her. Without taking his eyes from her, he held one hand out, fingers wide.

A small pairing knife lay next to his glass on the table across the room. It began to vibrate, slowly at first, and then faster and faster, until it rose from the table and flew across the distance to smack into his palm. His fingers closed around the handle.

Shea gasped, her eyes on the knife.

He released his cock on a hiss, and lifted his wrist so she could see, then pressed the knife blade against his skin.

CHAPTER 9

Shea was burning alive. Sliding two fingers inside herself, she felt Jesse touching her. She didn't know how he was doing it, but it was him using her wet heat to slide his fingers across her clit as she worked herself higher and higher. Her muscles strained, the heaviness in her womb building. Pinching her nipple, she couldn't stifle her cry as she felt it all the way to her core. The warlock had brought her right to the edge with his wicked words and hungry gaze. But she needed more.

When he pressed the blade of the small knife through the skin of his wrist, Shea's hips bucked beneath her hand. Her fangs ached to be the thing that sliced through that tan skin, bringing forth the bright red line of blood that appeared.

Making a clean cut horizontally across his wrist, Jesse leaned forward and braced his weight over her on one powerful arm. His sex hung thick and heavy barely an inch from where she needed him to be. He held the open wound over her mouth without touching her. "Drink, love."

Shea opened her mouth. Warm blood dripped past her fangs and onto her tongue. It was dark and sweet, with a hint of something wicked, just as she'd imagined. Shea moved restlessly beneath her own hands as his warm blood slid down her throat and his life force tore through her body. The waves of her orgasm rose higher and higher, until it slammed into her with an intensity that was almost frightening. She cried out, convulsing on the bed, feeling something hot and wet hit her chest and stomach as Jesse's words of encouragement joined her cries.

One word crashed over and over through her mind as she came—

MINE.

Her eyes shot open and zeroed in on the rugged male leaning over her. His head had fallen forward; his warm breath coming in ragged exhales to blow across the moisture on her chest.

Her lips pulled back from her fangs as her eyes fell to the rapid pulse on the side of his throat.

MINE.

She suddenly froze beneath him.

No. No. No! It can't be!

A ragged sob escaped from her throat as her worst nightmare came true. She was mated to a male she'd never be able to touch, or kiss, or hold.

Jesse's head snapped up. "Shea? Shea, what's wrong?" He ran his eyes over every inch of her, making sure he wasn't touching her anywhere, searching desperately for whatever caused her pain. "Did I hurt you?"

He had. He had hurt her horribly. But she couldn't answer him, could do nothing but stare up at him in horror. Everything he had done to her and Luukas and Keira...it all flashed through her head, one thing after another after another.

"Shea, talk to me, godsdammit! Or I will make you tell me."

She didn't know what to say. Didn't know what to do. She'd always known she had an unhealthy attraction to the warlock, but this—this was something she'd never expected. Would the fates really be so cruel as to mate her to someone she could never touch, and who could never touch her in return? Someone who she could never accept as her own?

Another harsh sob escaped her.

Jesse reached toward her face, remembered he couldn't touch her, and pulled at his own hair in frustration. "Dammit, Shea. Tell me what the fuck is wrong! Tell me right now, or I will come in and see for myself."

Scooting away from him, she pulled the blanket over her nakedness, looking anywhere but at him. It took her a moment to get a grip on her emotions, and her voice was thin when she finally answered him. "I'm fine. I'm just being stupid because I can't do what I really want." She tried to wipe the tears from her cheeks, but more kept falling. "I'm fine."

He was off the bed and across the room at a speed that should only be attainable by vampires or werewolves, of which he was neither. Pulling on his pants, he grabbed a box of tissues from the shelf in the nightstand and handed it to her. "You're not fine." He sat down on the bed beside her while she wiped at her face. "Please, talk to me, Shea. What did I do?"

She shook her head, unable to say the words aloud. "Nothing. You did nothing."

"Then what didn't I do?"

She just shook her head again. What the hell was she supposed to say? And what had she done to deserve this? And then another thought occurred to her, one that made her breath freeze in her lungs.

He'd given her his blood. She'd fed on the blood of her mate. Shea pressed her hands to either side of her skull and rocked back and forth. *No, no, no!* She couldn't leave him now. Ever. He couldn't leave her. She needed his blood to survive, would literally die without it. What the hell was she going to do?

Luukas, Nik—she couldn't go back there. Not with Jesse. They would never allow this male to be anywhere near them. And she couldn't say that she blamed either one of them. Luukas would never allow Jesse near *her*. She'd be lucky if he didn't kill him on sight. He wouldn't give her the chance to explain first. But what other choice did she have?

She would have to run, they would both have to run. It was the only chance she had to survive. Shea put her head in her hands and rocked back and forth.

What the hell had she been thinking? Coming anywhere near this male was a stupid, stupid, fucking mistake.

Shea suddenly realized that Jesse had stopped asking

her to tell him what was wrong. Lifting her head, she pushed her hair back off her face.

He was sitting eerily still, the expression on his face unreadable, golden eyes intense as she felt him probing around in her head.

She held up one hand, palm out. "No, Jesse! Don't—"

"Is this true?"

Shit. It was too late. She took a deep breath.

He knew. He knew everything she'd just been thinking. *Everything.*

Swallowing hard, she let her hand fall back down to her lap. "Yes," she whispered.

Rising from the bed, he returned to the other side of the room and picked up his sweater from the floor. Without a word, he shrugged into it and slipped his bare feet into his shoes.

Shea watched him, confused, as he headed to the door. "Where are you going?"

Pausing with one hand on the knob, he said, "I'm sorry that fate did not give you the mate you would've wished for." Then he opened the door and walked out, closing it behind him.

His cool collectiveness hurt her more than any touch she'd ever had to endure. As the door shut with a soft click, her soul shattered into a million pieces.

Jumping from the bed, Shea flung open the door and ran down the passageway after him with the comforter trailing along on the floor behind her. "Jesse! Jesse, stop!"

He was already at the end of the tunnel, heading back the way they'd come in.

Shea caught up to him easily just as he exited the

mountain. "Jesse, where are you going?" The rain was cold on her bare head and shoulders, the mossy ground sucking at her feet like a sponge as she followed him outside.

He didn't stop, or acknowledge her in any way as he made his way across the small clearing to the SUV where it was hidden just inside the tree line.

He was leaving her there?

In a spurt of panic, she rushed around him at vamp speed, placing herself between him and the driver's side door. He pulled up short, just in time.

"Shea, please get out of the way." His voice was quiet, controlled. Always so fucking controlled.

She shook her head. "No. I'm not just going to let you take off and leave me here."

"The sun is coming up soon. You won't have a choice."

The iciness that emanated from him made her blood run cold. She could sense nothing of what he was thinking or feeling, although she now shared his blood. She didn't know how he was doing it. "Jesse—"

"Move, Shea."

"No. Come back inside—"

Suddenly, his fist flew past her head and through the back passenger window. Golden eyes burned through her, glowing with fury. The muscles in his jaw jumped as he gritted out, "Get. Out. Of. My. Way."

Shea didn't move. His anger didn't frighten her, because she knew it was only a disguise to cover up what he was really feeling—hurt. She felt something akin to satisfaction that she had finally managed to break that calm façade he always wore like armor, although this wasn't the way she'd wanted to do it. "Come back inside and let me explain."

He tilted his head, a quizzical expression on his face. "Explain? Explain what, exactly? How I repulse you? How you hate yourself for being attracted to me? How you would rather the gods had mated you to a slug than me?"

Her heart squeezed in her chest. That's exactly what she had been thinking. "That's not all there is to it, and you know it."

"Ah, yes." He nodded, his brows drawn and his forehead creased in thought. "There's the problem of Luukas, your maker. You think he will kill me before you can tell him that you need me to survive, therefore ending your life in the process." He threw his head back and laughed. "I'm half-tempted to let him. Just to see his face when he realizes what he's done." In the next second, he grew perfectly serious. "Except that it will never happen, Shea. Luukas cannot kill me. And I know you already suspected as much. So, the real issue here isn't what Luukas thinks of me, but what *you* do."

He was right. She held one hand out in front of her in supplication, keeping the blanket from falling with the other. "I just wasn't expecting this." It was a lame excuse, and she knew it, but she didn't know what else to say.

"But, weren't you? Come on now, Shea. I felt it—this thing between us—the first time I laid eyes on you. I knew there was something there. I just didn't know what it was. Although, looking back, I should have guessed, especially knowing what was happening with the others. However, I'm not a vampire." His eyes came back to her. "Can you honestly tell me that you had no idea?"

Shea looked away, but it was impossible to hide the guilt that weighed on her.

"Yes. You knew." He released his breath on a heavy exhale. "And yet you came with me, anyway. What were you hoping to get out of taking such a risk?"

Wiping at a tear that fell from the corner of her eye, she shook her head. But there was no use denying it. She had known. She'd known the moment she saw him, with the hood of his robe covering half of his face and that silly bird on his shoulder. He'd protected her from Leeha, and she'd never questioned why he had done it. Not really. Because she'd known.

"The sun is coming up. You should get inside."

She shook her head again. "Not without you."

He narrowed his gaze in warning. "If you don't go inside now, I will carry you in myself, and I won't care how much you scream."

"Jesse—"

"Go, Shea. NOW."

The sky was beginning to lighten, the clouds clearing away, taking the rain with them. Shea looked up at him beseechingly, but was at a complete loss as to what to say to fix what she had done. And she wasn't sure she wanted to. For that would mean betraying Luukas and the others.

"There's nothing more to say," he answered her frazzled thoughts. "Not right now. I'll ask you again. Please, go inside."

The pain he was trying so hard to hide tore at her soul. The pain she had caused. "Are you coming back?" she whispered.

He just looked at her for a moment, his expression

unreadable. "I will have to. Eventually. If I don't want to let you die."

Shea swallowed hard. He was referring to her need of his blood. The first rays of the sun began to peek up over the horizon, still hidden behind the surrounding mountains. Her skin began to tingle and burn where it was exposed to the elements.

"Shea." There was a warning in his tone, and a stubborn set to his jaw.

"Okay. I'm going." Stepping to the side and out of his way, she paused to look over at him. She opened her mouth to say something, although she had no idea what it was.

But he didn't give her the chance. As soon as she was out of the way, Jesse wrenched open the door of the SUV and got inside. He started the engine and put his hands on the steering wheel, staring straight ahead for a brief second before throwing the vehicle into reverse and backing out of the hidden spot.

Shea pulled the blanket up over her head, staying where she was until he was out of sight. Then she ran back inside just as the sun broke through the trees.

Cruthú greeted her from her perch, her beady, black eyes looking past her for Jesse. When he didn't come, she flew over to where Shea had collapsed on the bed.

Shea sat staring straight ahead, numb from all that happened, until exhaustion overtook her and she curled up with the raven to sleep.

CHAPTER 10

Jesse floored the gas pedal, projecting the chaos raging inside of him onto the vehicle he was currently abusing. He flew down the dirt road through the mountain pass like the demons of hell were chasing him, and perhaps they were, at least theoretically.

Unconcerned with the danger he was putting himself in, Jesse sent the vehicle careening wildly around a corner. He was hard to kill, if not impossible. Unless the thing burst into flames, which wasn't very likely despite what the movies would like you to think, he would survive this day. And for the first time in his life, he wanted to survive. He needed to survive. His being alive didn't just affect him anymore. Shea's life now depended on him, too.

For a moment, the overwhelming responsibility of it felt like one of the boulders teetering on the edge of rock above the road had worked its way loose and landed on his chest.

The sun was well in the sky now, and for a moment he

felt a flash of fear. Had she listened to him and gone inside? Had she made it in time? But deep down he knew Shea was safe. He would feel it if anything happened to her.

Especially now.

The road began to climb, but Jesse didn't let up on the speed. Yanking the wheel to the right, he suddenly veered off the road and stomped on the brake, sending the back end spinning around in a tight circle. When the SUV finally skidded to a stop, the back tires were balanced precariously on the edge of a drop-off. Jesse got out and slammed the door behind him, leaving the vehicle rocking and small rocks cascading down the side of the cliff beneath the tires.

Walking to the edge, he stood beside the back tire and looked out over the valley below, breathing in the cool mountain air. The breeze had a bite of winter coming down from the snow-capped peaks towering above him, even though it was months away yet. The birds sang back and forth between the hemlock trees below, welcoming the new day. And the morning sun warmed the back of his bare neck.

Amongst all that natural beauty, Jesse clenched his fists at his sides, threw back his head, and released the pent-up frustration, anger, and hurt he'd been hoarding inside for months now. Flocks of black clouds rose from the trees as birds took flight in every direction. Small animals scattered, fleeing through the underbrush surrounding him. Even the wind picked up, spraying him with lingering raindrops that clung to the trees as it whipped around him.

A VAMPIRE'S CHOICE

When it was all out, and his voice was hoarse from screaming, Jesse closed his eyes and took a deep, meditative breath. A master at locking down his emotions, his fists slowly opened again as he pushed down and sealed away anything that lingered, deep inside where no one would ever see it. He had to be thus, or he wouldn't have survived as long as he had in this world of bloodthirsty vampires. Creatures who could tell exactly what you were feeling by the slightest uptick in your heartbeat, the faintest blush on your cheeks, or the tiniest whiff of fear, and would rip off your head before you could blink.

Once he had pulled it together again, Jesse put his mind back to the task at hand. He recalled what he had overheard in Shea's thoughts, this time from a more logical perspective, one that wasn't affected by things like sorrow or feelings of inadequacy. She was unhappy about what fate had decreed for her, and afraid of losing all those she cared about because of it. It was completely understandable. And as a vampire, those things she felt were so raw, so magnified, so overwhelming, she was unable to look past them.

He would have to help her.

Jesse began to pace back and forth, rapidly creating a list of everything he had learned about his female so far. Ideas were formed, ways to possibly ease her mind and spirit, and discarded just as quickly as he thought of them. In the end, he came to only one conclusion: she needed to learn to trust him, before their relationship could go any further, before she would allow him to help her. And he was determined that it would be so, whatever it took, for an endless lifetime without being able to touch his exquisite vampire was not going to work for him. As titillating as the past night together had been, it wasn't enough. Would never be enough. And he knew Shea felt the same.

But to earn her trust, he would have to tell her everything—who he was, why he was here, what he had done. And hope she would accept him for the male he was. It was not something he looked forward to. Jesse was not ashamed of any of it. He had his reasons, and they were sound. But they were not reasons that others would easily understand. And especially not one such as Shea.

It was good that she had agreed to come with him on this trip. They needed this time together to work out what was between them, before worrying about presenting their mating to the rest of the world. Yes, this was good. Shea would come to care for him, despite all he had done. He was certain of it. She had to. Fate decreed that it would be so.

Resolved in his decision and knowing that Shea would be sleeping, Jesse stayed where he was a while longer, enjoying the peace that being in the presence of nature always brought him. He would think more on what to say to his female on the drive back to his home. A way to convince her that this was not wrong, that *they* were not wrong. No matter what anyone else said or believed. But for right now, he needed the stillness to regroup. In the upcoming days, their survival would depend on his ability to control his reactions, inside and out. He could not allow his emotions regarding Shea to get the best of him, or he would ruin everything.

It was nearly noon by the time he climbed back inside

the SUV and eased it away from the overhang. The back tires skidded on the edge before they caught traction, but eventually they caught hold and he was on his way.

Back at his home, Cruthú pulled her head out from under her wing to greet him when he eased the door open and came inside. He smiled to see her settled on the bed within the curve of Shea's sleeping form, as she used to do when the vampire was his "guest."

He wondered what Shea would do if she knew how the bird snuck over there after she was asleep to snuggle with her. With a wild animal's intuition, Cruthú always knew right before she was about to awaken, and would return to her perch before Shea became fully conscious.

Jesse pulled his wet sweater over his head and off. The rain had returned on his way home and he'd gotten caught in the deluge on his way in. As fast as he was, it had soaked him through before he could get under cover. Quietly, he eased open his dresser drawer and got out a change of clothing—black fatigues and a black pullover. He picked up his boots, and with a whispered request to the raven to stay with Shea, let himself quietly out of the room.

He headed deeper underground through passageways he knew like the back of his hand. There was no need for lights. The darkness didn't frighten him. He felt at home in the shadows, much more so than in the light. It wasn't long before he heard water slapping against the stone sides of the underground spring, and a few seconds later he entered a small cavern.

With a wave of his hand, torches flared to life along the wall, illuminating the small room. The air was warm and damp, the water heated naturally from the spring below. This room was located directly beneath his own, and helped to keep the temperature regulated. It was the reason he had chosen it out of all the others Leeha had carved out of the mountain.

Removing the rest of his clothing, Jesse eased his body into the water and swam over to the far side with long, powerful strokes, until he encountered a natural shelf just beneath the surface of the water to sit on. There were bottles along the edge of the pool, and he picked one up and dumped some of the contents into his hand, then began to scrub himself clean, starting with his hair. It was getting long, and he made a mental note to take a knife to it in the near future.

A scene came to life in his mind: him sitting in a chair with a towel draped over his bare shoulders as Shea's long, elegant fingers ran through his hair, snipping off the ends. The peacefulness of it filled him with longing, but he would have to be patient.

Dipping beneath the surface, he rinsed his body and hair. A runoff carried the sudsy water away down to a trickling stream. He had no idea where it went. Maybe to hell.

When he was finished, he swam back over to the other side, intent on returning to Shea and getting some rest himself. He put his palms on the rocky edge, about to lift himself out, when something drew his eyes upward.

His lovely vampire stood in the entry to the cavern, wearing nothing but one of his black T-shirts. It hung to her mid-thigh, and he let himself enjoy the sight of her shapely legs. The dark color emphasized the paleness of her skin, her dark hair, and bright eyes. Cruthú was perched on her arm, her silky head cocked to the side as she stared at him with one black eye.

A lovely witch of the dark arts and her medium.

He eased his body back down into the water, unsurprised that she'd found him there. She was familiar with the cavern from her previous stay, although he had always given her privacy when she had used it to bathe. Yet, he didn't feel the need to do so now. "You should be sleeping, Shea."

She didn't argue with him. She didn't say anything. However, she didn't have to. He knew what she wanted. He could feel her need for him from where he was, and not only for his blood.

"Come inside. Would you like to join me?"

Her eyes flicked over the surface of the water, then to the steam rising from his skin in the flickering light of the torches. Still she didn't speak.

Jesse let her be. She was battling within herself again, and he didn't have to read her mind to know it. But she would have to be the one to decide, with no more coercion from him. After a moment, she took a hesitant step forward, then another.

He could make it easier for her by turning his back and swimming away, but he didn't. Instead, he followed her every movement. Jesse needed her to come to him willingly, and he wasn't going to pretend that the stakes were less than what they were by turning away. He didn't speak again until she was at the water's edge. "Would you like to feed?"

The change that overcame her was instant and furious.

Her posture tensed, changing into that of a hunter. Her lips pulled back from razor-sharp fangs that shot down into her mouth so fast they seemed to suddenly appear out of nowhere. Her features sharpened, the cheekbones becoming more prominent, the jaw sharper, and her green eyes glowed so bright they appeared almost white as they tracked his every tiny movement. Through it all, Cruthú perched on her arm, not so much as a feather ruffled in response.

Jesse, on the other hand, responded to the changes in his female in a way that was nearly as predatory. His entire body instantly hardened, his sex swelling painfully as a wave of lust burned through his blood until he had to grit his teeth so he didn't burst from the pool and drag her back in with him. His heart pounded and his breath left his lungs on a sharp exhale. The urge to expose the side of his throat nearly overwhelmed him. "Come here, Shea." He had to clear his throat to continue. "Come in with me."

"I can't." Even as she spoke the words, she squatted down next to his arm, her sharp gaze zeroing in on his pounding pulse.

In a flash of movement, Jesse raised his arm and brought the inside of his wrist down hard against the broken stone edging the pool, slashing the skin. Blood ran down his arm, a trickle of bright red that fed into the spring. "Come into the pool so you can feed."

The acoustics of the cavern made the preternatural growl appear to come at him from every direction at once. The small hairs stood up on the back of his neck, while at the same time he gripped his sex with his free hand to try to ease the discomfort of his erection. Shea flashed her fangs at him and cocked her head, her eyes glued to the wound.

Jesse waited with the patience of a thousand men, and he was soon rewarded when Shea lowered her arm so Cruthú could hop off and yanked his shirt over her head. She knelt before him like a goddess of old, bare as the day she was born: a vision of pale, seductive softness, accentuated by the shadows thrown from womanly curves. Her dark hair fell over her shoulder to cover one lovely breast, but as she leaned forward, the other swung free, begging for his mouth. Jesse had to clench his jaw to resist, but his eyes burned with hunger as they roved over every inch of her.

Lifting his wrist above her mouth, he turned it so the blood flowed sideways. It dripped between her lips and down the corner of her mouth.

Jesse watched, fascinated, as her tongue flicked out to catch his lifeblood. Something swelled with satisfaction within him, that he could provide for his female, that her very life depended on him.

Shea moaned, a sound halfway between pleasure and pain that tore at his heart. Swinging her legs out from beneath her, she dropped into the water beside him. "I want more."

Without even thinking about it, Jesse smashed his wrist down onto the rock again, reopening the wound until the blood flowed. But when he held his arm up, she wouldn't drink. "Shea?"

"I want more," she repeated. "I need more."

She wasn't speaking of her thirst anymore. Jesse heard the longing in her voice. It matched what was in his heart.

He dropped his arm beneath the surface. The water stung like holy hell, but he barely flinched, his entire being focused on the female in front of him. "I know. But until we figure out what's happened to you, this is the best we can do."

There was a flash of anger in her eyes just before she looked away. "It's not enough, Jesse."

She was angry with him for something he had no control over. "Shea, look at me."

After a slight pause, she did.

He fought the urge to pull back, away from her accusing glare. "You know that I had no part in this mating, right? What's happening between us, it's fate, not magic. I would never, ever, do anything to cause you any pain." The next part hurt like hell to say, but it was the truth. "If there was any way I could undo what has been done, I would do it. For you. So you wouldn't have to go through this. Please, believe me."

The anger slowly drained from her face, leaving only sorrow in its place. "I do. I'm sorry."

He let out the breath he'd been holding, but his mind spun. There had to be something more to this mating. Had to be a reason the fates had chosen *him*, of all creatures, to be her mate.

Could it be?

Shea held on to the edge of the pool. "What?"

"I want to touch you." His words made her eyes close, and when they opened again, he almost wished he'd kept his mouth shut, but he wouldn't take them back.

"I want you to touch me, too."

The words were spoken like a dirty secret. It angered

him. But now was not the time to deal with it. He shook his head. "No. I mean, I want to try actually touching you. Right now."

She pushed away from him so fast, a wave of water sloshed over the edge. "No! You can't!"

Refusing to give up, he eased toward her. "Just let me try, love."

"Jesse, no!" Her voice dropped to a whisper as tears filled her eyes. "Please. Don't."

"Shea, I only want to see if—"

She cut him off. "But I don't. I don't want to know. Because if you try and nothing has changed, it will only make it all worse." She shook her head. "I'm not ready to know."

He struggled to understand her logic. "But what if it doesn't?"

"It will."

"You can't know that."

Turning away, she dipped down under the water and came up on the other side of the pool near the runoff. Pushing her wet hair off her face, she wouldn't look at him.

"Shea…"

"No, Jesse. I can't. Not right now."

He sighed with disappointment, but gave her a nod. "All right." She wasn't speaking of physical pain. She was afraid of the emotional pain of finding out for sure that he, her own mate, couldn't touch her. "All right," he repeated. Turning away, he got out of the pool, and felt the weight of her stare travel over him. He dried off and got dressed, clenching his teeth as he pulled his pants on over his erection. Leaving his towel by the edge for his stubborn vampire, he called Cruthú to him and left Shea to her bath, going out into the passageway to wait for her.

Perhaps he would bide his time until she was sleeping, and then he would try. But he immediately tossed the thought aside. No. He wouldn't do that. If and when he tried his little experiment, he would do it with her permission. And only then. Because if he touched her and she didn't jerk away in agony, he didn't know if he could keep himself from ravishing her right then and there. And he would rather she was awake to enjoy it.

Shea joined him just a few minutes later, wearing his shirt again and still drying her hair with the towel. He didn't say anything, just turned and led the way back to his room. "Are you still thirsty?" he asked when they were nearly there. "I believe there's still some bagged blood around here somewhere I could find for you. It might help if you could manage to keep some down."

She made a face, but said, "That would be great. Thank you."

"I'll be right back." Leaving her in his room, he went to see what he could scrounge up.

A few minutes later, he returned with four bags of blood, the last of the stash.

Shea was sitting at the edge of the bed, near the foot in her favored spot. Like she was ready to run at the first opportunity. Seeing her there like that brought back memories of the last time she'd been there, and how beautiful he'd thought she was. She was even more so now, with her wet hair and bare legs and feet.

"This is all that is left," he told her as he set one bag beside her and put the rest on the table.

She picked up the bag, but didn't drink it. Only held it in her lap.

He cleared his throat. "I was thinking—"

Lifting her head, she waited for him to continue.

Setting Cruthú on her perch, he wondered why it was so hard for him to say what he wanted to say. "I wouldn't be opposed to you drinking from others." A fucking lie. "From women." Still lying. "If it would help ease the thirst. I don't want you to be malnourished." That, at least, was the truth. "I don't know that you will get enough, drinking from me this way."

Shea stared at him for a moment like he'd lost his mind, then she blinked a few times and looked down at the bagged blood in her lap. "Um...yeah. Okay." She shrugged. "I don't know that it will work, though. The others, when they would try to feed off someone who wasn't their...mate," She seemed to nearly choke on the word. "They couldn't do it. Not even Luukas."

The breath he didn't realize he'd been holding left him on a harsh exhale. "That's good, because everything I just said was a complete and utter lie. The thought of you being that intimate with anyone else drives me fucking insane."

The predatory stare was back. "I don't want to drink from anyone else. I've never tasted blood like yours before." After a tense few moments, she blinked, breaking the connection. Setting the blood on the nightstand, she stood up and got back under the covers.

Released from her hold, Jesse's knees very nearly gave

out. Seeing her at such a loss was ripping him up inside. He'd never seen her so disheartened, not even when he had imprisoned her in this very room. She'd always been full of life, which was maybe a strange thing to say about a vampire. But it was true. "Try to get some sleep," he told her. "I've arranged for a plane to take us to China. It leaves tonight."

She frowned up at him. "When did you do that?"

But Jesse just smiled. "Sleep, love. You'll need the energy."

"What about you? Where are you going to be?"

She looked down as she said it, her hands twisted in the bed sheet, trying to appear only vaguely curious. But he knew his answer was very important to her. "I'll be right here."

Her eyes closed, and without moving a muscle, Jesse dimmed the light with his mind until it was barely more than a nightlight. He went to the bed and pulled the blankets up over her, careful not to touch her skin. "We'll figure this out, Shea. Just give me a little time."

"You'd better hurry up," she told him quietly. "I won't last very long feeding the way we've been doing it. It needs to come straight from the vein, or it's no better than drinking from a bag. It only prolongs my inevitable death." Her eyes opened and met his. "Today is the first day of the rest of my short life."

Jesse's heart pounded in his chest. "What are you saying?"

"I'm saying I can't survive like this. So you'd better figure out how to fix what's wrong with me, and fast, or you're going to find yourself a widow in a few months—if we're lucky."

Jesse straightened as she closed her eyes again, horror freezing the blood in his veins.

What have I done?

CHAPTER 11

When Shea awoke, she didn't immediately open her eyes. Instead, she kept them closed, listening closely to her surroundings. Her breathing remained deep and steady, and she didn't so much as twitch a finger. As a vampire, *and* a female, it was a habit that had become so ingrained in her that she wasn't conscious of doing it anymore.

From the other side of the room, she heard someone at the table. No one needed to tell her it was Jesse. She knew the rhythm of his heart and lungs probably better than her own now. She'd spent many hours in this room all those weeks ago, listening to him when he thought she'd been asleep. But even if she hadn't heard him, she still would've known he was there. His scent filled the room, making her throat burn with thirst and her senses come alive. He smelled of nature and the dark, wicked sweetness of his blood. The lingering memory of his taste returned full force, and her fangs descended rapidly into her mouth, aching to pierce the taut skin of his throat.

"Would you like to feed?" His voice, low and husky, came to her ears.

Okay, maybe she wasn't as stealthy as she would like to believe.

"No," he replied to her unspoken thought. "You are. No one else would've known you were awake. Not even another vampire."

"Then how did you?" she asked as she rolled to her side and propped her head up on her elbow. "And I'm fine." She didn't bother to scold him for getting into her head again. He didn't seem to be able to help himself. And it would be his own fault if he heard something he didn't want to. "But, thank you," she added.

As usual, he dodged her question. "I'm going to take Cruthú outside to stretch her wings before we leave. I'll return in twenty minutes to get you. Will that be enough time for you to get ready?"

"It should be plenty, thank you." She started to sit up, and the blankets fell away. His eyes immediately dropped to her breasts. Though she still wore his shirt, the hunger in his stare made her feel naked. Her face heated, burning with embarrassment when she recalled what had happened earlier, and why he had such carnal knowledge of her body. Overcome with a sudden and irrational need for modesty, Shea pulled the blankets up to her chin and waited for him to leave.

"Twenty minutes." The words were practically spit at her from between clenched teeth as he stood to get the raven from her perch.

Shea knew her shame angered him, but she couldn't help it. It was wrong to want to be with him. He had done so many horrible things, not to her, but to others that she cared about deeply. And he made no apologies for any of it, so why should she feel bad for how she felt?

"Okay."

But he was gone before the word had left her mouth.

Breathing a deep sigh that was part disappointment and part relief, she rose from the bed. The soft material of his shirt felt abrasive on her hypersensitive skin. Shea was about to crawl out of her own skin with the blood lust, but the thought of gagging down the bagged blood did wonders for her cravings. Picking up her bag, she took it with her down to the cavern with the spring, where she brushed her teeth and washed up, allowing what was left of her thirst to fade before she got dressed.

When she finished, she picked up her stuff and seriously considered going home. But it was an impossible wish. There was no escaping the dark warlock now. Not if she wanted to live. The fates had spoken.

And if she never went home, would anyone really miss her? The only one who seemed to have an affinity for her at all, other than Jesse, was Dante. Yet, he had Laney now. He didn't need another female following him around.

Shea gave herself a mental kick. She was just being emotional. She was a Hunter, and a member of Luukas's council. Of course, they would miss her. Somehow, this would all work out. The guys would have to eventually understand, having mates of their own and knowing what the bloodlust was about. And besides, she'd only have to see him on the occasions she needed to feed. There were no tender feelings between them, only lust. It wasn't like she'd chosen Jesse on purpose.

That wasn't completely true. She may not have chosen him, but she had chosen to come here with him. And she had chosen to be intimate with him. And she'd also chosen to drink from him, knowing she had an unhealthy attraction to him. It was all right there in front of her.

Shea closed her eyes tight and tried to shake it off. It was too late for regrets.

Leaving the hot spring, Shea went back to Jesse's room and checked that she wasn't forgetting anything. No matter what happened, she had no intention of coming back here. Ever.

It was beginning to feel too much like home.

Spotting her hairband lying on the nightstand, she weaved her long hair into a thick braid and used it to tie off the end. Then she piled up the bags of blood in one arm, none of which she'd attempted to drink yet, and with a wrinkle of her nose and a sound of disgust, shoved them into her bag. With one last look around, she memorized the room that had brought her so much distress and so much pleasure.

The ride to the Vancouver International airport was tense and silent, other than an occasional click or croak coming from Cruthú in her cage behind them. Shea tried to keep her thoughts to blasé things, but by the way Jesse white-knuckled the steering wheel every few minutes, she wasn't very successful. They kept jumping back and forth between what the other Hunters were going to think when they found out, and how much she wanted to sink her fangs into the dangerous male beside her. Which would then flip her back to the shame she felt for lusting after the one who had caused so much pain and turmoil in their lives.

When they arrived at the airport, Jesse parked the SUV, but made no move to get out. He gripped the wheel and stared straight ahead. "You're killing me, Shea."

Fiddling with the seatbelt, she finally managed to get it off. "Maybe I shouldn't go. I should just go home." She wasn't saying it to be bitchy; she knew exactly how he felt because his shields were down. Perhaps it was his way of punishing her. Between the two of them, they were creating a tornado of emotion within the small space, and it was slowly ripping the skin off them both to expose the bloody guts churning beneath. The only one who appeared unaffected was Cruthú.

"You must come with me."

"Why?" The word tore from her throat.

"Because I'm going, and I don't know how long this will take or when I'll be back. And you need me."

"I only need your blood."

He finally turned his head to look at her, and raised one dark brow as if to say: *And your point is?*

Blowing a loose strand of hair from her face, she admitted to herself that she wasn't balking at the mission ahead of them, but at the thought of spending so much time alone with him. It was going to be pure torture.

His voice was gentle when he spoke. "You're not the only one feeling that way, Shea." Then a harsh laugh escaped him. "I've dreamt of you every night since I let you go, do you know that? I sat in that fucking room in that fucking mountain breathing your scent in my bed, and I ached to have you back with me. Physically *ached*. Only to find out I can't touch you when I finally convince myself to come after you. I can't *touch* you, Shea."

She stared at his profile, silent tears running unchecked down her cheeks.

"This can't be it for us, love. It can't be. Please, give me the chance to make it better. To fix it. I'll fix everything, I swear it to you."

"There are some things you can't fix, Jesse."

When he turned to her, his golden eyes blazed like her memories of the summer sun. "I can, and I will. For *you*." He raised a hand toward her face, before letting it fall onto the seat between them. "Please don't cry, Shea."

With a sniff, she looked away and wiped the tears from her cheeks. "I'm sorry." She didn't know what she was apologizing for.

"Come on, the plane is waiting."

Shea wiped at her face one last time, and got out of the vehicle. Jesse grabbed their two small bags in one hand and Cruthú's cage in the other, refusing Shea's offer of help. With a nod, he indicated for her to walk ahead of him.

Shea headed for the small, private jet, grateful the rain had tapered off. Out of the corner of her eye, she saw another plane that had just taxied to a stop a good distance away. But it barely registered until she heard Jesse's soft curse behind her, followed by a shout in the distance.

"Hey! Get the FUCK away from her!"

The voice was horrifyingly familiar, and was followed by the sound of boots pounding across the blacktop.

"Shea! Run!"

She closed her eyes, frozen with one foot on the step, praying to any god that would listen that she wasn't hearing what she thought she was hearing.

"What are you going to do, Shea?" Jesse's voice sounded right next to her ear. Before she could speak, he answered the question for her. "Let me strongly advise you against what just flashed through your mind. I really don't want to kill them."

Her breath froze in her lungs. "Please, don't hurt them."

"Then make them go away."

She felt more than saw him back away so she could get off the steps. When she was out of the way, Jesse took the stairs two at a time, depositing their bags and Cruthú inside, before coming back out to stand at the top of the stairs with his arms crossed over his chest, his attention completely focused on her.

As if in a dream, Shea turned to face the two vampires running toward her at little more than a fast, human pace. Even with the perceived danger she was in, they wouldn't do anything to blow their cover with so many human witnesses around unless they absolutely had to. Even if they wiped the memories of everyone there, there was always the chance that they could miss someone. She waited where she was until they were within hearing distance. "I'm fine. I'm not in any danger." She didn't raise her voice above its normal volume, knowing they would hear her.

Nikulas slowed to a lazy jog and then stopped a few

feet away from her, a look of bafflement distorting his Hollywood good looks. "Are you rigged or something?"

"What?"

"Are you rigged? Like with a bomb or something?"

Shea rolled her eyes and shook her head. "No. I just told you I'm not in any danger."

Aiden stood next to his friend, a similar expression on his striking face, but was quickly distracted by the sight of Jesse calmly waiting for her at the top of the stairs like a king overlooking his subjects.

Aiden's grey eyes burned silver-hot and a low growl reverberated through the air, raising the hair on the back of her neck. "What the bloody hell are you doing with this one, Shea?"

Shea couldn't blame Aiden for the hatred that spewed from his eyes. The demon that had been meant to possess her had ended up in Aiden, with Jesse's help. Yet, Aiden couldn't blame her for something she'd had no knowledge of at the time, and with Leeha dead, Jesse was the only left one left to take the brunt of his wrath.

Nikulas also glared at the male standing calmly at the top of the stairs. The muscles of his jaw tensed with rage, Aiden being his best friend and Luukas being his brother and all. Jesse had wronged them both beyond forgiveness. Shea was surprised they were even bothering to stop to hear her argument, though being out in the open, there was really no other option.

"I'm going with him," she told them, proud at how clear and strong her voice sounded.

"What the fuck for?" Nikulas never took his eyes from

his enemy. "Is he blackmailing you? Fucking with your head?"

She sighed. "No. He asked me to come with him. He gave me a choice. Jesse thinks he knows where the demon's blood is, and I'm going with him to try to stop them from getting it."

Aiden threw back his head and laughed, the sound somehow more terrifying than funny. "Stop them?" He laughed again before getting control of himself. "Don't be an idiot, Shea. The bloke doesn't want to stop them. He *created* them!"

"You don't have to do this, Shea," Nik told her. His attention flicked back to her, and he held out his hand. "Come on. Come with us."

She longed to be able to take that hand, but she couldn't even if she wanted to. Closing her eyes, she shook her head. "I'm going, Nik." Her voice was no more than a whisper. "Please tell Luukas that I'm sorry." She knew better than to ask that they not tell the Master Vampire. That wouldn't bode well for either of them when Luukas found out. And he would find out, eventually. As she turned and started up the short stairway, she couldn't bring herself to look up at the male that was silently waiting at the top for her. She couldn't stand to see the look of triumph on his face.

"Shea." Aiden's voice cut across the short distance between them like a shard of glass.

She stopped, but didn't turn around.

"If you go with this bloody wanker of your own free will, don't bother to come back."

Pain erupted in her chest, and she did spin around

then. Aiden's face was hard, his eyes clear of the shadows that preluded the presence of the demon inside of him. It was so unlike his usual self she could only stare in shock for a moment. She looked to Nik for help, but he crossed his arms over his chest, and averted his face in disgust.

"Come, Shea," Jesse ordered quietly, but not without sympathy.

Shea stared in horror at the two males she'd known for more years than she could count. They were her family, the only one she'd ever known since she'd been reborn. "You don't mean that," she whispered. "Aiden?"

They held their ground and refused to look at her, Aiden visibly containing his rage.

"Luukas won't agree with this," she burst out. "I'm a Hunter, and part of the council. I'm only trying to help."

"Shea," Jesse's tone held the hint of a question.

With the onslaught of their hatred burned into her heart, she turned and ran up the stairs.

CHAPTER 12

Jesse glanced at Shea's exquisite profile. After waiting for the sun to go down once they'd landed, they were now in the back of a cab, heading to the room he had booked at the New World Dalian Hotel not far from Zhongshan Square, where, from what Shea had told him in as few words as possible, the demons had dug up Aiden and Grace. He'd considered getting separate rooms, but had quickly discarded the idea. He wanted Shea to get used to being near him. No, he wanted more than that. Much, much more. This was not the time to give her space.

Of course, it would be easier if she would deign to speak to him. Or even look at him, for that matter.

After they'd boarded the jet back in Vancouver, Shea had found a group of seats as far away from him as possible and had spent the entire eighteen-hour trip staring out the window as they'd chased the night across the ocean. When the sun came up over the horizon, and the shades were pulled, she stared straight ahead.

Jesse watched her, fascinated with how completely still vampires could be when they didn't have to keep up the charade of blending in with the humans. She wouldn't respond to his inquiries or acknowledge his presence at all, really. Except to tell him to "please, shut up and go away" when he'd relocated to a seat across from her to get her to talk to him. He'd acquiesced to her request, knowing there was nowhere she could go, and had done his best to stay out of her head.

But he was impatient for her to accept what was, and more than once he cursed Leeha and her spite over Luukas' rejection. The spite that led her to torture not only the male who'd rejected her, but to force Keira to curse every vampire he was close to—namely his Hunters. He hadn't thought much of it at the time, but now it affected him personally.

Jesse glanced over at Shea again. He couldn't seem to help himself. His eyes were forever drawn to her stunning visage. Every tiny movement and nuance entranced him more than any spell she could weave. Weariness and sorrow sucked the animation from her features, and he knew she was not yet resigned to her new reality. He wished he could wave his magic wand and make it better for her. But this was something she was going to have to work through herself.

Now, Shea stood silently by his side as he got their key and paid for the room. Speaking perfect Mandarin, he thanked the desk clerk and headed to the elevators with their bags and Cruthú. He knew Shea followed him by the many sets of male eyes that couldn't seem to keep from staring at a point just behind him. As he understood their fascination, he couldn't really hold it against them. She was a contradiction in motion—soft and tough, elegant and awkward, alluring and terrifying.

And she was stunningly beautiful.

Setting Cruthú down on the muted, striped carpet, he used the key card to unlock their room and allowed Shea to go inside first. As expected, she dug in her heels and spoke to him for the first time since they'd left Vancouver.

"I'd like my own room."

"No. You're staying with me, where I can keep you safe."

She quirked one eyebrow. "I'm a vampire. I am perfectly capable of protecting myself."

Jesse wasn't going to stand in the hall arguing with her. Picking up Cruthú's cage, he left her there and went into the room, propping the door open with her bag. Setting the raven on the dresser and his bag on one of the double beds, he went over to the window to check that it had sufficient curtains to block out the daytime sun. As a precaution, he had asked for a north facing room. It wasn't much, but at least the rays wouldn't shine directly in the window.

Satisfied with the window covering, he moved his bag to the bed closest to it and went over to open the cage so Cruthú could get out. She flew up to his shoulder with a croak of thanks, and clicked in his ear.

"I know. It was a long trip. I'm very sorry I kept you in there so long," he murmured as he stroked her silky feathers. He heard the door click shut, but resisted the urge to look in that direction. He knew it was hard for Shea to give in; he wouldn't make a big deal about it. She set her own bag on the nearest bed and went into the bathroom. He heard the water come on in the sink.

When she came out, she sat down and traced the pattern on the white comforter with one elegant fingertip. Jesse gave her the time to work out what she wanted to say.

"There are two beds."

It amused him that the beds were the first things she was worried about. She appeared unable to decide if she was happy about their sleeping arrangement, or disappointed. He tried to hide his smile, but was unsuccessful. So, he made a pretense of setting Cruthú on the sitting chair by the window and bent down to unpack his things. "Of course. I want to keep you near, Shea. However, I wouldn't want to cause you pain, even accidentally, as we sleep. And I am much more comfortable in a bed than trying to sleep in a chair." Opening one of the dresser drawers, he started putting his things away.

She rubbed her forehead with her fingertips.

"I only need the drawers on this side." He indicated which ones with a nod, as his hands were full of clothes. "You're welcome to use the rest."

"I normally just live out of my bag when I travel," she told him.

A survivor through and through. Always ready to run. Why was he not surprised? "Well, if you change your mind, there's plenty of room."

"Thank you."

Her voice cracked, and Jesse spun around on his heel, clothes forgotten. "Shea? What is it?"

She shook her head.

Angry that she still refused to open up to him, he helped himself to her thoughts, and quickly got the gist of what was upsetting her.

Basically, everything. The entire situation.

"I wish you would talk to me, Shea. Please talk to me."

But she just looked away.

Patience. He needed to have patience. "I'm going to take a quick shower. I would ask that you not leave this room." Once he'd ascertained that she wasn't going anywhere, he went into the bathroom. Leaving the door cracked open just enough that he would see her if she ignored his request, he quickly and efficiently got cleaned up and dressed in black cargo pants and a forest green, short-sleeved pullover. When he came out, Shea was still sitting right where he had left her. And she was still worrying over things that were out of her control. It wouldn't solve anything.

The remainder of his unpacking forgotten, he went to sit near her. She stiffened—her automatic response whenever he got too close, it seemed—but didn't move away. Jesse had the passing thought that if he were a normal male without his many abilities, he would be quite convinced that this female wanted absolutely nothing to do with him. Luckily, he was not a normal male, so he knew exactly what was upsetting her.

"Shea, I will fix this between us. And the others will come around. You'll see. They're just angry right now, and striking out." He supposed he would do the same, were the situation reversed. "And understandably so."

She looked up at him then, and her green eyes were shining with unshed tears. "I hope you're right."

"I am," he told her with maybe a little too much confidence.

One corner of her mouth turned up in the barest hint of a smile. Then she sniffed and took a breath. "So, what do we do now?"

"Now, we go find out the location of the demon's blood. But first"—he stopped her from getting up—"we feed you."

At his words, she immediately recoiled and shook her head. "No. I'm fine."

But Jesse was adamant. "You're not fine, Shea. You're pale and shaky, and your lovely eyes are beginning to look too large for your face. You need to feed." His tone would brook no argument, and for once, she didn't push it.

"I brought the bags. I'll drink one of those."

His heart dropped, and he had to quickly hide his disappointment. But he pushed aside his own feelings of rejection, happy that she would be getting some nutrients, even if he wasn't the one providing for her. Giving her a nod, he left her to her meal and went to clean Cruthú's cage. He had eaten on the plane. It would hold him over until he could find a store to stock the room.

"So, how are you paying for all of this?"

At least his vampire was still talking to him. This was good. "I am quite wealthy," he said without preamble. He wasn't bragging, but said it as a statement of fact. "Vampires aren't the only ones who know how to work the system." Setting the last few things inside, he shut the drawer and turned to Shea just as she tipped a bag of blood up to her mouth.

Her face screwed up in disgust, but she managed to take a few swallows. "Oh my gods, that's disgusting."

He eyed her steadily, his mouth twitching only slightly as he said, "I'd be more than happy to slit my wrist for you."

Shea glanced down at the wounds from the day before. They were still healing, and she quickly looked away. She shook her head, holding up the bag in her hand with a grimace. "I'll manage with this. It's practically the same thing."

The mood for teasing left. "You'll have to drink from me again eventually, Shea. You know this as well as I do. I will find a way to cease the pain it causes you to touch me, if it even exists. The substance in that bag won't sustain you for long."

"No, but it will do for now."

"Until you can bring yourself to deal with the shame of being mated to me? Or until you allow the thirst to kill you?"

"Jesse—"

But he held up a hand, palm out. "No. Don't bother. I need to make a call. Shower if you'd like. I'll wait for you downstairs in the lobby. Do not leave the hotel without me." Leaving one of the key cards on the bed next to her, he pocketed the other and left the room, silently telling Cruthú that he would be back soon.

One day soon, his vampire would be begging for his lifeblood, and with a solemn heart, he knew that he would give it to her without hesitation. He would give her anything.

Except the demon blood.

Punching the button to the elevator, he whipped out his cell phone just as it started to ring. "I just arrived, and will be going soon," he told the creature on the other end of the line. "I have someone with me. She is not to be harmed in any way, shape, or form, or the deal is off." Hanging up, he put the phone back in his pocket just as the elevator doors opened.

Jesse stepped inside. As the doors slid closed, he let his shoulders slump with exhaustion as his head fell forward, chin resting on his chest.

CHAPTER 13

Mammot, or Steven, as he now liked to be called, punched the button on his cell phone, ending the call with the warlock. As he stuck it back in his pocket, he glanced down at the vials of blood laid out on the table before him: hundreds of them, wrapped in cloth to protect them. The dark one would not be finding this blood, nor would he be bringing that bitch anywhere near it.

The monks had taken good care of it, updating the containers that held it as more modern material became available. Pulling the phone out again, he pushed the pattern of numbers he'd memorized a few weeks before. He held it close to his ear, but not touching, as the skin in this vessel was apt to break off at the slightest provocation.

"Do you have the blood?" The voice at the other end of the line sounded bored.

"I do," Steven told him. "It was exactly where you said it would be. And I did your little spell before we left."

"Did it work?"

"Yes."

"Perfect. How soon will you be on a flight?"

Steven leaned back in his chair and pulled aside the ugly curtain. He looked out the window of his borrowed apartment, watching the tourists dodge the businessmen as they hustled up and down the street. The sun peeked out from behind the clouds, hitting his fingers with a beam of sunlight. They promptly began to smoke.

He dropped the curtain with a curse, shutting out the daylight and rubbing the back of his hand on his jeans. These fucking bodies. They may last longer than the humans they possess, but being unable to go out in the sunlight was not conducive to getting things done. "That might be an issue."

"Why is that? You don't need money."

"No, that's not it. But we've been in these bodies for a long time. And they're beginning to smell. Even if we broke up into smaller groups, the sight of us walking through a crowded airport will be sure to cause panic with the humans, which in turn will alert the vampires—and the warlock—to our exact location."

There was a great sigh on the other end of the phone. "I will send a plane. Get the others together and meet it on the tarmac. I'll tell you exactly where after it has landed. Don't go into the building. We wouldn't want to upset the human's delicate sensibilities."

"What of the warlock?"

"Play along with him. Don't give him any reason to

think you're not going to carry through with your end of the deal. Once you are back here and returned to your original forms, and your power, I will deal with him—once I'm certain you don't plan to fuck *me* over as well."

Steven picked up a vial, rolling it between his fingers. "You don't have to worry about that. We want the same thing. There is no reason for me to betray you."

"Be sure to remember that. I'll call you when the plane lands." The connection cut off.

The blood spun within the vial, coating the clear sides before running down to join the whole.

CHAPTER 14

Shea found Jesse in the bar just off the lobby. He didn't acknowledge her when she sat down one stool away from him, but she knew he was more than aware of her presence, just as she was of his. She stared at his strong profile. The neon lights cast shadows in the hollows of his cheeks, making them appear sharper than normal. "I'm not going to apologize," she told him.

Pushing away the glass in front of him, he gave her a tight smile. "I wouldn't expect you to, Shea. You can't help the way you feel." He stood up. "Are you ready to go?"

"Don't you want to finish your drink?" There was a good two fingers of amber liquid left. Whiskey, from the smell of it. This was the second time she'd found him with an untouched drink in front of him.

"No. I'm good. We need to go."

Shea slid off the stool. "Where are we going?"

The tense smile was back. "To pay our respects to a certain group of monks."

"Are they dead?"

"Not yet." Extending an arm to the side, he indicated for her to go before him. "There's a rental car waiting in front of the hotel," he told her.

Shea headed out the front doors with the warlock close on her heels, but she waited until they were alone in the car before she asked the question that was burning in her mind. "You're going to kill them? The humans we're going to see?"

"Only if they don't give me what I want."

"The location of the demon's blood."

"Yes."

A horrifying thought occurred to her. "Do you expect me to help you? They're innocent humans, and monks are male. I wouldn't be able to touch them, even if I wanted to. Which I don't."

He gave her a sideways look. "Ridding ourselves of a few human lives is a small sacrifice to make to save the world."

"But we don't have to hurt them. You can read their minds, and I can make them forget we were ever there. There's no need for violence."

"A pacifist vampire? What are the odds?"

It took her a moment to realize that he had gotten over his pique and was teasing her. "They're holy men," was all she said.

She felt Jesse's eyes on her, but didn't feel the need to elaborate. It's not that she was religious. The gods knew, after all she'd been through in her life, she didn't believe there was any higher power looking out for her. Yet, she felt an affinity with others who lived a holy life. And monks believed all life was important, even the tiniest insect.

Perhaps they would even see the value in a deranged existence such as hers.

Shea turned away to stare out the window. He could make fun of her all he wanted, she wasn't killing anyone just for the sake of doing so. So, instead of arguing more, she tried to get her bearings as to where they were. If she remembered correctly from the last time she was here, it looked like they were just leaving the residential areas. The city had changed a lot over the years, but the monk's location had not. "Isn't the Temple like, a few days drive from here?"

"We're not going to the main temple. There's a small group just outside of town at a smaller temple near Dalian Xijiao National Forest Park. They're the ones we're going to see."

"Oh."

He was quiet for a few seconds, and out of curiosity, she tried to open herself up to what he was feeling. But if he was experiencing any nervousness or disquiet of any kind, he was blocking it from her again. She'd never met anyone who could do that. It was disquieting.

"Or maybe I'm just not nervous," he responded to her unspoken thought. "May I ask you something?" he added before she could scold him for reading her mind—again.

"Sure. But I'm not promising I'm going to answer you."

He smirked a bit at that. "Fair enough. What was your life like before you became a vampire?"

"My life?"

"Yes. I'd like you to tell me about your human life."

"I was a lady's maid, for a very rich and spoiled lady in London." And she was. At least for a little while.

He glanced at her with a small frown. "You don't sound like a Londoner."

"That's because I was born in France."

"Ah, yes. Makes more sense. You still have a slight accent."

Shea would swear she had lost her accent a lifetime ago. As a matter of fact, she tried very hard not to sound French. But perhaps she was not as successful as she believed.

"Did you like being a lady's maid?"

"I didn't like or dislike it. It was what it was. My employer was kind, and I was grateful for the income."

"Why did Luukas turn you?"

Memories, long forgotten, flashed through her mind at warp speed. Lost in the nostalgia of times past, she simply said, "Because I asked him to."

Jesse kept his voice even and his foot easy on the gas pedal, as though he knew how fragile her attention was. "Why would you ask something like that?"

"So I could kill her." The words were out before Shea realized she'd spoken them aloud. Frowning, she looked over at Jesse, but he was staring straight ahead.

"Kill who?" He sounded neither shocked nor horrified, just genuinely curious. His eyes went back and forth between Shea and the road as he waited for her answer.

"The lady I served."

"And did you?"

"Yes."

"Are you glad?"

She took a deep breath, and looked directly into his stunning golden eyes. "Yes," she said. "I am. It had to be done." His face wavered before her. Shea blinked hard, and felt a single tear slide down her cheek.

He searched her expression, and then he nodded once. "Good." Looking forward again, he added, "We're almost there."

Shea directed her attention back to the road. She'd never told anyone that before. Not even Luukas. The Master Vampire had turned her because she'd told him she was sick and pleaded with him to save her. One taste of her blood and Luukas had quickly figured out that she was lying. However, to this day, he'd never questioned her choice.

Yet, it was surprisingly easy to share that most intimate detail of herself with Jesse. "She was my sister." The words came out with no coercion.

Jesse nodded, as if he had known this all along. And perhaps he had and just wanted to see if she would tell him. Fool that she was, she'd played right into it.

"You're wrong. I didn't know," he said softly. "Not until just now."

She'd had enough. "Get the fuck out of my head," she told him through clenched teeth.

"Shea...." He paused, inhaling a quick breath and releasing it again. "I'm sorry. You're right. I haven't respected your wishes, and I apologize." He paused, and when he spoke again, his words were rushed, like he didn't want to say them but felt that he needed to. "It's hard for me to be patient, to feel any kind of separation from you, even if it's simply something you don't want me to know." One side of his mouth lifted in a small smile. "Particularly if it's something you don't want me to know." He glanced over at her. "I'm so used to doing it, I don't realize that I am at times. With the company I'm used to keeping, it was necessary for my survival to know what others were thinking. I promise I'll try to stop…for you."

She sighed audibly, feeling like a complete bitch. "Jesse, I just—" She trailed off, unsure how to say what she wanted to say, or even what it was.

"I know. It's all right."

No more was said, for they turned down a gravel road that discouraged conversation, and soon arrived at their destination. The temple at the edge of the forest was surrounded by leafy trees, the stones weathered and covered with creeping vines, but alive with the ancient spirits of the monks who had come before. A light mist blocked the light from the torches burning on either side of the doorway, and made the entire scene dreamy and mystical. Shea kept her voice to a whisper, afraid of disturbing the peace and solitude of the place. "Are they expecting us?"

"No."

"Then how do you know they're here?"

Jesse gave her a look that seemed to say, "You really need to ask me that?" then got out of the car.

With another quick look around, Shea joined him.

Walking with a confidence she didn't feel, she followed him to the entryway and into the interior. The first room they arrived in was dark, only the dim light from the torches outside coming through the doorway to give the faintest illumination. Being a vampire, Shea could still see quite well, but there wasn't much to see. The stone floor and walls were barren, except for a table-like structure toward the back.

Stopping in the middle of the empty room, Jesse called, "Come out, come out wherever you are!" He repeated the words in Chinese.

"Maybe no one is here," Shea said when she heard no sounds of alarm, and no one came running.

"They're here." Walking toward the back of the room, he ran one finger along the top of the table. Holding it up, he showed her the lack of dirt or dust.

"Mystical cleaning sprites?" she suggested.

He smiled at her little joke, an honest and open smile that made the skin crinkle around his eyes and laugh lines appear on his cheeks, and Shea couldn't tear her eyes away from the sight. His eyes roved over her face and landed on her parted lips. They stayed there, his amusement fading, replaced with the scent of his lust for her.

Shea's breath caught in her lungs and she turned away, uncomfortable with the intensity of his attention.

"I know you're here!" Jesse shouted a few seconds later. "Don't make me come find you."

She was just about to suggest that maybe, quite possibly, he had been wrong this time, when a slight movement caught her attention out of the corner of her eye. Turning her head, she saw a man. He stood serenely with his hands tucked into his sleeves, and did not seem at all surprised by the sight of unexpected visitors. Wearing not the red and yellow robes she was used to seeing on the monks in town, but dark gray with a white sash, he was nonetheless still an impressive figure. Shea glanced quickly around, wondering how he'd gotten into the room without her seeing him, as there was only the one doorway and he was standing against the far wall.

"What can I help you with?" he asked in perfect English.

"Oh, good," Jesse responded. "You're here."

The monk flicked his eyes over to Shea, then back to Jesse. If he knew that she wasn't human anymore, he gave no indication of it. "Do you need assistance?"

Though it was obvious he was asking if they're car broke down or some such business, Jesse answered with the affirmative.

"Yes, actually we do. I'm here for the location of the blood. The demon blood," he clarified.

A slight pause was the only indication that the monk was surprised by the request. "I'm sure I do not know what you mean." He didn't move from his spot by the wall, or show any type of discomfort or panic.

"I think you do. Also, I promised this stunning female that I would not kill you for it. Please don't make me rescind that promise."

Brown eyes held steady as they met Jesse's golden gaze. The monk was obviously taking his measure, and his next words confirmed that he had correctly determined the type of male he was dealing with, and that it would do no good to lie. "I cannot tell you the location. I have made a vow that cannot be broken."

Jesse sighed, crossed his arms over his chest, and regarded the monk. It didn't take him long to decide his next move. Turning to Shea, he cocked one eyebrow. "I gave him a chance."

Her heart skipped in her chest. "You promised."

His features grew softer as he looked at her. "So I did." Dropping his arms back down to his sides, he stalked the monk with long strides that quickly took him across the stone floor. Leaning down until they were face to face, he said, "Tell me the location of the blood, or I will retrieve it on my own. And being that I'm certain it's buried deep within the gray matter of your brain behind lock and key, I cannot guarantee the condition you'll be in when I'm finished."

"Jesse."

He held up one hand, asking for her silence.

The monk stared up at him impassively.

"All right, then," Jesse told him. He glanced back over his shoulder at Shea. "I'm sorry, love. But we don't have time for this. I have to do what I have to do. I promise I will try my best to leave him intact."

Shea watched as Jesse gave the monk his full attention. She wasn't overly concerned at first; Jesse read her mind all the time. It didn't hurt her. However, she soon realized that there were different ways of sucking out one's thoughts.

Jesse's head tilted to the side as he focused on the monk, and soon the male's eyes grew wide, then rolled back in his head. She heard a clacking noise, and realized his teeth were chattering, though there was no chill in the air. His jaw slammed together, and his head fell forward. The entire process took less than a few seconds.

"Got it," Jesse announced. Striding back over to Shea, he left the monk standing by the wall, his eyes blank and a trickle of drool running down his chin. When he reached her, he appeared sincerely sorry as he said, "I tried to harm him as little as possible, I swear it. But these men are masters at the art of mind control, and this was a secret he didn't want anyone to find."

Sorrow and anger filled her as she watched the stoic male slide down the wall to the floor. His robe pooled about his shrunken body. "What will become of him?"

"He may recover somewhat, enough to live a simple life. I don't believe it's necessary to remove his memories of us, however. There's nothing left."

He was so matter of fact, so cold about it all. Filled with disgust for what he'd just done, Shea turned away and headed back out to the car.

Jesse caught up to her quickly. "And there is that look again."

She didn't respond. She had nothing to say to him.

With a burst of speed, he got in front of her, appearing so fast that Shea had no choice but to stop. She tried to go around him, but he threw out his arms.

"Get out of my way," she snarled.

But though he lowered his arms, his body remained tense and alert, ready to cut off any means of her escape. "Shea, it had to be done. It was necessary."

"Not like that," she gritted out.

"Yes. Exactly like that. There was no time to try to cajole the location from him. *We have no time.* The demons have all the clues. This monk is one of the few who are still alive with the knowledge of the location. We'll be lucky if they haven't already been here and have gotten to their original blood before we ever make it there. It may already be too late."

"Then why are we even here?" She threw up her arms. "Why coerce me into coming on this trip with the false hope of stopping them?"

His chin rose as his teeth clamped together. "There is still a chance. If we hurry."

She stared him down. "Then what are we waiting for? This is why I came with you. The *only* reason." Her tone was sarcastic.

"Shea."

This time when she walked around him, he didn't stop her.

CHAPTER 15

Nikulas was not looking forward to this conversation. Not one fucking bit.

He and Aiden were supposed to be out searching for pods of demon-possessed vampires running amok. But instead, they were back in Seattle, gearing up to tell Luukas that one of his Hunters was consorting with his biggest enemy behind his back.

At least he assumed it was behind his back. No, no. There was no fucking way Luukas had given Shea his blessing to go hang out with that fucking warlock. Not after what that son of a bitch had done to him.

"Stop it, mate. Your face gets all wonky when you do that. I can practically see the smoke coming out of your ears. You're going to burn out the few brain cells you have left."

Nik looked at his best friend in disbelief. "How can you fucking joke around at a time like this?"

"Who's joking?" Aiden said, then knocked on Luukas's

apartment door.

Rolling his eyes, Nik listened for his brother or Keira to come to the door. But the footsteps that sounded were neither of them, but rather Emma's, his mate. And they sounded...off. Something was wrong. Pushing Aiden out of the way, he kicked the door in, busting the lock and crumbling the door jam.

Emma slid to a stop just out of the way of the door, putting her hands on her hips and scowling at the two males as they burst into the apartment. "Really, Nik. You've gotta stop destroying your brother's doors."

But even though she was scolding him with a hint of amusement, he could see the strain around her eyes. He reached her in two long strides. Scooping her up into his arms, he held her tight against his chest, and breathed a sigh of relief when she wrapped her arms around his neck. "I've missed you, sweetheart."

"I've missed you, too, blood sucker."

He laughed at her reference to when they'd first met, but immediately got serious again. "What's wrong? What's going on?"

"And where is Grace?" Aiden squeezed past them until he could see the entire apartment. He lifted his chin and smelled the air. "She's not here. Where is she?"

Emma tried to pull away, and Nik released her with more than a little reluctance. "Grace is fine. She went to your place to feed Mojo."

Turning on his heel and telling them, "I'll be back," Aiden stepped over the broken door and headed to the stairs, bypassing the elevator.

Once he was gone, Nik turned back to the love of his

life. Taking her small face in his hands, he pressed a kiss to the freckles on her nose. "Now, please tell me what's going on, Em, before I imagine the worst and lose my fucking mind."

She gave him a sad smile. "It's Luukas."

His breath froze in his lungs. "What's happened?"

Emma shook her head, her eyes filling with worried tears. "We're not really sure. But something's wrong with him. He's been getting weaker and weaker since you've been gone. Keira has given him as much blood as she dares, sometimes forcing it upon him, and making sure he gets enough rest, but nothing is helping. It's like he's"—she gave a little shrug—"fading away."

Nik pressed the heels of his hands over his eyes. "It's the fucking demons."

"The demons?"

He dropped his arms back down to his sides. "Well, not the demons, but the bodies they're possessing. The bodies are rotting, slowly."

Comprehension lit her hazel eyes. "And they're the bodies of vampires that Luuk created. Oh, my God." She stared up at Nik in horror. "He's weakening because his creations are dying."

"Yeah." Nik turned away, fists clenched at his sides. "Losing one or two here and there he can take. It would only set him back a day or so. Losing fifty at once—" He couldn't imagine any kind of life without his overbearing older brother. "Fuck."

"What do we do?" Emma wrapped her arms around her middle. "Nik? What do we do?"

Wandering over to the window, Nikulas stared out at

the lights of downtown Seattle. But he wasn't really seeing the beauty of the city that had been their home for many years now. His jaw ached, and he realized he was grinding his teeth. He knew what they needed to do. If they didn't stop those motherfuckers, he was going to lose his brother...and his best friend. Aiden was old and strong, and perhaps his body was lasting longer because his demon preferred to stay dormant, but soon, even he would be a walking, rotting corpse. "We have to send them back to hell. And we need to do it five fucking minutes ago. We're running out of time."

He felt Emma's hand on his back, and her touch gave him strength, as it always did. Reaching back, he caught her hand in his and pulled it around to kiss the pulse on her inner wrist, breathing in the sweet scent of her.

"Go see your brother," she told him. Then her forehead wrinkled up in that adorable way it did. "Wait. Why are you even here? I thought you and Aiden were going to be gone another three days, at least."

Shit. He'd nearly forgotten. "Shea is hanging out with that bastard warlock. We came home to tell Luukas." It took him a minute to notice that his female wasn't showing the sufficient amount of surprise he would expect from such a pronouncement. Suddenly, she had his full attention. "Emma? Do you know something that I don't?"

"No. Well, not really. Just that that explains why we saw Shea ducking down into the passenger seat of an SUV the other day. Grace and I didn't recognize the guy who was driving."

"And you didn't bother to tell anyone?"

She gave that little shrug again. "We just figured she didn't want us giving her the third degree when she got home."

He stared at the woman he loved more than anything in this world or the next, and wondered if he'd ever understand the female mind.

"Nikulas? What are you doing here? Did you find something?"

Nik's eyes locked with Emma's before he turned to find his brother leaning against the doorjamb of his bedroom. He looked tired and thin, but his grey eyes were still as sharp as ever. And as they spotted the damage to the front door, Nik almost wished they weren't.

"What the fuck is it with you and my doors?"

Nik ran a hand through his blond hair. "Yeah, sorry about that." He didn't bother telling his brother that he'd done it because he knew something was wrong. It wouldn't make anyone feel better to point out the obvious. "I'll have it fixed first thing."

"You'd better." Luukas made his way over to one of the overstuffed chairs and sat down. "Now tell me what's going on. Why are you back? And where's Aiden?"

"I'll just go hang out with Keira," Emma told him, rising on her tiptoes to give him a quick kiss on his jaw. "Come get me when you're done."

He promised her he would, and then he joined his brother, taking the chair on the opposite side of the coffee table. Leaning forward, he rested his elbows on his thighs and laced his fingers together. How to tell Luuk what was going on....

"Shea is with that fucking warlock." There. That was subtle.

The temperature in the room suddenly dropped at least fifteen degrees, yet Luukas's expression didn't change one iota. "I'm sorry. I don't think I heard you correctly. Would you please repeat that?"

"You heard correctly," Nik assured him. "Aiden and I just saw them at the airport in Vancouver, getting onto a private jet."

Luukas sat back in his chair. Other than the white-knuckled grip he had on the armrests, no one would be able to tell how upset he was if they didn't know him. But Nik knew him almost as well as he knew himself, and he knew his brother was hanging on by a thread. "He found her somehow, and is forcing her to go with him."

Nik was shaking his head before Luuk finished the sentence. "No, Luuk. She was there of her own free will."

"But how can you be sure of this?"

"Because we spoke to her. I tried to get her to come with us, and she wouldn't. We watched her get onto the plane without any coercion."

Luuk burst up from his chair with a show of speed that was surprising, considering his appearance. He started pacing back and forth in front of the floor-to-ceiling window, moving so fast a human wouldn't be able to track him. "He must be blackmailing her. Forcing her to go with him. Shea would not betray me so readily."

"I don't think so, bro."

"But you don't know for certain."

"No, but I know what I saw. And I'm telling you she was not being forced onto that plane. No one can force

Shea to do anything she doesn't want to do, not without going to extreme lengths."

"But you don't know that for certain," Luukas insisted.

"No, but—"

"You don't *know*," he emphasized.

Nikulas took a deep breath and gave in. "No. I don't know for sure."

Luukas stopped pacing. With his back to the room, he stared out the window much as Nik had done just moments before. "I'm not going to condemn her without proof."

"I understand." Nik rose to go. "I just wanted to let you know what was going on."

"Thank you," his brother told him.

But Nik could already tell he was losing him. Fuck. Maybe he shouldn't have said anything, and just handled it himself. He thought Luukas was getting better after the years of hell he'd been through, but maybe this reminder was too much for him.

"I'm gonna get Em and go."

There was no response.

He'd better get Keira out here. She was the only one who could pull Luukas from the depths of his own hell once the terrors engulfed him.

CHAPTER 16

Jesse gripped the steering wheel of the rental car, trying to think of something he could say to bridge this gap between him and Shea. But nothing came immediately to mind.

Dammit! He needed more time. More time to bond her to him. More time to make her understand what it was he had to do, and why.

But they were out of time.

"Where are we going?" Her tense voice broke through the silence. It was the first time she'd spoken since they'd left the temple.

"To the airport. We're flying to Shaolin Temple, or more specifically, to the Forest of the Dagobas."

"Is that where the blood is hidden?"

"Yes. The clues show different dagobas throughout the Forest. We must find them, and where the path to each connects. Where they come together. That's where the blood is buried."

"And what are we going to do with it once we find it?"

How to answer that without giving it away too soon? "What we have to do."

She fell back into her brooding silence, but not for long. "What about Cruthú?"

Jesse fought back a smile. Much as Shea denied it, she was as fond of the raven as the bird was of her. "She'll be fine. I paid the hotel an obscene amount of money to take good care of her until we get back."

He felt Shea's eyes on him, but she said nothing else, eventually turning away and gazing out the window again for the remainder of the trip.

Leaving the car at the rental place at the airport, he got them both through security without any issues and then left Shea seated in a waiting area while he confirmed the jet would be ready. While the pilot ensured all checks were done, he turned around and leaned back against the counter, ignoring the looks he received from both females and males as they rushed to their gates. His attention was completely taken by the female waiting for him in a seat overlooking the concourse.

She sat completely still, not fidgeting as humans often did. The lack of color in her clothing did nothing to deter from her beauty—just the opposite, in fact. It only made one focus on her striking features. Her long, dark hair was pulled away from her face. The thick braid lay over one shoulder, and contrasted beautifully against her pale throat and cheek. Again, he ached to touch that porcelain skin. He would bet anything that it was as soft and smooth as silk.

As Jesse watched, a young human man edged closer to her, his eyes hungry as they went from her face to her chest and back, and Jesse felt a flash of heat go through him. It took him a moment to realize it was possessiveness.

As the boy eased closer, Jesse pushed himself away from the counter and went to stand directly behind Shea. He said not a word, but knew the moment she sensed his presence by the sudden alertness of her muscles, the flush that stole across her chest, and the way her body seemed to sway toward him while barely moving at all.

The young male's lips parted and his pupil's dilated as he observed the changes in her. Narrowing his eyes, Jesse shot daggers at this one who dared to so much as *look* at his female with such thoughts in his head. The only thing that saved the young male at all was that his thoughts were completely without menace toward her, but only the natural attraction of boy to girl, human to vampire.

Keeping one eye on the young male, Jesse leaned down as close as he dared to whisper in Shea's ear. "Come, Shea. The jet should be ready." A rush of satisfaction cooled his ire as the male finally took notice of him, his eyes widening as he took a step back. Jesse supposed he probably shouldn't have thrown that particular threat into the male's head, but what fun would that be? As the human retreated a bit more, Jesse's attention went back to the female who had claimed him as her own.

Shea closed her eyes for a split second, and as Jesse straightened, he noticed goose bumps along her skin. With a tight smile at the young human, who couldn't seem to help but linger by the windows, he waited while Shea rose gracefully from her seat and walked around the row of seats to join him. As she headed toward their gate, Jesse took his place behind her, blocking the human's view.

He was acting no better than an adolescent, but he couldn't seem to help himself. It frustrated him to no end that he couldn't show the world that she was his the normal way: holding her hand, touching her arm, a sweet kiss. But this is what it would have to be until he found a way to reverse the curse.

"You're acting like a dog."

Jesse dropped his eyes to the seductive sway of Shea's hips as she walked in front of him. "A dog?" She was absolutely right. But he didn't have to let her know he agreed with her.

"Why don't you just piss on me and get it over with?"

"Don't tempt me, love. How else will everyone know that your vampire blood has claimed me as yours?" That remark was a bit snide, but Jesse couldn't help it. After all, the only reason he was acting this way was because she had decided he was her mate.

He studiously ignored the little voice in his head that was trying to remind him that *he* had claimed *her* the moment he'd first seen her.

They arrived at the door that would lead them out to the concourse and the private jet that would take them to the temple. Shea stood stiffly, waiting for the attendant to swipe her badge and allow them access.

Although he had promised to try to resist, Jesse touched his mind to hers, just briefly. The corners of his mouth tipped up when he heard her silently tell him, quite distinctly, to go to hell. She was becoming more sensitive to him, beginning to sense when he was in her thoughts. Jesse could only imagine the level of intimacy they would obtain if...no, not if—*when*...physical contact was added to the mix.

Shea breathed an audible sigh of relief when the door opened and they could go out to the jet. As expected, the attendant didn't ask to see IDs or boarding passes, and they left the terminal without any deterrents to stop them.

Twenty minutes later, they were strapped into their plush leather seats across the aisle from each other as the jet taxied down the runway. Leaning back in his seat, Jesse folded his hands across his stomach and closed his eyes. His thoughts jumped around from what he needed to do, and what his heart wanted him to do.

Jesse knew if he carried through with his plans as they were, there was a very good chance that he would lose Shea forever, fated mate or not. It wouldn't surprise him at all if she chose starvation and death over being with a liar and a traitor.

He couldn't say that he would blame her, but giving up his vampire was not an option for him. And neither was giving up what he had worked so hard for, risked his own life for, when he was so very close to achieving that end.

There was a slim chance she would understand. If she gave him the chance to explain his reasoning—and they were damn good reasons—and if he could do so in a way that would make her understand *why* it had to be this way, she would stay with him.

He would need to assure her there was nothing for her to fear, that he would be able to protect her. That he was the *only* one who would be able to protect her. Hell, he'd even protect her entire vampire family if that was what it took.

Jesse feared very few things, but for reasons he was only beginning to understand, losing Shea terrified him. He would make her understand.

He didn't know how long he'd been lost in his thoughts when there was suddenly a loud pop from Shea's side of the plane. The air whistled through the small engine outside, so loud, he could barely hear his own thoughts. A few seconds later, the cabin began to shutter, and Jesse's stomach flip-flopped as the nose of the plane dipped and righted itself again.

His immediate concern was for Shea. She had a white-knuckled grip on the arms of her seat, and her fangs were revealed with a hiss as she stared back at him with fear in her wide, green eyes.

Jesse unbuckled his belt, catching himself with one hand on the ceiling as the plane bucked again.

"Where are you going?" Shea reached over as if to grab his hand before remembering herself and renewing her death grip on the armrest. Jesse noticed the metal had bent with the strength of her panic, and now held the imprint of her small hand. She would break his bones if she held onto him like that.

And he would relish the pain just to be able to hold her.

"Jesse?"

With a quick shake of his head, he came back to the

real world. "I'm going to speak with the pilot. I'll be right back."

"Jesse, please don't leave me back here by myself." Though her voice sounded calm, he knew she was anything but.

With one hand on the ceiling and one on the back of his seat to steady himself against the jostling of the aircraft, he gave her what he hoped was a reassuring smile. "I'm sure he has everything under control. I just want to find out what's going on."

Leaving Shea strapped in her seat, Jesse made his way to the cockpit, moving quickly to avoid smashing his head into the ceiling. They were losing altitude. This couldn't be good. With the heel of his hand, he struck the door separating the pilots from the passengers just above the lock. It flew open, smashing into the wall behind it.

The scene within was something right out of a bad action movie.

Ignoring the co-pilot, who was frantically trying to get a hold of the tower over the radio, Jesse went straight over to the pilot. He had to raise his voice to be heard above all the commotion. "What the fuck is going on?"

Never taking his eyes from the instruments, the pilot shook his head, the movement spastic. "I don't know! We've lost the electrical—"

Jesse leaned down to speak directly into the man's ear. "I thought you performed all of the checks on this aircraft?"

Panicked eyes swung his way for a fraction of a second. "I did! I swear to you. This aircraft is in perfect condition."

"Then how the hell did we lose power to the electrical system?"

"I don't know, sir. But right now, I'm just trying to keep this plane in the air until I can find somewhere to land. I would suggest you get back to your seat and let us do our job."

Jesse straightened, slightly taken aback by the no-nonsense tone that had replaced the fear in the man's voice. A tiny inkling of respect for the middle-aged human crept into his original opinion of him. With a glance at the pasty co-pilot, who was still on the radio and still ignoring him, Jesse made his way back to Shea.

"What's happening?" she asked him before he even had a chance to sit down.

He longed to sit next to her, to reach over and take her hand, but all he could do was try to keep his voice calm. "It appears we're having some issues with the electrical system. The pilot is looking for a safe place to land."

The nose of the plane dipped forward suddenly, and Jesse's eyes widened as he watched the wing outside of Shea's window peel away from the body of the jet with a thunderous sound.

Shea's head whipped around to look out the window. "Oh my gods. It's gone. Jesse, the wing is completely gone!"

Jesse sat down and snapped his seat belt buckle closed, his heart pounding, and his jaw clenched with frustration that he was unable to do anything to protect her. Less than a second later, the plane dipped sharply to the side, and this time, it didn't right itself. The overhead compartments opened and the yellow cups came tumbling out.

The pilot's voice came over the intercom. "Brace for impact! Repeat. We're going down. Brace for impact!"

The last thing Jesse remembered was Shea's hand reaching for him across the aisle.

And his regret that he didn't sit beside her.

CHAPTER 17

"I've lost the signal."

Nine sets of eyes turned to stare at him.

Luukas tapped a few keys on the keyboard. Giving up, he sagged back in his chair. "Shea's gone. I've lost the signal."

Aiden got up from his spot in front of Luukas's desk and came around to stand beside him. "Let me give it a go."

Bracing his palms on the desktop, Luukas slowly stood, trying not to wince as he gave up his chair for Aiden. His joints ached and his muscles felt like an old man. He could feel Keira's eyes on him, and with extreme effort, he straightened until he stood tall. Even though all he wanted to do was hunch over his desk. Or maybe crumple into a heap on the hard floor.

As Aiden worked his magic on the computer, Nikulas rose quietly from his chair and slid it over toward his brother, then leaned against the glass wall behind Emma and crossed his muscular arms over his chest. He didn't say anything, didn't even look Luukas's way, and for that, the Master Vampire was grateful. He was sick and fucking tired of everyone fussing over him.

Well, the females fussed over him. The guys let him be to do what he could, and when he was worn out, like now, they slid him a chair. Or grabbed something from across the room for him without his having to ask. Or answered his cell phone and screened his calls. All without the sad eyes, concerned words, or awkward silences. Releasing a tired sigh, Luukas sank into the chair that was offered to him and waited in silence with everyone else to see what Aiden could find out.

After Nikulas and Aiden told him about seeing Shea at the airport with the warlock, Luukas had attempted to contact her a few times. His calls went directly to voicemail every time. If it wasn't for the GPS tracker on her cell, he would've thought she'd already ditched the phone. But apparently, now that she knew that *he* knew what she was up to, she didn't see the need. So, although she wouldn't answer his calls, he knew exactly where she was every fucking minute of every fucking day.

Until about ten minutes ago when he'd gathered the Hunters and the witches into his office for a meeting and logged on to check her location.

"This may take a bit, but I'll try to get as close to her last location as I can."

Aiden's brow furrowed in concentration, lending shadows to his grey eyes. It gave Luukas a start, until he looked closer and realized it was only his expression, and not the demon inside of him coming to the surface that caused the shadows. With a relieved intake of breath, he nodded, and turned to the silent group gathered in his office. "Let's get on with this."

All eyes swung his way, except Keira's. For Keira's eyes had been on him the entire time, as always.

He tried to suppress his irritation with his witch. She was only worried about him. And she was right to do so, for there was plenty to worry about. At times, Luukas wished it would all just end—the nausea, the fatigue, the muddled thoughts—just get it the fuck over with. Then he wouldn't have to see that look in her eyes anymore. It was the look she'd given him when he was chained to the wall in the bowels of that fucking mountain. Like he was weak. Like he was fragile. Like he was something to be pitied.

He cleared his throat. "Witches. Update me on your progress."

Keira spoke first, keeping her voice low, like she knew his head was pounding. And hell, maybe she did. "Emma is good. We've narrowed down her strongest skills. Along with sending objects flying across the room at Nik when he gets on her bad side—" This was said with a teasing note. "She is now able to immobilize him, or any vampire, where they stand while keeping her emotions under control. Even the strongest of you."

Dante, the oldest and strongest vampire there other than Luukas, growled out something that sounded like grudging agreement.

Luukas nodded. "Good. And Ryan?" He turned to

Christian's mate where she sat quietly to the side, her copper hair bright against her pale skin.

Keira began to speak, but Luukas held up a hand, cutting off whatever she'd been about to say. "Ryan?" He wanted the witch to speak for herself. He understood the other vampires still weren't quite comfortable with her, except for Christian, of course. Making her speak for herself would help draw her out of her shell, and help the others get more used to her being there. Having any animosity in the group would cause problems they couldn't afford to have.

"Honestly, I've been struggling. The entities...Well, Christian's blood makes them quiet." Her sense of relief was almost palpable. "But now I'm trying to control when they speak to me and when they don't. I've got them to stop screaming at me incoherently, but they still talk over one another." She shrugged.

"Tell him what else," Grace piped in.

Ryan took a deep breath. Luukas had the feeling he made her nervous.

"I can read the spell that Grace's parents left for her. Well, not me, *them*."

"Yes, Keira was telling me about that."

"What's going on?" Nik asked.

It was Emma who answered him. "Ryan's spirits can read that old spell Grace has. We know what it is now."

"And what is that?"

"It's the spell that will send the demons back," Ryan told him.

Aiden stopped typing, his eyes flicked from Ryan to

Grace, and Luukas could see the hope he desperately tried to hide.

Luukas sat back in his chair and steepled his fingers beneath his chin, turning over what she'd just said. He was well aware of the condition she'd been in when Christian had met her. She'd been an addict, using the drug to quiet the spirits that insisted on gathering around her. The vampires couldn't see or hear them, but the other witches confirmed they were there.

And now they knew the spell. "You told me once that they're protective of you, is this correct?"

She nodded. "Yes. If someone they don't like is trying to hurt me or another person I care about, they will stop them."

"These spirits, they can physically hurt people?"

"Yes. They've done it before." She paused. "They seem to do whatever they think will make me happy."

"Will they kill?"

He suddenly had her full attention. "Yes," she whispered.

Luukas turned to look out the window. The city of Seattle was shrouded in mist this night, the lights of the ferries crossing the Sound like ghost ships.

Christian stood up and came over to his desk. Bracing his hands on the edge, he leaned in toward Luukas, his topaz eyes dark with worry. "I know where you're going with this. And with all due respect, there's no fucking way I'm letting her put herself in danger so the entities will help us."

Cocking his head to the side, Luukas stared Christian down until he backed up and lowered his eyes. He may be weakening, but godsdammit, he was still the Master here. And they would all do well to remember that fact.

However, he wasn't completely without heart.

"I would never put your mate in any true danger, Christian. You should know that. However, if she agrees, her help would be greatly appreciated. As a matter of fact, I don't know that we will succeed in sending the demons back to hell without it."

CHAPTER 18

Something wet trickled down Shea's forehead and over her nose. It gathered at the tip for a second before it fell, landing in the dirt beneath her cheek. Shea spit grass and leaves from her mouth, ran her tongue over her gritty teeth, which hurt, and tried to lift her hand to wipe away the stuff on her face. A burst of red-hot pain shot through her shoulder and upper arm for her efforts. Trying the other hand instead, she rubbed clumsily at her face with stiff fingers. They came away covered in blood. Her blood. For a vampire, this was an unusual way to wake up.

With a moan, she gathered her legs and one good arm beneath her and attempted to haul herself up onto her hand and knees. After a few tries, she managed to stay there. Her hair, pulled from her braid, hung in her face to skim the ground beneath her. Shea spit blood and dirt out of her mouth.

Throwing her weight to one side, Shea landed on her

bum. Even that small feat had her catching her breath. The air was warm and humid, and hard to breathe. She peeled her sticky hair from her skin and shoved it out of her eyes, glanced around, and quickly took in her surroundings with eyes that were still sharp despite the unusual amount of pain she was in. When she registered nothing but trees, and heard only the sounds of small nighttime creatures hunting for their next meal, she turned her attention to her right arm. A piece of bone stuck through the skin halfway between her elbow and her shoulder, and the limb hung awkwardly from her shoulder joint.

Fuck *me. Fixing that is gonna hurt.*

With another quick scan of the area around her, she lurched to her feet and took a moment to test out her legs before she tried to walk. Other than some deep cuts that were well on their way to healing, but still stung, they seemed to be working fine. One boot was lost somewhere in the brush, and her jeans looked like Freddy Kruger had tried to pull her down through the dirt, but otherwise her bottom half felt okay.

She only stumbled the first few steps as she weaved her way to the nearest tree. Bugs swarmed around her face, attracted to the blood, and Shea shook her head to dislodge them. Gripping her limp wrist with her opposite hand and clenching her jaw, she yanked down. A scream of pain tore from her throat despite her efforts to repress it. Holding her broken arm steady, she repeatedly slammed her shoulder into the trunk until she managed to knock her joint back into the socket. Sagging against the rough bark, Shea took in oxygen as she squinted out of the corner of her eye for something to use as a brace and a sling. She wouldn't need it for long; her injuries would heal pretty fast. Just long enough to keep everything in place while her body did its thing. When she didn't see anything offhand that would work, Shea used her good arm to pull off her shirt. She clamped the cotton material between her teeth and ripped until she had enough homemade bandages for what she needed, then carefully put what remained of her shirt back on. It was now an uneven crop top, and an ugly one at that, but it covered her breasts, so it would do.

Setting her broken arm was a little more difficult. It had already begun to heal, and lining up the edges of bone was an experience Shea hoped to never have to repeat. As a matter of fact, Shea had to stop twice to avoid passing out again while she did it. When she finished, she was panting, and sweat ran in rivulets down her back. Orange spots danced in front of her eyes that stung from sweat and blood, making her nauseous, but somehow, she managed to stay conscious. Once the feeling passed, she wrapped one of the bandages around the broken area, and made a sling out of the rest.

Immediate needs taken care of, she wiped at her eyes and tried to get her bearings.

Jesse.

Flashes of the crash hit her hard and fast. Jesse's face when he realized the pilot had lost all control of the plane. The horror and frustration in his golden eyes as he looked at her, knowing there was nothing he could do to stop it.

Though he'd tried. Shea vaguely remembered hearing words in a language she'd never heard before leaving his lips. Words he'd screamed louder and louder as nothing happened. Finally, he'd fought with the buckle of his safety belt, the chanting replaced by curses. Shouting at Shea to stop as she'd done the same. She'd gotten her belt off first, just as the plane hit the tops of trees.

Lurching away from the rough bark, Shea began to search the area around her. "Jesse!" Her voice was rough and hoarse. From screaming? But she kept calling out for him anyway. "Jesse! Where are you?" In a full-blown panic now, she broke out into a run, covering as much ground as she could. Branches scratched her face and arms through what was left of her sleeves, but at least the gash in her head was healing and the river of blood had slowed, allowing her to see.

However, she saw no sign of the dark warlock.

Fear curled its icy fingers around her heart. Not for herself, but for the male who had managed to make her feel like a woman again for the first time in a long time, without even touching her. The threat to her own life if he hadn't survived the crash never even crossed her mind as she staggered in circles around the area where she had landed, widening the circumference with every pass. She stopped every few minutes and called for him, but never heard so much as a rustle of leaves to give her a hint as to his whereabouts.

"Jesse." His name came out on a sob as she stopped to take a closer look at a piece of metal from the plane. She had no idea what part it was. She was just searching for something—anything—that would give her the slightest hope that he was still alive. Pushing her hair out of her face again, she turned in a circle. In the distance, about a hundred yards from where she stood, she saw something glinting in the moonlight. Something large.

Busting her way through the fallen trees, she came upon what was left of the cabin. There was no way of knowing if it was the front or the back. She called his name as she peered through the broken windows. There was no sign of him. Shea scaled the side of the jet with a strength she didn't know she possessed in her weakened state, and made her way over the top. She dropped down to the other side, and found herself standing in what used to be the aisle.

The smell of blood was strong. Jesse's blood.

The other half—where she had been sitting—was completely gone. A few of the seats were still attached, seat cushions scattered about, but most were ripped from the floor and either in pieces or gone completely. She took her best guess as to where Jesse had been sitting. A wave of numbness washed over her. The seat was torn nearly in two, the top half hanging into the aisle by one armrest.

A single tear cooled her hot skin, and Shea wiped it away distractedly. His body wasn't there, which meant he may be all right. Maybe, somehow, he'd gotten his belt off and had walked away from the wreckage and was out there looking for her.

And maybe tiny pieces of his body are lying scattered around this fucking forest.

Shea picked her way through the wreckage until she was outside the body of the plane and standing where the cockpit used to be. Only now there was nothing there at all.

She backed away from the crash site, and continued to

walk in no particular direction. A vague thought came to her that she needed to find shelter before the sun came up, but it was there and gone before she could fully comprehend it.

Planting one foot on top of a half-burned, fallen tree, she lifted herself up and fell to the other side. Her legs gave out when she landed, and she caught herself on her one good arm. Something to her left caught her attention. A movement. She cautiously turned her head, thinking maybe an animal had found her.

A long branch—the width of a broom—stuck up at an angle from the forest floor, it's large, green leaves waving in the light breeze that did nothing to relieve the mugginess of the night. It didn't seem natural, the way it swayed. Shea wondered why it didn't fall over. Relieved it wasn't an animal, she followed the length of the branch down to its base.

The end of the branch impaled a body through the gut. A body lying prone, covered in leaves and dirt, causing it to blend almost perfectly with its surroundings. A body wearing pants as dark as the night and a shirt the same color as the forest around it. Shea couldn't even see his face. It was covered by the fallen log. The one she'd just jumped over.

Her stomach lurched. She'd just put her weight on the tree that was crushing Jesse's face. She forced one foot forward, followed by the other, her eyes never leaving the body lying there as still as death. "Jesse?" The name that passed her lips was no more than a breath.

Sinking down to her haunches beside him, she reached out for his hand. But before she could make contact with his skin, she pulled hers back with a hiss of frustration and anger. A scream of rage started low in her lungs and forced its way out, startling the creatures sleeping in the trees around them. Without thought, her good hand shot out and slammed into the log, knocking it off him with one strong push.

But just as fast as it had come on, the rush of adrenaline left her. Afraid to look, but more afraid not to, Shea slowly turned her head to find out how bad the damage was. When her eyes landed on his perfect face, marred only by a few scrapes and one small gash above his right eye, she nearly sobbed with relief. His head was not crushed as she had feared. And when she checked out the log again, she saw why.

Right where it had covered his face and head, there was a natural curvature in the trunk.

Shea scooted up by his head and held her hand in front of his mouth. She felt nothing but the heat of the night. So, she leaned down as close as she could to his chest. Closing her eyes, she tried to calm herself enough to listen.

And then she heard it. Faint, but there. The sound of his heartbeat.

Thank the gods.

Relief flooded through her, so hard and fast she became momentarily lightheaded. If his heart was still beating, there was a very good chance that she could save him. She just needed to pull the branch out of his stomach, and get him to feed from her before his heart stopped completely. Her blood would heal him if she got enough in him before he bled out. If by chance she missed that window of opportunity, she would have to turn him without his knowledge to save his life. And she would be doing it without permission from Luukas. Or more importantly, from Jesse.

"Hang on, Jesse. Just stay alive. I'm going to save you."

At the sound of her voice, his eyelids fluttered, but didn't open. Shea opened her mind, trying to reach him that way, but she couldn't hear anything but the thudding of her own pulse.

She stood up, and took a deep breath. Though there was blood, it didn't appear the tree had gone completely through. That was good. She only had two hands. Placing one booted foot on his chest, she gripped the branch with her good hand. It would have to be pulled out in one try. He would begin to bleed out right away, which meant she would have mere seconds to get her blood into his system and help his body heal itself.

"I'm so sorry," she whispered. Adjusting her grip on the trunk, she added the hand from her bad arm as leverage, and with a grunt, yanked the offending thing from his stomach.

The delicious scent of his warm blood rose up through the muggy air and surrounded her, and Shea growled low in her throat. Tossing the sapling to the side, she dropped to her knees beside him. Blood rushed from his body like a gurgling stream, soaking the ground where she knelt. Raising her wrist to her mouth, Shea bared her fangs and ripped open a large wound. She immediately held it over his mouth as she clumsily tried to lift the bottom of his shirt and pack it into the wound without touching him.

Her blood dripped onto his closed lips and ran down the sides of his jaw.

Shea's eyes widened in horror. "Jesse! Open your mouth! Open your fucking mouth!" But her words fell on unconscious ears. Leaning over, she listened for his heartbeat. She heard nothing. "Jesse!" Without thinking, she gripped both hands together and brought them down hard onto the center of his chest. She listened again.

His heart gave a weak thump.

"Yes!" Ripping open the wound in her wrist again, she pried her fingers between his teeth and opened his mouth, then pressed her wrist against it, forcing it to stay open. As her blood finally made its way into his mouth, she again gathered his shirt together and held it over the wound. Then she watched and prayed to any god who would listen.

Seconds ticked by that felt like years. And still, she watched for the smallest sign. With a frustrated sound, she pulled her wrist away from his mouth only to tear it open again. When she noticed her blood pooled inside, she started massaging his throat to make him swallow, and pressed her wrist back between his lips. "Drink, damn you. Drink!"

His throat moved beneath her fingers. Or had it?

She pulled her hand away, pressing it to his stomach again. Her eyes were glued to his throat as she ripped open her wrist for the third time and offered it to him again.

A moan, weak with pain and barely audible, rose to her sensitive ears. She felt suction on her wrist. Not much, but it was there.

"Yes. That's it. Drink, Jesse." A sob escaped her as emotions that had been running so high she had to shut them down to do what she needed, suddenly came rushing back. She kept pressure on his stomach wound with her hand on his shirt, and watched as he drank from her with more strength every second.

With eyes filled with tears, Shea looked over the entire length of him, searching for more injuries. When she returned to the site of her wrist on his lips, she froze.

Her wrist was on his lips.

Touching them.

Touching them directly.

Startled, she jerked it away from him. Then immediately put it back. He needed more blood to heal from such a grave injury.

I can touch him. I can touch him.

Shea crouched beside Jesse's blood-soaked form, one hand holding his bunched-up shirt bottom to the hole in his gut, and the other pressed to his lips.

Good gods, I can fucking touch him.

Small tremors overtook her, gradually building until she was shaking so badly that she could barely hold her wrist steady as he drank with weak pulls. She lifted his shirt from his wound. The hole in his gut was shrinking, the sides knitting together. It would probably be safe to stop now. She couldn't afford to lose too much blood herself while her own body was still healing. She could stop now.

But she didn't want to.

If she didn't, he would know.

Jesse's eyelids fluttered. With a hiss of frustration that

she hoped would be mistaken for pain, Shea pulled her wrist away before he became fully conscious again. Falling back to sit on the wet leaves, she patted his stomach with his shirt. It was nearly healed.

She watched his face. His tongue touched the blood on his bottom lip, and he moaned. He would wake up soon.

Scooting a few inches away, she crossed her legs and waited. Her hands curled into fists in her lap as she remembered the softness of his lips on her skin. Her eyes drifted down to his stomach. The muscles had felt firm and hard, even injured as they'd been. She wished she had taken the time to touch the skin that covered them. It was smooth and hairless, except for the small trail that led down to his manhood, she remembered from their day in his room. She wanted to trace that trail with her fingertips. And perhaps her tongue.

She reached for him with trembling fingers.

Shea pulled her hand back into her lap and twisted her fingers together before he woke up to find her molesting him like some innocent virgin. But she kind of felt like one. It had been so long since she'd touched a male, and since she'd felt the roughness of a male's palms on the most sensitive parts of her.

Would it be so bad for him to know she could touch him? What would he do?

He would overwhelm her. She'd barely survived their one night of not touching with her heart and soul intact. She would never be herself again if he knew.

But what would it feel like to have him kiss her, run his hands over her? To feel his weight pressing her down into the ground, to feel him inside of her….

A VAMPIRE'S CHOICE

It had been so long since anyone had been inside of her, at least not with something that wasn't made of plastic and ran on batteries.

Shea shook her head. Her brains must be rattled from the crash. He was her mate, yes. A great joke from the gods, that they chose *this* male among all the billions on earth to be hers. He wasn't good, or kind, or even a normal human. Deep down inside, he was evil. He did horrible things. He'd tried to kill Luukas, for gods' sake. The others—her only family—wouldn't understand, would never accept him. Being with him would allow her to live, but would ruin her life. She'd never be able to go back to her home, to the ones she had come to love as her own during all the years they'd lived and fought together side by side. Nik and Aiden and Christian—they were like brothers to her. Even Dante, ornery as he was. They were her very own dysfunctional family.

Jesse would never respect her like that. He craved her, yes. Wanted her body. But he didn't respect her mind, or her fighting skills, or—

"You're wrong, love."

The words were spoken so quietly, she never would have heard them if she wasn't the supernatural creature that she was. Fear shot through her veins, immobilizing her where she sat, and she immediately emptied her mind of everything she'd just been thinking. Slowly, she raised her eyes to meet his.

They were dull with pain and disappointment, but they were open. And he was alive. Shea allowed a small feeling of relief in.

A tiny smile lifted the corners of his mouth. "Thank you for saving me."

"You're welcome." He stared at her until she frowned down at him. "What?"

"You look beautiful."

The dude had completely lost his mind. "I seriously doubt that. I'm filthy and covered in blood and dirt. I look terrible. As do you."

His smile widened, then slowly fell. "I thought I would never see you again, Shea."

She had no smart comeback for that one. For a little while there, she thought she would never see him again, either. It had terrified her to the point she'd had to shut down her emotions to save him.

He tried to sit up, and Shea automatically reached out to help him, but stopped before she forgot herself and touched him. Agitated, she drew her legs beneath her and kneeled beside him, ready to jump away at a moment's notice. He couldn't know that she could touch him. She wasn't ready for that yet. "Maybe you should just rest for a bit."

Using the small saplings around him, he hauled himself up. He gave her a strange, sideways look as he caught his breath. "We don't have time." Feeling for his phone and not finding it, he started looking around in the leaves. "Have you seen my phone? I need to make a call."

"No, I haven't. I was a little busy keeping you from bleeding to death."

Jesse stopped patting the ground around him and reached for her. Shea nearly let his fingers graze her cheek —she ached to let him—before remembering to pull away.

His hand stayed there for a few seconds, suspended midair, as though daring her to change her mind, before it dropped back down to the leaves. He had a strange look on his face, one Shea didn't want to analyze too closely. Clearing her throat, she rose to her feet none too gracefully. Closing her eyes, she waited for the head rush to subside. When she opened them again, Jesse stood beside her.

"You need to feed, Shea. You gave me too much blood."

She stepped back. "I'm fine. Just a little woozy. You need it more than I do right now."

Again, he looked at her strangely. Shea stared back at him, not wanting to give him any reason to think anything had changed. She would analyze her feelings more when he wasn't so intent on reading her, for she could feel him probing around in her head, much as she was trying to keep him out.

Finally, he looked away. "All right, we need to move. See if we can at least find some water, and shelter before the sun comes up." Those golden eyes, brighter every moment, flashed back to her face. "You will tell me if you get too tired. Or if you need me."

The double entendre wasn't lost on her. "I'll tell you if I need to feed." Glancing up at the stars, she started walking in the direction the plane had been heading as she adjusted her homemade sling.

Jesse was suddenly beside her. "Shea."

She kept walking. "Yes?"

"*Thank you.*"

She gave him a tight smile. "Don't get too full of yourself. I need you around if I'm to survive now. Let's not forget that." She paused, then forced herself to say, "I wouldn't have saved you otherwise." The lie lay heavy on her tongue. But she didn't take it back. She couldn't. If she did, she would be accepting him as hers. Accepting what he was. And what he had done. And what he may do in the future.

And that was something she couldn't do.

CHAPTER 19

She can touch me.
    She can fucking touch me.
Jesse walked beside and slightly behind Shea, shamelessly listening to every random thought that passed through her bewildering female brain. And more than that, he could *feel* her so much more now. Feel every emotion she was feeling.
It was fucking amazing. It was like he was a part of her, and she of him.
He wondered if it was the same for her, with him?
Shea.
He directed his thought at her, and smiled when she stumbled over a non-existent root. She glanced at him out of the corner of her eye, frowned, and kept walking. With the streaks of blood on her face and in her hair, she was nonetheless stunning. Like a satanic princess.
And she could hear him. Hear his thoughts when he

directed them at her. Or could she hear everything as he could?

I want to lick her sex until the taste of her is seared in my brain.

He thought it only to himself, not to her. A truth that would shock her into reacting if she could hear it, judging by the way she'd stumbled when he'd only called her name. But there was no reaction this time. Shea wiped her brow with her sleeve and trudged on, pushing a tree branch out of the way and holding it so it wouldn't smack him in the face.

So, she couldn't hear everything. Good. That was very good.

Much as he wanted to submerse himself in her every thought and emotion for the next year or so, there were more important things he needed to be thinking about right now. They hadn't found his phone, or hers. And though they were traveling as fast as their battered bodies could go, they needed to find shelter and rest. It would make them incredibly late to their destination. But hopefully, he would still find the blood before the demons figured it out. He needed every advantage he could get in dealing with them.

"There."

Jesse looked where Shea was pointing. There was a hill just ahead and to the left. It jutted out over a small creek that was little more than a trickle, but must become a raging river when the rains came. Enough that it carved out a small alcove into the side of the hill. Little more than an overhang, really. "Will that be enough?"

She eyed the sky, then looked back at him. "It'll have to

be. The sun is coming up. Worse case scenario, just bury me in the dirt." She grinned, but he knew she was perfectly serious.

Jesse nodded. "Okay. Let's go."

When they got to the overhang, he saw it was a little deeper than he had originally thought. Unless the sun decided to change which side of the earth it rose on, she would be out of the direct rays.

Jesse would make sure of it.

"Go ahead, Shea," he ordered her.

But she didn't do as he told her. Instead, she dropped down to her knees beside the creek and tasted the water. She nodded. "It's good," she shot over her shoulder. Then she cupped her hands and started drinking in earnest.

Jesse hadn't realized how thirsty he was until just that moment. Or how tired. He nearly fell to the ground beside her, and followed her example. The water was icy and crisp and tasted delicious.

Downstream from him, Shea removed her sling and splashed water on her face and as much of her body as she could, even rinsing out strands of her blood coated hair. When she finished, she pushed herself up to her feet without looking at him, and shuffled over to the overhang. She crawled all the way to the back and lay down.

Jesse pulled off his blood-soaked shirt and submersed it in the water. He scrubbed the material with pebbles from the bed, getting out as much of the stain as he could. Then wrung out the water and stood. Hanging the shirt over a low branch to dry, he followed Shea inside. He was glad that Cruthú hadn't been with them in the crash, yet a part of him wished she was there. If she were, he could send the raven with a message. Instead, he had to reassure himself that they would be able to move much faster once they got a good day's rest.

And the demons would not be going anywhere until the sun went down.

Shea lay down with her back to him, her arm bent beneath her head for a pillow. He waited until he heard her breathing even out. It didn't take her long, and he wasn't surprised. He knew she was much more exhausted than she let on.

Jesse sat cross-legged and rested his palms on his knees. Once he was certain she was asleep, he closed his eyes and spoke in low tones, calling on forces that most wouldn't dare get near. When he opened his eyes, the sun was coming up, but the air around their little cubby was thick with protective layers, blocking out the rays so completely it was nearly dark inside.

Now they decide to answer.

The entities were fickle.

Lying beside Shea, he wrapped an arm around her and pulled her limp form close to him. Resting her head on his own arm, he curled his body around the back of hers, and ignored his instant hard-on.

There would be plenty of time to ease that ache when she could bring herself to accept his part in her life. He wouldn't attempt to take her until then.

Trying to ignore the warmth of her skin and the way her curves fit so perfectly against him, Jesse closed his eyes and willed himself to sleep.

* * *

A VAMPIRE'S CHOICE

JESSE WOKE FIRST. Disengaging Shea's limbs from his own, he had already washed up in the creek, put his now dry shirt on, and was sitting in the opening keeping watch when she finally regained consciousness.

"What time is it?"

Her whiskey voice—even huskier than normal after sleeping so hard—raised chill bumps along his skin. Jesse glanced up at the sky. "About nine, judging by the position of the moon." He twisted around to face her, and caught his breath.

The battered female from the night before was gone. In her place was a woman who, although still covered in dirt, was haunting in her perfection. Even the unusual paleness of her skin and shadows under her eyes, caused by her lack of feeding, did nothing but add to her ethereal beauty.

Some may say her chin was too pointy, her forehead too wide, her cheekbones too sharp, or her bottom lip too full. She was tall for a woman, nearly as tall as Jesse, but he knew from cuddling up to her as she slept that she fit against him like she was created just for him.

And she was. He'd known it from the first time he'd sensed her in the altar room, before he'd ever seen her face.

To him, she was perfect.

"Why are you staring at me like that?" She pushed her dark hair from her face with arms that were both working perfectly, fussing with her appearance. Though there was little she could do, and there was no need.

"I was just thinking that you look pale, Shea. You need to feed."

She was shaking her head before he'd even finished saying the words. "I'm fine. I'll be fine."

"You're not 'fine'. And we're never going to get out of here if you keep refusing to drink from me. There's no bagged blood lying about for you to choke down."

Lines appeared between her elegant brows as she scowled. "I should have searched near the portion of the plane I found—"

Jesse burst up from the ground, his tolerance at an end. "Fucking hell, Shea! Stop! Just stop." He lowered his voice and inhaled deeply, embarrassed that she had brought out such a reaction in him. But he was tired of keeping it under control, especially around her. "Just…stop," he told her, calmer now.

His vampire had shot to her feet when he had, and now stood slightly bent over to avoid banging her head on the top of the overhang. Pointed, white fangs were bared under a raised upper lip, and green eyes glowed with the sharp focus of a predator. They were fixed to his every move. He had startled her with his outburst.

Raising his hands in front of him in supplication, he kept his voice low and even. "I'm sorry I startled you, but you must feed, Shea. And I feel wonderful, thanks to you. I can afford to spare a little of my blood for you. You're no good to me the way you are right now. You're weak, and unfocused. If we had to defend ourselves, I would be too busy worrying about you and we would both be killed."

She had settled down during his speech, and seemed to deflate before his eyes now that the rush of adrenaline was gone. Her eyelids drooped with exhaustion, despite the deep sleep she'd just had. Even the act of standing up seemed to be too much. Her thoughts bounced around in her head, making no sense.

"I'd like a little privacy. Please."

He nodded. "I'll take a little walk. But I won't be far, so just call out if you need me. I'll hear you." He didn't bother to tell her that he would hear her even if she whispered inside of her head without ever speaking a word out loud.

As a matter of fact, she didn't even need to do that much. With her blood inside of him, he was tuned in to her every emotion. If she felt the slightest sliver of fear, he would know.

Shea gave him a nod, and headed outside. He watched her kneel at the bank of the creek and cup her hands to drink, then he turned and did a quick check of the area. Opening his senses to any intruders, he listened closely, but he sensed nothing other than the usual nocturnal animals. Satisfied that she would be okay alone, he told her he would be right back, and returned to the crash site. It didn't take him long. Jesse could move at a speed that shouldn't be possible for a human.

However, he wasn't a human. Not completely.

It took him a total of five minutes to find the one blood bag that had survived the crash. He also found the pilot and co-pilot. The cockpit had broken off from the rest of the plane and they appeared to have died instantly. Jesse left the bodies there to feed the scavengers.

He stared at the plastic bag of blood in his hand, his lip curled in distaste. If Shea wanted to feed, she would drink from him, and only from him. Gripping the opening with his teeth, he tore it open and dumped the contents onto the ground at his feet. He watched the red liquid soak into the dirt to mix with that of the pilots, and felt not an ounce of remorse. He had plenty of blood for her. She didn't need this. She only needed him.

Five minutes later, he slowed down as he came within sight of their makeshift camp. He saw Shea sitting beside the creek with her arms wrapped around her knees. She didn't move a muscle as he walked up to stand behind her, though he knew she was aware of his approach through his new connection with her.

She didn't look at him. "Did you find any of the blood?"

Jesse narrowed his eyes at the back of her head. Was she in his head more than she let on?

"I saw you take off in the direction we had just come from, so I assumed you went back to the crash site to look for blood."

Ah.

"No." The lie slipped easily off his tongue. "I didn't find any of the blood. I would imagine it was destroyed during the rough landing." He felt her probing inside his head, and by the clumsiness of her approach, he could tell she didn't realize yet she was doing it. He raised his guard, blocking his thoughts.

Her shoulders lifted and lowered as she took a deep breath. "All right, then."

Even though she had just agreed to drink from him, in so many words, she made no move to do so. Her continued stubbornness angered him more than he'd like to admit. Lowering himself onto his haunches beside her, Jesse held his wrist out in front of her face. Blue veins showed clearly beneath the unmarred skin. He waited to see what she would do. Would she continue the charade? Or would she mark him with her bite as they both so longed for her to do?

Her upper lip twitched, and the blood lust emanating from her became his. It flooded every cell of his body, a mere shadow of the hunger she had to be feeling. He knew she was starving, and still, she resisted.

Jesse clenched his jaw. She wanted to pretend that he was so distasteful to her? She could deny it all she fucking wanted. He knew better. Without taking his eyes from her, Jesse made his offering irresistible.

Shea inhaled sharply as the skin on his inner wrist split open, as if an invisible knife of the sharpest steel slowly cut its way through his skin. Blood rose to the surface, pooling there briefly before running down his wrist, where it paused to gather into a good amount, then dripped onto her lap.

"Tilt your head back, Shea," he commanded. Jesse was done with her games. He'd fucking force-feed her if he needed to.

Her tongue flicked out to wet her dry lips, and he thought she would refuse again, but then she tilted her head back. With a sideways glance, she parted her lips. Her tongue ran over the tip of one fang, then the other, teasing him with the vision of her bite.

"Good girl." Jesse moved his wrist over her waiting mouth, and as the first drops fell between those sweet lips, he growled deep in his throat—a rumble of satisfaction. It was an indescribable feeling, knowing that he alone provided the only sustenance she needed. That he was the single reason she still survived.

And as for his vampire, the moment his blood hit her tongue, her eyes rolled back before closing completely as her spine straightened and her mouth opened wider. Her appearance altered as he watched: color replacing the pallor of her soft skin, her limbs fleshing out, and her breasts swelling. Her legs moved, restless, as she moaned. Her entire body begged for his touch. The changes were subtle. Most people wouldn't even notice. But Jesse did. He noticed everything about her.

Like the way she looked at him now as she drank, eyes burning with need. Jesse smiled as his body hardened in response, and she quickly looked away. He sighed, but didn't push her more. She was feeding, and that was enough for now. He fed her until she was satiated, although she tried to wave him away before she'd had nearly enough.

When she finished, he rinsed off his arm in the creek, the cut gone when he pulled it from the cold water.

"How did you do that?" Shea had gotten to her feet, and stared down at his wrist in disbelief.

He shrugged, a casual movement meant to throw her off the scent. "Just a simple parlor trick." He shouldn't have shown her that ability. It would make her too suspicious. He'd done it without thinking. He should've left the wounds as he'd done before. Little did she know, it was only the tip of the iceberg as to what he was capable of. "Are you feeling better?"

She nodded, still staring at the smooth skin, a tiny crease between her brows. "A little, yes. Thank you."

Turning away, Jesse started walking. "Good. We need to get going." He heard her following him. "If I'm not mistaken, we're not very far from our destination. If we hurry, we can make it there tonight. Are you up for a run, Shea?" She didn't respond, and he looked back over his shoulder to check on her.

He caught her staring at his ass, and he smiled. "Shea?"

Green eyes flashed up to his. "Yes. I can run."

Ah. So, she was listening after all. "You're thinking about me naked."

Her footsteps faltered. "I am not."

Jesse could practically feel the daggers aimed at his back, and glanced back to find her narrowed gaze focused right between his shoulder blades. "It's nothing to be ashamed of, Shea. I think of you naked all the time. The sight is scalded into my brain. I'll never forget it as long as I live." This last was said with respectful fervor, all teasing gone from his tone.

"Jesse, please."

He stopped and turned. They had no time for these games, but he couldn't seem to stop himself. "Please what, Shea?"

She stopped walking as well, and now stared up at him with pleading eyes. "I can't do this right now."

"This is what you keep telling me." He studied her lovely face, lowering his guards as he did so. Her emotions flooded through him: confusion, lust, need, denial. So many emotions, all tumbling over one another. Jesse sighed. "All right. Are you ready to run?"

Her relief flowed through him. "Yes."

"If you get tired, you must tell me. Understood?"

She crossed her arms and narrowed her cat eyes. "What about you? Won't you get tired?"

He smiled. "With your blood running through me? I feel like I could shift the earth off its axis if I wanted to. I don't think I'll be getting tired anytime soon."

She rolled her eyes. "Let's just go and get this over with."

So you can leave me? He kept the thought to himself. Honestly, he didn't want to hear her answer. He didn't need to. He knew that's what she intended. But he would face that obstacle when he came to it. Right now, they had other things to worry about.

Turning on his heel, he took off at full speed, dodging tree trunks and hanging branches. Shea caught up to him within moments.

CHAPTER 20

Shea watched the muscles flex in Jesse's back as the dark warlock crouched down to cup his hands in the clear water. They'd been running for hours, following the small creek they'd camped by during the day and yet, he was barely winded. No human she had ever met could run like a vampire or shifter. Not even with vampire blood inside of them. So, why could he? She'd tried to ask him, but he'd just shrugged it off, mumbling something about the powers of dark magic.

Shea let it go. For now. The Forest of Dagobas should be close. Once they found what they were looking for, she would have to face reality. Until then, she'd live in the little fantasy world they'd created by taking this trip together.

She wasn't looking forward to it—reality. For then she would have to face the raw truth of her situation: she would have to leave her family. There was no getting around it. Luukas would kill her himself before allowing

Jesse to be anywhere near him or Keira, and she couldn't say that she blamed him. And Nikulas and Aiden would hold her down while he did it. She was the weak link now. Jesse's link. *She* was how they would take their revenge against him.

But not if Shea succeeded in doing what she'd decided to do. It was her one small thread of hope in this otherwise hopeless situation.

Jesse's spine suddenly tensed, and she quickly cloaked her thoughts. It was easier to do now that she had some of her strength back. She needed to be careful. If he discovered what she was up to, he would stop her. Shea wasn't fooled by their mission to save the world. Jesse didn't want to save the world. He wanted to save himself. And she didn't have to read his mind to figure that out. He was up to something, and she had the feeling she wasn't going to like it, so Shea was taking matters into her own hands.

She just needed to keep him convinced that she believed him for a little while longer.

But even knowing what he was, her stomach twisted at the thought of deceiving him, leaving a hollow ache in the middle of her gut. She hated that she had to do this. She didn't love him, not yet, but she was undeniably drawn to him more than anyone she had ever met before. Even before she'd tasted his blood and knew that he was hers. She wanted to ask him who he was, where he had come from, and the real reason he had gotten mixed up in Leeha's shenanigans. She longed to understand what made him tick.

But it would be better to keep her distance. He was not a good male. He had no conscience. No empathy for others. He ruined lives without a care, and killed without thought.

Like you are so innocent. You tore off the head of your very own sister.

The memory momentarily sobered her.

No, that was different. Shea had had no choice. Her sister was dead long before Shea took the life from her body. It had been the only way to stop the thing she had become.

Lost in thought, she didn't notice that Jesse had stopped drinking and was now standing a little too close for comfort, staring at her intently with those eerie, golden eyes. She was so much in her own head that she jumped when he spoke.

"Are you ready to go?"

His gaze was steady, and when Shea met it with her own, the connection between them was like a million threads binding her body and soul to his. They would stretch, but they would never break. Not until one of them was dead.

She nodded her head. "Ready."

Jesse held a hand out to her, dropping it with an irritated expression when she pointedly crossed her arms over her chest and then walked past him. Little did he know that her own hands were clenched into fists as she fought the urge to place her hand in his. "It smells like rain. We'd better get going."

"Shea."

"If I remember correctly, we're only about an hour away." She glanced up at the sky, but couldn't see anything but clouds. However, she didn't really need to.

Her vampire instincts would let her know when it was getting close to sunrise. "We should have just enough time to find the blood and get to shelter if we get a move on it."

"Shea—"

She exhaled sharply. "We don't have time, Jesse."

Snapping his mouth shut with an audible click, he stared at her. She thought he was about to say more, but then he nodded. "You're right, of course. Let's go."

Shea sped up to an easy jog, then a full-out run when she heard Jesse's light footsteps behind her. They ran the rest of the way in silence, other than the soft sounds of their footfalls. Shea concentrated on her breathing to keep herself from obsessing about things she had no control over. Things that fate, bitch that she was, had taken into her own hands.

And things that she hadn't thought about in a long time.

Jesse pulled ahead of her about halfway through. She knew it was more of a protective thing than to prove that he was faster, and so she let him. Now he slowed to a normal sprint, then a jog, and finally eased to a halt. He came to stand in the shadows of a tall oak tree, nearly completely concealed in moonless night, staring straight ahead.

"Shea, please come here."

His voice was low, just above a whisper. He sounded strange. Shea picked her way through some underbrush and went to stand beside him. She studied his strong profile. "What is it?"

He never took his eyes from the area in front of him.

"Look there"—he pointed with his chin—"and tell me what you see."

Shea directed her gaze to the area he'd indicated, then further out, and further still. "I see a clearing...like a field. Only the grass is mowed, and even worn down to dirt in places." She looked back at Jesse. "What am I supposed to be seeing?"

"The Forest of Dagobas. A graveyard for monks and abbots, and among the tombs possibly even some students from the monastery practicing Kung Fu in their orange robes. But most importantly, *dagobas* that vary in levels and have inscriptions. Inscriptions that will point us to where the blood of the demons is buried."

Squinting her eyes, Shea walked forward a few steps. "But there's nothing here. Are you sure we're in the right place?"

"I'm fucking positive." He sounded strangely calm about the whole matter. "Please don't go any further."

She stopped, but stayed where she was. "Why?"

"Because I don't know what the fuck is going on here, and I would prefer that you stay by me where you'll be safe."

"Maybe they are there, and we just can't see them. It's really foggy." She looked back over her shoulder, but he was still staring straight ahead with narrowed eyes and a clenched jaw. Shea could practically hear his mind spinning as he tried to figure out what was going on. "Maybe they're just being cloaked?"

He shook his head distractedly. "No. They're gone."

"But how can an entire graveyard just up and disappear?" She started in the direction of the clearing. "I bet they're just cloaked." Holding her hands out in front of her, Shea took short steps, feeling with her hands and boots for the structures as she stepped out from the cover of the trees.

Jesse appeared in front of her like a wraith. Later, Shea would swear she could see right through him for a split second before his form solidified. She gasped, her arms dropping to her sides. "What the hell was that, Jesse?"

He ignored her question. "Back up, Shea. Now."

She did, stepping back carefully so as not to trip as she kept one eye on him and one eye on the ground until she was out of the clearing and back in the darkness of the forest.

"I told you to stay by me," he gritted out. "You *need* to listen to me. There are forces here. Things you don't want to fuck with."

She stared at his hardened expression. "How do you know?"

"Because I can sense it. There is dark magic at play here. And I don't know what may have happened if you walked out into the middle of it."

He was angry with her for not listening to him. But underneath that anger, she saw fear. Gut-wrenching fear. "I'm sorry," she whispered. "I'm only trying to help."

The fight slowly drained out of him. He closed his eyes and took a deep breath. "I know. I'm sorry for speaking to you that way. It was uncalled for." He turned away and began to pace back and forth in front of her.

"Jesse, it's okay. We'll figure something out." Suddenly exhausted, she sank down onto the ground, crossing her legs in front of her. "Maybe the demons got here first. We can track them—"

"We don't have to track them. I know exactly where they're going. But it wasn't the demons who did this."

She looked up at him, confused again. "How do you know?"

He just shook his head and kept pacing.

"Jesse, how do you know?"

With a great, suffering sigh, he stopped. He looked down at her, chewing the inside of his cheek. The interior battle he was fighting within himself would barely have been noticeable to anyone else, as not a single muscle twitched to show it. But Shea could feel the turmoil inside of him. He scrubbed his face with his hands, looked at her again, and finally dropped down to his knees in front of her, his legs giving out like he was as exhausted as she was. He knelt there, not saying a word, only looking at her with heartbreak darkening his brilliant eyes.

Shea felt something wrap around her lungs, and squeeze. "What is it?" Her voice was shaking. She'd known this time would come. The time he would feel ready to expose himself to her, to tell her who he truly was. But she wasn't ready. Not yet. For when he told her, there would be nothing stopping her from hating him completely. There would be no excuses for the things he'd done. No acts of kindness, however small, that would make her think more of him.

"I need to tell you something. And I don't want to."

"Then don't."

"I have to. It isn't right to keep this from you any longer."

She waited, every cell in her body wishing he would keep his mouth shut. And for a moment, she thought he'd heard her wish and he would do just that. For he said nothing for a long time. Just knelt there, staring, with that look in his eyes.

Shea was getting more nervous by the second. She'd never seen this look. And she knew that she was only seeing it now because he wanted her to. He only ever let her in when he wanted her there. Any other time he was completely unreadable. He was a master at disguising his emotions, internally and out. "All right, fine. Then tell me."

He gave her a tight smile that wasn't really a smile at all. "You're not going to like it."

Shea couldn't take it anymore. "Jesus Christ, Jesse. Just tell me."

He took a deep breath, his hands clenching and unclenching on his lap. "First, I want you to know that this had nothing at all to do with you. And I would have protected you at all costs. *With my own life.* Nothing would have happened to you or your family. I would have made sure of it."

She swallowed the bile rising in her throat. "What are you talking about? Why would anything happen to any of us?"

He looked straight at her. There was no fidgeting, no nervousness, just a damning stillness. "I'm not here to stop the demons, Shea. I'm here to help them."

She should've been surprised, shocked, at the very least disappointed, to finally hear him admit it. But she was none of those things. He wasn't a good male, and he'd done way worse things before she'd met him. So, she felt nearly nothing at his confession. Not shock. Not disappointment. Nothing at all.

Some sense of morbid curiosity led her to ask, "Why?"

"I need them to help me with something. Or, actually, someone." He didn't go into any further explanation, or offer any more details.

"Is there no one else who can help you?" She was reaching, and she knew it.

"No. There is no one else. The demons are the only ones with the power and the…reach…to help me."

Shea plucked at a blade of grass that had somehow managed to grow there within the trees, reaching for sunlight within the darkness of the forest. She honestly didn't even want to know what he meant by that statement.

"You don't seem surprised," he said after long seconds had passed.

She sighed. "I'm not. I only wish I'd been wrong."

"Don't you want to know who it is I need their help with?"

"Not really, no." Because if only the demons could stop him or her, they were talking about a creature of indescribable evil and power. Worse than Leeha at her finest.

Worse than Jesse.

"You're not going to sit there and argue with me? Try to win me over to the good side?"

"Nope." Shea was a realist. Jesse was who he was and she wouldn't be able to change him, she knew that. No matter how badly she wished he was someone else. No matter how she wished he was someone she could admire. Someone she could respect. "I only wonder why you bothered to drag me along if you had no intention of helping me." She still couldn't look at him.

"You know the answer to that."

Yes, she did. He'd done it for his own selfish reasons.

"I lied to you. I'm very sorry."

The apology was simple, but heartfelt. She could feel how much he meant it, and she realized that this was the real reason she hadn't been surprised by his admission. The connection between them had told her all along that he wasn't being truthful with her.

Yet, she'd come along anyway. And worse, she'd stayed. Even after she'd fed from him. Even after her senses had become so tuned in to this male that she could no longer fool herself about who he was.

Shea knew it was time to be honest with herself. She'd come with him because she wanted to explore this thing between them. And she'd stayed because she wanted to be with him, no matter the consequences. Not because he was her mate. Not because she could touch him, which she'd only recently discovered. And not just to have him around as a feedbag. But simply because she'd always known she belonged with him.

They belonged together. And there was the truth she'd been fighting. All out in the open.

"You don't hate me." The thread of hope was fragile, but Shea could hear it.

She shook her head. "I don't hate you." Then she shrugged. "No more than usual, anyway."

His laughter rose through the treetops, dispersing the air of tension that had surrounded them at his confession. The sound washed over her, soothing her wounded ego.

She leaned back against a tree and waited out his amusement. The thought occurred to her that perhaps she should come clean about her own intentions, as long as they were going there, but something stopped her from saying the words.

"Ah, love. You never cease to keep me on my toes." Jesse still had a twinkle in his eye as he rose to his full height, but it quickly diminished as he again looked out over the barren area where the dagobas should be.

Shea also rose, needlessly brushing the leaves and twigs from her dirty jeans. "You know who did this?"

"I do. But the joke is on them."

"What do you mean?"

He turned to look down at her. Carefully, he reached out and moved a strand of her long hair that had blown into her face with the humid breeze.

Shea shooed him away and tucked the wayward strand behind her ear. "Jesse, what did you mean by that?"

"Because it doesn't matter. I will still get what I want."

CHAPTER 21

Back at the hotel two nights later, Shea watched Jesse as he greeted Cruthú and freed the raven from her cage. Her body was attuned to every breath, every muscle movement, every beat of his heart. She craved the taste of him, the feel of him, even dirty as they were. Many times since leaving the clearing where the dagobas should've been, she'd found herself reaching for him, the blood lust nearly as overwhelming as the longing for his touch. But each time, she'd drawn back.

They'd made it back to the shelter that night with minutes to spare. Shea had immediately curled up beneath the overhang and fell into an exhausted sleep. She'd dreamed that she'd felt Jesse's arm wrapped around her waist, and his hard body curved around hers, keeping her warm. The sensations were so real, that when she woke, she swore she could still feel him there.

But when she rolled over and looked for him, he was sitting cross-legged out by the creek. Trying to stem the rise of disappointment, she rose and joined him. They'd made their way out to the road, and "borrowed" a car to drive back. Jesse drove the entire distance straight through, the trip made mostly in silence. When the sun rose, Shea hid under thick blankets they'd found in the back to protect her from the sun.

The raven scolded him for leaving her for so long, and Jesse apologized to her with soft words, treats, and scratches under her feathers. The bond they had was obvious, and if Shea were to be completely honest, she was a bit envious of it.

Okay, a lot envious.

Which was ridiculous. Cruthú was only a bird. A pet. And she was very sweet when she wasn't trying to steal Shea's diamond stud earrings. "Where did you find her, anyway?"

Jesse glanced over at Shea, and for a moment, his eyes shone with the complete love and devotion he felt for his pet before a veil of caution dulled their shine.

A wave of disappointment came over her at the loss. It made no sense at all, but Shea wanted him to look at her that way.

"I didn't. She found me." He set the raven down on top of her cage, murmured a promise that he would take her out to fly just as soon as they got cleaned up, and sank down onto the edge of the bed near her to take off his boots. "Cruthú helped me get out of a sticky situation when she was just a young raven and I was first attempting to infiltrate the vampire world. She saved me." A shadow of a smile ghosted about his lips as the bird bobbed her head, as though in agreement. "And then she wouldn't leave." When he met her eyes again, he appeared almost shy. "I'm glad she was so stubborn. She's my best friend. My only friend." This last came out so low only a vampire would be able to hear it.

Shea's heart ached for him, for the loneliness he must suffer. She frowned at herself, and shook it off. He'd chosen this life he led, witch or no witch. If he lacked friends, it was no one's fault but his own. "What made you get involved with Leeha?"

She didn't expect him to answer her, but this time there was no hesitation. "She had the altar that housed the demons that I needed. The easiest way to get to them was to work with her to do so."

"You weren't afraid of her?"

"Of Leeha?" One eyebrow lifted. "No. She was no threat to me."

Shea was confused. "If she was no threat to you, then why did you do the things you did? Why live there with her? Why do what you did to Luukas? Why not just go in there and get the demons out yourself?"

"Because I needed her to create the vampires for them to possess. I'm capable of accomplishing many things, but I can't create a creature of darkness."

"Why not just use humans?"

"Because vampires can be tracked by their maker. And, as you know, human bodies don't last very long once possessed. If I'd just set them loose upon the world, they would body hop so much, there would be no way I could possibly keep track of them, nor would I have any way to control what bodies they used. The elderly, children—it wouldn't matter to them."

Beloved sisters, Shea thought.

His gaze narrowed in on her, perhaps catching something in her thoughts or expression, but there was more she needed to know before he got distracted.

"I'm still not quite getting it. You could've released them, let them possess whoever they wanted to, and then told them where to find their original blood right then and there. Why the long wait?"

"It wasn't time. There were things that needed to happen before the demons regained control."

Before the demons regain control. Those words didn't cease to terrify her. "'Things' like what?"

He didn't answer her right away. "Just 'things'."

She sighed in exasperation. "Fine. Don't tell me. I'm going to take a shower."

Jesse sidestepped into her path. "I only don't tell you 'things' for your own safety, Shea. Never because I don't think your questions are important."

Strangely enough, she believed him. "I really just want to get clean and changed."

"Take your time in the shower. I'll take Cruthú out to stretch her wings, and when I return I need to call room service."

Shea had just picked up her bag and was heading into the bathroom. She came to a sudden stop as his words sunk in. Her head whipped around. She'd totally forgotten that he needed food. "Oh my gods! Jesse, I'm so sorry. You need to eat. I completely forgot."

He gave her a bemused look. "Don't look so crestfallen, Shea. I'm a man grown, among other things, and perfectly capable of getting my own meals. Besides, it wasn't your fault that we crash landed in the middle of the forest and not near a 24-hour diner."

She saw a trace of humor in his eyes at that last part. It was true, but it didn't make her feel any better. "I still should have thought about it, at least."

He gave her a look that she couldn't interpret. "Please don't beat yourself about it. I appreciate the concern, but there's really no need. I should have planned better."

Still feeling guilty for something that had been beyond her control, she hovered where she was, wanting to say more, and unsure why.

After a moment, Jesse had stepped closer to her, and waited patiently for her to give him her full attention. Shea's gaze hovered at the tanned skin of his throat, before eventually making its way up to his face. Golden fire blazed down at her, as unexpected as it was hoped for, imprisoning her where she stood. Shea caught her breath at the tension that erupted between them.

"Is this how our life together is to be, Shea? Polite conversation and the occasional slit wrist?"

"I don't know how else to be," she whispered. She couldn't look away, couldn't think, could barely breathe. His scent—of the darkest side of nature, male desire, and blood—swirled around her as Jesse lowered his head until his lips were less than an inch from hers. He froze, his eyes traveling over her face, and then lowered his head closer.

Closer.

Shea's fangs shot down, preparing to feed. Her mouth watered and her body trembled with hunger and need. She told herself to back away, to put distance between them, before she gave too much away and he discovered the power he wielded over her with the lust for his blood...and his body. Her head screamed at her to do so. But her muscles refused to obey.

With a helpless sound, she leaned in the last fraction of an inch and touched her lips to his. Just barely. Just a small taste.

She heard a sound of desperation, and realized it came from her. But she didn't even have time to appreciate the heat of his lips on hers before he was pulling away, leaving her cold and alone again. With a triumphant expression, he held out his arm to the raven and left Shea standing there in the middle of the room, her bag on the floor where she'd dropped it. With a horrified feeling, she realized...

He knew.

The bastard. He knew he could touch her, and he'd never said a word. Fear flashed through her, followed swiftly by a surge of longing so intense it made her lightheaded, only to be replaced by irritation that he hadn't told her, and then the fear was back. It was all too much to process at one time.

Shea shuffled into the bathroom in a sort of daze and closed and locked the door. She shed her ragged, dirty clothes and turned on the shower as hot as she could stand it. The water scalded her sensitive skin, but she barely felt it as she washed the dirt and blood from her hair and skin. Standing in the spray, she let the water rinse the soap away. But as she watched it circle the drain, she let her mind wander.

Anticipation filled her. He knew. There was no reason

for games anymore. No reason to keep him at bay. She was here. She was with him. The damage was already done. There was no reason to deny him now, or herself. Shea ran her hands up her stomach to her breasts. Her nipples were hard and responsive, aching to be touched, the skim of her palm shooting sparks to her lower belly. Her body longed for him in ways she'd never experienced before, and for a vampire who felt everything a hundred times more intensely than humans, that was really saying something.

But Shea couldn't in good conscience just fall into his arms. He was playing with her. With his secrets and his lies and his inability to stay the hell out of her head. But gods, her throat burned with thirst, and her body ached to be fucked.

It occurred to her that she if she could touch Jesse, she should be able to touch any male. He had obviously fixed whatever was wrong with her, perhaps when she was sleeping, and she was half-tempted to leave him here alone at the hotel while she did a little experimenting. She had years of good hetero sex to catch up on.

But even if she didn't already know what had happened to the others when they'd tried to do the same, the thought didn't appeal to her in the slightest. She didn't want anyone else. Sick as it was, she wanted the dark warlock.

But did she dare be with someone like him? Truly be with him?

She had the disturbing feeling that it didn't really matter what she wanted. Her vampire side had chosen its mate, whether she approved of the choice or not.

A VAMPIRE'S CHOICE

Shea shut the water off and grabbed her towel. She scrubbed her skin until it was pink and dry, then dug out a T-shirt and her favorite pajama pants. Once she'd dressed, she combed out her long hair and left it to air dry.

When she left the bathroom, Jesse still wasn't back, so she clicked on the TV and tried to get comfortable in the bed. But she was so jazzed up, she couldn't even focus on what she was seeing.

She was mindlessly flicking through the channels when there was a knock on the door. Shea muted the station she was on and flashed over to the door. "Who is it?"

A voice called out in accented English, "Room service, ma'am."

Shea opened the door and backed out of the way so he could come in and set the tray down. She tipped him handsomely, and thanked him in Chinese. The young male smiled in surprise, bowed, and left her alone. Shea locked the door behind him.

Glancing at the time, Shea frowned slightly. If Jesse had already ordered room service, then where was he? She glanced down at the covered dishes on the tray, and two things came to her at the same time: Jesse hadn't ordered anything before he left, and there was no aroma of food coming from the tray.

Shea flew backwards across the room so fast her head slammed into the door. Unlocking it, she left the room, smiling at the couple across the hall who were entering their room as she padded barefoot to the elevator.

She met Jesse in the lobby, coming back in with

Cruthú. It struck her that no one was paying them a bit of mind—a man in torn clothes, covered in blood and dirt, with a large raven on his shoulder. But right now, there were other things to worry about.

"Shea, what's wrong?"

"Did you order room service when you came downstairs earlier?" She kept her voice low.

"Yes, I did. Has it arrived? I'm starving."

No, I didn't. What is wrong?

Shea blinked as he smiled pleasantly and walked past her to the elevator.

Act normal. And come with me.

Holy shit. He can talk to me in my head?

Yes, and you can speak to me, as you already know. Now, walk, Shea. Quickly. We're not alone here.

She gave him a brilliant smile. "Oh, good. I'm hungry, too."

Don't overdo it, love.

Sorry. She glanced at his profile. He walked steadily toward their destination. Not rushing, but not wasting any time either. *Have you always been able to talk to me this way?*

No. Only since you gave me your blood.

So, that *was* him she'd heard saying her name after the crash.

Yes.

Okay. She'd already had enough of this shit. She'd never have a moment's peace again, not even in her own mind. *Get out of my head, warlock.*

Shea walked calmly beside him, not saying another word until they got into the elevator. Once the doors closed, she released the breath she'd been holding pent up inside of her and spun toward him.

But Jesse shook his head in warning, a subtle gesture, and glanced up briefly at the camera in the corner.

Changing tactics, Shea reached out to pet the raven. "Where have you been? I didn't think you were going to be so long." Gods, she sounded like a wife.

"Cruthú was enjoying the time outside. I'm sorry if we worried you."

The bell above the doors chimed, and they slid open a few seconds later. Shea followed him out and to their room.

Stay in the hall until I tell you it's safe to come in.

She nodded, even though she was walking behind him and he couldn't see her, and watched him as he walked inside after handing the raven off to her. Leaning against the wall, she waited with one eye on the window at the end of the hall. The sun was going to come up soon.

"Come in, Shea."

Hurrying inside, she stopped just inside the door. Jesse stood in front of the tray, hands clasped behind his back. The cover from one of the dishes floated in front of him as he studied the contents beneath.

"What is it?"

"Only a message."

"From whom?"

The cover floated down to the tray, covering the plate before she could get a good look. Without a word, Jesse turned away and walked over to the windows. He tugged on the curtains, closing them tight against the coming dawn.

Shea was about to ask him again when he spoke.

"Someone you would rather not know about." He finished fussing with the curtains. "I'm going to take a shower." Grabbing some clean clothes, he went into the bathroom and shut the door.

Shea stood where she was, her eyes on the tray. Less than a second later, she stood in front of it, lifting the cover with her free hand. An earring lay in the center of the plate: a diamond stud.

Her hand went immediately to her left ear. She felt the jewelry there and checked the other side. All she felt was her earlobe. Shea looked at Cruthú, but the bird tilted her head jerkily to the side and stared back with one black eye as if to say, "Why are you blaming me?"

Shea took her over to her cage and gave her some food. How could he just say something like that and then go off to take a shower, knowing she stood out here burning with questions. She turned off the TV and listened to the sound of running water coming from the bathroom. What the hell was taking him so long?

Leaving the raven eating in her cage with the door open in case she wanted to come out again, Shea burst into the bathroom. "What does this mean? Who had my earring, Jesse?"

"It's cold out there, Shea."

She closed the door behind her. "And what are they trying to warn us of, exactly? Are they coming after you? After me? What?"

The water shut off and the curtain yanked open. Shea's next words dried up in her throat as Jesse reached for the white towel folded on the cabinet above the toilet. He didn't bother to cover himself with it as he stepped out. Water dripped from his dark hair and beaded on his skin, flushed from the heat of the shower. The muscles in his arms flexed as he dried his hair, leaving it in a wild disarray of dark waves until he ran one hand through it to get it into some type of order. His body was lean and hard, with just the right amount of dark chest hair to make him a man rather than a boy. And in case she had missed that fact, his penis hung thick and long between his hips, fully erect.

Gods, he was a fine specimen of a male.

Shea watched him dry off, her body instantly reacting to his. She should apologize and leave, allow him his privacy while he got dressed, but she found herself unable to turn away. Her tongue wet her lips, teasing the tips of her fangs. They ached painfully at the sight of all that bare skin, the blood flowing just beneath the surface. She wouldn't have to bite very deep to get to it. She tried to swallow, but her throat was dry. A low growl started deep in her core and rose to her chest. An involuntary response that still surprised her a little after all these years.

Her prey stood not four feet away, calmly wrapping the towel around his waist. One corner of his mouth lifted when the predatory sound filled the small room. The smirk fell from his face and his hips jerked forward slightly as his hand brushed the now hidden bulge. His body swayed toward her, instead of running away, as if pulled by the sound of her hunger. Shea noticed every draw of breath, every tiny movement. She was no longer thinking clearly, was no longer rational. She was a predator, and she was starving.

Jesse ground his jaw together and looked at her, his eyes full of the golden fire she'd only glimpsed earlier, but he didn't come for her.

"If you want me, vampire, I'm right here. But it must be your decision, because we both know once this starts, it's not going to stop."

Shea flicked her eyes over his body once, twice, before coming back to his face. The wanting was so much more than before, the blood lust so much stronger. Her every cell attuned to him. She could hear the blood rushing through his veins. The dark power in him called to something in her she could no longer deny. Yet still, she hesitated.

"I want you, Shea." His voice was raw with emotion. "I have since the first moment I saw you. And yes, I've known since the plane crash that you could touch me. But I didn't say anything because I wanted this to be your decision."

Water dripped from the ends of his hair and landed on his powerful shoulders. Shea watched them run down the ridges of muscle. She tried to force herself to focus on the reason she'd barged in there. Tried to stop watching the drops as they traveled a crooked path down his chest and over his abs to disappear into the towel.

Only then did she remember about the earring.

He answered her unspoken half-thought. "The earring is nothing to be overly concerned about. It's just a message that they know you are with me. You lost it in the plane crash. I noticed it was missing when you first found me."

"Who sent it?" She could barely get the words out. Her

body trembled with the effort it took to stay where she was.

"Mammot—Steven, as he now likes to call himself. He's the leader of the demons that were released, the one organizing them."

"How do you know it was him?" Her voice barely sounded like herself. But she needed to concentrate. It was important to know.

His intake of breath drew her attention to his chest. "I could sense his aura on the earring." He shrugged. "It's the only way I can explain it. But you are in no danger. Please trust me when I say that."

She gave a short nod to let him know she understood. Her hand fumbled for the doorknob behind her. She needed to escape. Before she did something she would regret. She hadn't had enough time to think this through.

But her hand stilled on the knob. For deep down, she knew there would never be any real escape from him. Not if she wanted to survive.

His eyes flicked down to her hand on the doorknob. "Shea."

Her name was a plea on his lips. A surrender. A submission. But not an order.

"Please. Come to me." He held out one hand to her, then it dropped back down to his side. "It has to be your choice." The words sounded rushed, like some last remnant of decency was forcing him to still give her a choice. A choice that didn't exist.

She wanted to. Gods, how she wanted to. Her body swayed forward. Through the red haze of her lust, she thought of Luukas and the others. The Master Vampire would never take her back. Not with Jesse in tow. Too much had been done. He would see her actions as a betrayal. He would never forgive her. She would never be able to go home.

A tear slid down her cheek.

Jesse searched her face, his jaw clenched. His head fell forward in defeat. Sorrow and frustration emitted from him in waves. But when he lifted his chin a few seconds later, the fire was replaced by a grim acceptance. "I can't change who I am, or what I've done, or what I have yet to do." He paused, took a deep breath. "I've told you how I felt. It must be your choice."

Blood lust fogged her thoughts, yet her vampire instincts were razor-sharp. And right now, they told her to hunt. To feed. To *claim*.

She took a step forward. Stopped. Her head twitched to the side. Pulling her lips up into a snarl, she flashed her fangs at him in a last desperate warning. Coherent thought was nearly beyond her now.

Jesse stood with his feet braced apart, the white towel slung low on his narrow hips. He was breathing hard, his arms at his sides, his hands balled into tight fists, his eyes alight in sinful triumph at every second that passed with her still in the room.

Shea was losing the fight. The rest of the room faded away as her focus zeroed in on her prey. Another growl ripped from her throat, but he showed no fear. Not even a twinge of nervousness.

"I'm not afraid of you, Shea. I *crave* you. The weight of your body, the satin of your skin, the silk of your hair. Even the craziness of the thoughts that bounce around in your head." Golden fire flashed from his eyes. "The very idea of those razor fangs of yours slicing into my throat excites me. And the only thing I fear is that I will come too soon while you feed, before giving you any pleasure." His eyes narrowed in challenge. "What are you waiting for, vampire? You need blood. You need to be pleasured." He opened his arms wide. "And I'm right here."

He had a point.

Shea slammed into him, the force of her momentum sending him flying backward. Yet, instead of catching himself, his arms wrapped tight around her as he fell, taking her with him. They landed hard in the shower with her lying on top of him. Grabbing a fistful of his hair, she wrenched his head to the side and sank her fangs into his throat.

Jesse cried out in pain and pleasure, his fingers digging into her flesh. But he didn't pull away, or even try to. Instead, he cranked his head over even farther in the small space, giving her more room to latch on to him.

Shea moaned as his dark blood flooded her mouth, arousing more than the blood lust as her body responded to the feel of him...the taste of him. She swallowed, and it was like taking a shot of raw power. It rushed through her system, flooding every cell, every muscle, filling her with his dark sorcery.

She was invincible.

Another strong pull, and her blood lit on fire. She wanted him. Gods, how she wanted him. But she was thirsty, so she drank. She drank while he moaned with pleasure beneath her, his hands running all over her body now. Slipping under her shirt and down the back of her loose pants.

"Shea, stop. Stop. Ah! I'm about to come." His hips rolled up, and she felt the hard length of his erection against her thigh.

Lifting her head, she released him from her bite and licked the wound clean as he moaned in disappointment and relief. Then she reared back, quick as a snake, and struck again. Pulling hard on his vein, she groaned with pleasure and adjusted her hips until she felt him right where she wanted him, and then she began to move.

His muscles tensed, his body jerking beneath her as he lost control and came into the towel. Her name left his lips on a cry as he rocked his hips against hers, holding her tight against his body.

Shea growled with need and sucked harder. His blood filled her, his arms held her close, and his raw cries sounded in her ear until she wasn't sure where she ended and he began. But it wasn't enough. She wanted more. She needed more. Withdrawing her fangs, she again licked the wound clean.

But before she could bite again, Jesse cupped her face in his large palms and brought her mouth to his. He kissed her with desperation, heedless of her fangs cutting his lips, until they were breathing the same air and Shea's heart pounded in rhythm with his.

She needed more. Needed to feel his skin on hers. Needed to feel him inside of her. She felt his cock swell beneath her at the thought and knew he was in her head even as he was taking control of her body.

Suddenly, Jesse sat up, bringing her with him. Cupping

one arm around her bottom, he stood with her in his arms. He was stronger than one would think. The bathroom door slammed into the wall behind it as he flung it open, and Shea pulled her T-shirt off and dropped it on the floor between kisses as he took them over to the bed. She smiled as he stole a glance to check the curtains, and her gaze dropped hungrily to the pulse in his throat. She tore her eyes away as he looked back and caught her.

"Go on, love. Take all you want. I can handle it."

CHAPTER 22

Jesse moaned as she bit him again, those sharp teeth sliding effortlessly through his skin and into the vein. When she sucked, he felt it all the way to his balls. His arm tightened around her back, pulling her closer.

If he were to die by vampire, he didn't think there was any better way to go.

Somehow, he managed to yank his towel the rest of the way off and get them both onto the bed without breaking her hold on his throat. The blood he had remaining concentrated in his cock, and he pressed his hips into hers. The softness of her skin was warmer than he'd imagined, the feel of her feeding from him the most erotic thing he'd ever experienced. But it wasn't enough, wasn't nearly enough. "Let go, love. Just for a second. I need to be inside you."

She made a sound of protest, but released her bite.

Jesse wasted no time in getting her pajama pants off.

Tossing them onto the floor, he took a few seconds just to gaze upon her, part of him wondering what he'd ever done to deserve her. She was all soft curves and long legs. He wanted to take his time—explore her, make it last—but even though he'd already come once, his body had other ideas.

Kneeling between her legs, he pulled her up until her face was inches from his and moved her into position on his lap. With one hand around the base of his cock and one hand on her hip, he found her entrance. As soon as she figured out what he was doing, she sank down without pause. Jesse slid into her warm sheath until he was entirely inside of her. Her husky voice cried out in his ear, and he worried for a moment that he'd hurt her. But she was wet and ready for him, her body squeezing him tight as she rose up and came down again.

He threw back his head as she moved her hips, exposing his throat, and Shea struck. Gripping her hips, he let her feed while he started a steady rhythm, not rushing, enjoying the feel of this female he'd waited so long for. His heart thumped with strong, steady beats, pumping his blood through his veins for her while his breath came in short bursts of air.

But too soon, he felt his orgasm rising. Taking her with him, he rose up and leaned forward. None too gently, he laid her on her back and moved into position. Her teeth tore through his skin until she had to release him, but he barely felt the pain. Bracing one arm on the headboard and one on the bed, Jesse fucked her as he'd dreamt about ever since that first day in the altar room—fast and hard and quite thoroughly. His balls tightened up against his body and his cock swelled, filling her until she was almost uncomfortably snug around him. He gritted his teeth, but there was no way he could hang on, or wait for her. It was too late. He couldn't stop.

Turning her head, she bit his wrist. Jesse grunted at the slight pain and pumped harder as she strained beneath him, her hips meeting his thrust for thrust. She drank, sending electric shocks straight to his groin. Her fingers dug into his hips, urging him on. He memorized every sound she made, every look, every touch. And when she came, with her body arched and her fangs bared, it was the most erotically beautiful thing he'd ever seen. Her name tore from his lungs as he joined her, burying himself deep until he was spent. Catching his breath, he collapsed on top of her.

When he could finally lift his head, he gazed down into her green eyes. They were filled with concern.

"Are you all right? I didn't mean to take so much, I was just so thirsty."

His head buzzed like a swarm of bees had taken up residence, and his body felt weak and satiated. "I feel wonderful, Shea."

She scowled up at him. "Then why are you slurring your words? Get off me and I can help you."

"No. I like you right where you are."

She stopped wiggling around and settled underneath him with a sigh. She searched his face, and he suddenly felt exposed, like somehow by taking so much of him inside of her she saw right through to his black soul. With a soft kiss to the tip of her nose, he hugged her to him for a minute before he rolled away and sat up. "Shea, I need to tell you some things. Things I should have told you right from—"

"No, Jesse. Don't."

He looked over his shoulder. Her long, dark hair spread over his pillow, and those mysterious cat eyes fixed on the ceiling. She didn't try to cover herself, or hide from him.

One slender hand slid across the comforter until she touched his hip with the tips of her fingers. He understood her need for the contact, and didn't want to say anything that would ruin this moment between them, but she needed to know. Needed to know who exactly she'd mated. Especially now that things between them were changing. This female was a gift he didn't deserve. He may not be what she'd always dreamed of, but he never wanted there to be a reason for her to mistrust him.

Anyone else. But not her. "I have to. I don't want secrets between us anymore."

She sat up and pressed against his back. He closed his eyes at the feel of her soft breasts. The simple gesture was nearly his undoing. She dropped a kiss onto his shoulder. "I don't care who you are."

"Yes, you do," he whispered.

She sighed. "All right, I do. But, there's not much to do about it now, is there? Fate has chosen you for me, and I don't seem capable of fighting her whims or controlling myself enough to commit a slow suicide. I need your blood to live. And I want to live. It is what it is."

Her words cut him to the quick. She sounded so matter of fact, so resigned to her fate. Twisting around to face her, he dove into her thoughts. She was lying, her casual attitude hiding what she truly felt. It was much more than that to her. "Don't hide from me, Shea. Don't do that."

She pulled back and narrowed her eyes. "If you don't like what I'm thinking, then get out of my head."

"I can't. Not when you insist on lying to me. How else will I know how you really think or feel?"

Getting up from the bed, she marched into the bathroom and slammed the door.

Jesse gave her some privacy. He could use a little himself. Pulling on a pair of boxer briefs, he went to the window. The sun was just cresting the horizon, and he quickly dropped the curtain back into place. It worried him that Shea was so exposed up here. The slightest breeze from the ventilation could take her away from him forever.

Taking a deep breath, he quieted his thoughts. Speaking to the dark souls that hovered around him, he ordered them to guard the window. When he looked again, a large dark shadow blocked the sun's rays from coming into the room, just as they'd done in the small cave. He turned away as the bathroom door opened, a bit easier than it had been closed.

Shea leaned in the doorway, gloriously nude, and regarded him with a guarded expression. Her hands twisted in front of her. "I don't want to hear what you have to tell me. Not right now. I'm still trying to get used to this. To us." She paused and looked down at her bare feet for a moment. Her dark hair hid her face, and Jesse resisted the urge to move it out of the way. When she lifted her head, she gave him a small smile. "Can we talk tonight? And just take today to enjoy being together?"

A sense of relief filled him. "Yes. We can do that."

She nodded. "Good. There are things I need to tell you, too."

Ah. So, they were getting to that. "I know."

CHAPTER 23

Keira waved at the doorman of her apartment building, pulled up the hood of her raincoat, and walked out into the Seattle drizzle with Emma, Grace, Ryan, and Laney. He would tell Luukas she'd snuck out as soon as the sun went down, but she'd be back by then and could show him no harm was done. As far as he needed to know, she and the other girls just needed a little daylight and went to get a coffee.

Which was true, and which they were.

What he didn't need to know, is they decided to meet at the coffee shop down the street instead of the one he'd had newly installed in the building specifically to get away from listening ears. It was the middle of the day, there were tons of people around, and it was perfectly safe, despite what her overprotective mate thought.

Normally, Keira wouldn't do something like this. Luukas, although getting better, wasn't completely healed from his years in Leeha's company. And perhaps he never would be. He totally freaked out every time she so much as mentioned doing anything other than sitting around the apartment under his watchful eye.

But after everything they'd been through, she wasn't about to lose him now.

She held the door open for the other girls and they filed in and ordered their drinks, then claimed the sitting area in the back corner of the shop. The brown, faux leather chairs there were thick and comfy, and it set back from the counter and the other customers.

Keira waited until they'd all gotten comfortable. "Okay, ladies. We can't be gone too long, the guys are gonna freak later as it is."

"Right, though?" Grace said. "Aiden almost didn't want me to hang out with you guys this morning. He wanted to 'snuggle'. It took some doing to convince him we could snuggle all he wanted once that damn demon was out of him. He tolerates our girl time, but he doesn't really get it."

"Well, Nik gets it, but mostly he just finds the stuff I can do amusing." Emma rolled her eyes.

"If I can manage to get away from Dante, I don't want to hear any complaining from any of you," Laney teased.

"She has a point," Ryan told them.

They all nodded in agreement and took sips of their coffees.

"Okay, then," Keira told them. "Let's get a plan together. The guys are all vampy and powerful and blah, blah, blah. But we all know it's going to be up to us to send the demons back to hell where they belong."

"So, um, how exactly are we going to do that?" Emma asked with a shudder.

Keira gave her sister a sympathetic smile. Out of all of them, she had the most scars from her run in with those things. Literally. "If you don't want to do this, Em. You don't have to."

But Emma firmly shook her head. "No way. I'm in. I'm not hiding under the blankets while you guys go risk your lives. While Nikulas is out there facing these things." She smiled at the other girls. "Besides, we're stronger together, right? We've learned that in our little lessons. Imagine what we'll be able to accomplish if we really cut loose."

Laney squeezed Emma's hand and turned to Keira. "So, how're we gonna do this?"

"With Grace's spell," Keira told her.

"I thought no one could read that spell," Laney said.

"Ryan can. Or, rather, her spirits can."

All eyes turned to Ryan.

"Really?" Laney asked her. "They can translate it?"

"It appears that way," she answered. "I get the sense it's a very old language. Not all of them know what it says, but a few do. I wasn't sure what it was at first, but eventually I figured out it's not just a spell. It's *the* spell. The one that will send them back to the altar."

"The spell is strong," Keira told them. "It will take all of us together to summon it. But with all our skills combined, I think we have a good chance at success." She nodded at Emma. "When the possessed vampires converge at the altar with their original blood, we'll be there, and we'll be ready."

"What if they rip us apart before we manage to bind them to the spell?" Ryan asked.

But Keira shook her head. "They won't. We'll be

protected within the circle. Grace will bring the salt. Right?"

Grace whipped out her phone and started typing a note to herself. "Buy salt. Lots and lots of salt."

"The guys will be there, just in case, and Emma can freeze them," Keira continued. "Once they're contained, Laney, we'll need you to exorcise the demons out of the host bodies. Ryan will translate the spell for us, and we'll bind our magic and execute the spell. Once the demons are gone, Grace and Luukas will save who they can."

"You make it sound so easy." Grace took a deep breath.

Keira wouldn't lie to them. "It won't be easy. Not at all. We're taking our lives in our hands. One slip, and the circle could break or our magic could come unbound and it will all be over. Are you all ready for this?" She looked at the circle of faces surrounding her. Her family.

"Do we have a choice?" Emma asked.

"I don't," Grace told her. "I want that damn thing out of my mate."

Emma leaned over and took her hand. "We all do, Gracie."

The rest of the girls piled their hands on top of Emma's.

CHAPTER 24

When the sun finally set that night, a pounding on the hotel door woke Shea and Jesse. Shea bolted upright with a hiss, and in the twilight, Jesse saw the glint of her fangs. He calmed her with a hand on her arm, got out of bed, pulled on his pants, and went to the door to look through the peephole.

Mammot stood on the other side. Jesse should have known by the stench. An old hooded coat hid the demon's features, and when he turned his head to look down the hall, the bones of his teeth were exposed through the rotted flesh of his cheek. The body the demon inhabited was dying, which meant the others weren't far behind. They were going to have to move fast.

Jesse came back inside and found his shirt. "Shea, I need you to go into the bathroom and stay there until I come get you."

She was already out of bed and digging around in her bag.

Stepping into a pair of cotton underwear, she pulled them up over her hips and bent over again to pull out a bra. "I'm not hiding in the other room. I'm staying out here with you."

He pulled a black T-shirt on and prepared to force her into the other room if need be. "Don't argue, Shea. Please. He will know you're here, and he knows who and what you are. But I can perhaps convince him not to fuck with you just yet. Now do as I say. Please."

She stared at him. "What do you mean, you know 'who and what' I am?"

"Let's not play this game right now. We don't have time, love." And with that, he shoved her toward the bathroom. "Lock the door and turn on the shower." His tone left no room for argument.

He waited until he heard the click of the lock and the water, then he narrowed his eyes at the door. She would hear everything that was said, despite the running water. Shea could hear a human heartbeat four blocks away.

Jesse didn't like this. It wasn't the way he wanted her to find out. He sighed heavily. There was nothing to do for it now. He would just have to do damage control as best as he could once the demon was gone.

A moment later, he released the chain and invited the demon into their room. The morbid appearance didn't faze him. He'd seen much worse. "What are you doing here, Mammot?" He didn't bother to ask how the demon had found him. He was a demon, after all, and had abilities that nearly rivaled Jesse's own.

"Where is she?"

Jesse crossed his arms over his chest. So, it was getting

straight to the point. "She's not a concern to you. Her being here has nothing to do with our deal."

Mammot cocked his head slowly to the side. The action caused the rotting skin of his face to gather in loose folds. "No concern?" he mocked. "You have a descendent of the holy bloods here and you expect me to not be 'concerned'?"

"She doesn't know what she is, other than a vampire." Not completely true. "And she is only here because it was the only way I could make sure she never found out. At least, not until the ritual is performed and it's too late for her to do anything about it."

The demon leaned in until he but a few inches from Jesse's face. Cruthú clicked her beak from her cage, angry at the threat to him. Jesse held up a hand behind his back without taking his attention from the demon, telling her it was okay. He stayed where he was, even though he wanted to recoil from the smell.

"Give her to me," it growled.

Jesse stared down the fires of hell standing before him. He had no fear of hell. Or of the creatures it birthed. "No."

Mammot straightened. If it were smart, it would leave the subject alone. But apparently, its skin wasn't the only organ that was rotting. "The bitch is coming with me, witch."

Jesse smiled as an icy-hot rage filled him. Everything else left his mind except the need to protect his female. "You take one step farther into this room, and I will rip you apart where you stand and toss the bloody pieces of you out of that window." It wasn't a bluff. Having the demon in chunks would do nothing to mess up Jesse's plans.

Mammot/Steven eyed him with his one good eye. "You wouldn't dare. You need me. You need us."

"I will still get what I want. This body does not need to be whole to be effective."

"Perhaps I'll find a different body. You're lucky I haven't already. For as you can see, these vampires are not so resilient once their creator is dead. And then what will you do, witch? Come after us? Send us back to the altar?" He laughed at the idea. "I think not. Not after you've spent so much time and effort helping us to get this far."

"The time I've spent with you and your dead mistress is naught but a flash in the pan during my long life. And patience is something I've had to learn along the way. I need you, yes, but not as much as you need me. If this doesn't work out, I will only find another way to get what I want. So, let's not push it, Mammot." Jesse purposefully called it by its original name, because he knew it pissed it off. "Now let's stop worrying about things that are no threat to you, or me." He walked away, turning his back on Mammot to prove to the demon how little it threatened him. Getting a water out of the small refrigerator, Jesse twisted off the top and took a drink. He kept his back to the demon, unafraid that it would sneak up on him. Jesse would know what it was going to do before it managed to fully develop the thought. "Where is the blood, Mammot?"

After a tense few seconds of silence, Mammot/Steven said, "We have it."

Jesse glanced at the bathroom door. He could imagine

Shea pressed up against it, her ear to the door. He turned to face the demon again. "The blood, where is it?"

"It's safe."

Jesse needed to get his hands on it to ensure his plan was going to work. "You need to give it to me so I can prepare it for the ritual."

The demon crossed its arms over its chest. "Why can't you prepare it there?"

Jesse didn't have the time or the patience for this bullshit, but he kept his voice level. "Because there are things I need to do with it, and because it will take time. I need to re-activate the life force in the blood cells. It's been stagnant for many years." It was a bit more complicated than that, but that was the gist of it. "I need time, and a quiet place to prepare it. I will bring it with me to the altar. Safe and sound and ready."

Mammot/Steven grunted at him, but didn't agree.

"Hand it over, Mammot. We don't want to take any chances that even one of your idiot followers happens to get an idea in its head and takes it upon itself to take the blood to someone else. Or worse, spill it back into the earth while they knock each other around in one of their never-ending disagreements."

The demon didn't like it, but it finally agreed. "All right. Fine. I will bring it back here. Tonight."

"When?"

"In one hour."

Jesse gave him a nod. "You need to leave now."

Mammot didn't so much as twitch a finger. "You know, I'm not afraid of you, witch."

Jesse pinned it with an unflinching stare. "Perhaps you should be, demon."

The water shut off in the bathroom, and Jesse knew—without having to read her mind—that Shea was about to come out. "It's time for you to go," he told Mammot. "I will meet you in the alley behind the hotel in an hour to get the blood."

The thing still made no move to leave. "How do I know I can trust you?"

Jesse set his water down and laced his fingers together in front of him. "You don't. But what choice do you have?" When it had no response, he walked past the demon and opened the door. "You'd best hurry if you're going to be back here in an hour."

Mammot/Steven walked out into the hallway, pulling its hood down to hide the rotting face from the humans. "One hour."

"I'll be waiting."

Once it was on the elevator, Jesse closed and locked the door. He turned to find Shea directly behind him. He wasn't surprised. He'd known she was there without needing to look. He could feel her.

She didn't say anything. Didn't ask any questions. Just watched him with those green, green eyes.

Jesse returned her stare without flinching. "There are things you need to know about me."

The life appeared to drain from her face as he watched, but she nodded. "Yes. It's time to talk."

CHAPTER 25

Shea stared at the male she had come to have such complicated feelings for in such a short amount of time, and she dreaded this conversation they were about to have. Right now, those feelings could sway easily one way or the other, and she didn't know what she was more terrified of: that she would come to hate him...

Or love him.

But either way, it was time for her to know. Perhaps it wouldn't be as bad as she feared. "You're not a normal witch."

He took her hand and pulled her along with him to the bed. Sitting her down, he knelt on the floor in front of her, still holding her hand. His thumb rubbed the delicate bones of her knuckles.

To Shea, he looked like he was praying. And perhaps he was.

"No. I'm not just a witch. I am half witch on my mother's side. The Moss side."

"Moss?"

"Yes, my name is Jesse Moss."

"You're related to Keira and Emma...?"

"Yes. And Grace. And Laney. But mostly to Ryan."

Shea was still trying to wrap her head around it. "Ryan?"

"Ryan is my sister. We were separated by our mother when she was too young to remember."

Well, that explains why I don't like her. "So, you said you're only half witch. Witches mate with humans all the time. As long as one parent carries the magic it will pass on to the child. Your other half is human?"

He sighed. "No."

Staring into his golden eyes, she was almost afraid to ask. "What is the other half, Jesse?"

His stare didn't waver. "My father is djinn."

Shea frowned. She couldn't have heard him correctly. "I'm sorry? What?"

"I'm half witch, from the Moss coven, and half djinn. And not the good kind. As is Ryan. Although, from what I know of her, my genes are stronger."

"Djinn. As in genie."

"Yes."

"I didn't realize there was more than one kind of genie."

He shrugged. "There are two types. Good and evil, to keep it simple. My father is from the wrong side of the tracks, so to speak."

Shea's heart sank with every word. "Good gods. That's the darkness in you."

"Yes."

"That's the power in you."

"Yes."

"That's why I feared you."

"Yes." He glanced down at their joined hands. "You don't seem surprised by my admission."

He was right. There was no surprise. She knew of the djinn. Her father had taught her of their existence and their ways. They were to be feared more than demons, and avoided at all costs if you happened to run across one. Even for someone of her bloodline. They were more powerful than a Master Vampire, were capable of sorcery witches could only dream of, and they weren't to be trusted. If he had all of that, on top of the normal magic a true witch possessed….

She looked away, unable to hold his gaze any longer. Her heart pounded in her ears. Yet, she couldn't bring herself to remove her hand from his. His touch was a drug to her, a drug she couldn't resist. And she didn't want to.

"I can taste it in you. The darkness."

"You like it." It wasn't a question.

She turned back to him. "Yes." The word was said more in her mind than out loud, but he heard her.

"And it brings you shame."

"Yes."

"Because of who *you* are."

Shea nodded. "I shouldn't crave your darkness. I should want to destroy it."

"But you don't want to destroy me."

"No." Her voice cracked.

She closed her eyes as shame flooded through her, making her reel. Everything she'd done in her life, everything she'd fought for, everything she'd been forced to do, went directly against her being with Jesse. Yet, she couldn't make herself turn away. Even without the vampire bond to its mate, she had craved him like no other. Just to be in his presence, to hear his voice.

Tears ran unheeded down her cheeks. "I shouldn't be with you. Yet I went against everything I'd been taught —*everything*—to do just that."

"I'm so sorry I've caused you so much confusion and pain, Shea." His words rang with honesty, and his own pain for causing her any suffering. "It was never my intention. I tried to stay away after you left. I did. I sat in that room alone, and I dreamed of you every second. But I didn't reach out, not once. Because I knew I was no good for you. I knew it before I discovered who you really are." He reached out to touch her face. "But the moment I heard your voice on the phone, my resolve fell to pieces." He dropped his hand, and sat back on his haunches. "I paced my room for days, worrying about you, and trying to talk myself out of coming to you. But in the end, I couldn't resist the pull. I just…I wasn't strong enough. And for that, I apologize. I should have been stronger, Shea. I should've been strong enough for both of us." He ran his hand through his dark hair. "I should have left after seeing you at that club and reassuring myself that you were safe."

Shea listened to his words, but more importantly, she felt the turmoil within him. The blood bond between them was so strong now they were almost as one person. And knowing his feelings for her were as turbulent as hers were for him was her undoing. She wanted to reach for him. But there was more that needed to be said. More that needed to be out in the open.

"I'm not so innocent myself," she said. "I have blood on my hands. And I'm not talking about some poor person I accidentally drained when I was new to this life." She cringed a bit. "Although, that did happen once or twice before I got the hang of feeding."

"You're speaking of your sister."

Shea nodded. "Yes. And let me tell it. Don't pull it out of my head. I need to say it. I need to say it to you."

"All right." He took her hand between both of his. "Tell me what happened with your sister."

Shea took a deep breath. The only other person who knew what she was about to say was Luukas. She'd told him the night she'd asked him to turn her, once it was done and he knew she'd lied about being ill. "I belong to a long bloodline of people. Some would call us special, others think we're cursed."

"What do you think?"

She thought about that. "I think we're a little of both. Our line has been around for thousands of years—way before the Christians created their book and worshipped their God. We are the true holy people. We are the ones who fought to keep demons from this world, and the ones who send them back when they escape their hell."

She thought back to the beginning of her human life. It seemed so long ago. "Every generation has three children. Two girls and one boy to secure the bloodline."

"I've heard of your kind, but always wondered if it was only a tale creatures like me were told to keep us in line, since we're not afraid of anyone else."

"And did you fear me when you figured out what I am?"

He smiled. "No."

Shea narrowed her eyes at his egotistical attitude, and repeated his own words to him. "Maybe you should."

"Perhaps." He stared into her eyes for a moment, and Shea felt him poking around in her head. "Tell me what happened to your sister."

The teasing mood left her as quickly as it had come on. "I had to kill her."

"Why?"

"She was possessed by a demon."

Jesse frowned. "But why the vampirism? If you come from the holy bloodline, why did you go to Luukas?"

Memories of Elise came flooding back. Her sister had meant everything to Shea. She'd been her best friend, her confidant, her partner in life.

And the only possessed person she wasn't able to kill. "I couldn't kill her because we shared the holy blood. It's forbidden. The blood doesn't allow it. So, I went to Luukas and asked him to turn me."

Understanding crossed Jesse's features. "Because the vampire side of you doesn't discriminate against who its victims are."

"Exactly." Shea wiped more tears away. "But I had to do it, Jesse. There was no other way to free her. The demon had found its way into her somehow. Into one of us! One of the bloodline! And it wasn't leaving anytime soon. It was only biding its time, figuring out a way to kill us all, including the host body—my sister."

"I'm so sorry, love. I'm so sorry that you had to go through that."

Shea swallowed hard and took a haggard breath, pushing the memories deep down into the furthest recesses of her mind. It was the only way she could live with herself. When she'd convinced Luukas to turn her, her only thought had been to save her sister's soul. She hadn't thought twice about it. There was no one else to do it. She had to be the one to take her sister's life. Because she loved her so much. Just as Shea would have wanted Elise to do the same if the situation had been reversed.

"You have nothing to feel guilty about, Shea. You did what you had to do."

She focused on him again. "Is that what you're doing, Jesse? What you have to do?"

He was quiet for a long time. "Yes."

"And what is that, exactly?" When he stayed quiet, she prompted, "I showed you mine, it's only fair that you show me yours."

He laughed at the saying. "I thought I'd already done that."

She rolled her eyes. "Stop trying to deflect my questions. I want to know everything, Jesse. No. I need to know everything. If we are going to be together, I need to know." She backtracked a bit. "That *is* what you want? For us to be together? Truly together?"

Still on his knees, he was suddenly mere inches from her face, before she'd even seen him move. "Shea, I can't begin to tell you what it's been like for me these last few days, having you with me. Having someone else want to be with me...no. Not just 'someone'. *You.* Having *you* want to be with me. However much you fought against it."

"Then tell me why you're helping the demons."

Ah, yes. That. She heard the words though they were not spoken aloud.

"Yes," she said. "That."

Jesse shrugged. "It's simple really. I have a family member who is running amok. I need to stop him."

"And you need *demons,* creatures from the furthest depths of hell, to help you."

"Yes. They are the only ones with enough power to do it."

Shea tried to imagine someone so powerful Jesse would need demons to take him out, rather than just doing it himself. It was hard to imagine, even though she had a feeling she'd only seen the merest hints of what he was capable of. "Your father?"

"My father," he confirmed. "The newest High Priest of the Moss coven."

Shock rocked her to the core. "Your father is the High Priest? The one the others are running from?"

"Yes. And with good reason."

Good gods. "So, I still don't understand what the demons have to do with it."

"The demons are the only creatures with power as completely evil as my father's. Once they are in their original forms, and have all that power back, they've agreed to help me kill him."

"But he's your father—"

"And he's completely insane. He needs to be removed from this dimension and back to his own. The demons will take him there. And in return, his power will become theirs."

"And your end of the deal is you've agreed to bring them back, and help them reclaim their place in this world." Lines of worry creased her forehead. "And this is why you need to protect me and my family."

"Yes."

She shook her head. "But humanity won't survive such an invasion, Jesse. And then how will the vampires survive?"

"I don't care about other vampires. I care about you. And Luukas and the others have all found their mates, as have you. I will protect my family, also."

"But how? If the demons can take out your father, what's to stop them from taking *you* out?" She tried to keep the fear from her voice, and failed miserably.

"I am not a pure blood djinn. I am also part Moss witch, the most powerful coven of white witches ever to exist. I am light and dark, good and evil. And as such, I am something for the demons to fear."

For the first time, Shea was beginning to understand the full magnitude of the male in front of her. "And every other creature that exists," she whispered. "Oh, my gods." She got it now, why fate had chosen him for her mate.

Because they were the same. Good and evil. Both two sides of the same coin.

"I can protect you, Shea. I *will* protect you. If you will let me. But please understand, this is something I must do. My father must be stopped."

Shea barely heard what he was saying. Her holy blood was drawn to his magical blood, and her vampire blood to his djinn. Light to light. Dark to dark. Together, they were much more powerful than on their own.

It was how it was meant to be. Relief flooded through her, to finally know, finally understand why he had been chosen for her.

Her attention was pulled back to him when he took her face between his hands. "Shea. Tell me. Out loud. You've decided."

Shea's eyes traveled over his handsome face, from the dark waves of his hair falling over his forehead, to the slight unevenness of his nose, the sculpted lips, sharp edge of his jaw and back up to those amazing eyes. Even now, she felt the tug of desire between their physical forms, but she also felt the tug of her heart.

Her thoughts jumped to Luukas. After what she had just learned, was she ready to cut ties with the vampire that had created her, and make a life together with the male that made her forget everything but him with nothing but the slightest touch? Because no matter what Jesse chose to believe, Shea knew that is what it would come down to.

She felt pulled in two different directions, yet one was so much stronger than the other. "Yes. I've decided."

His lips parted, but for once, no words formed. However, Shea didn't need to hear the words. She felt his wonder, his lust, and his overwhelming joy. Warmth glowed from his eyes like liquid gold, along with possessiveness and triumph. Her breath caught at the intensity of everything he was throwing at her.

Suddenly, a wall was thrown up between them. Not physically, but emotionally. Jesse's expression closed off and the heat faded swiftly from his eyes, until they became as cold as stone. Jesse was once again the enigma she had first met all those weeks ago in the altar room. Unemotional. Self-Contained. Frightening.

She reached out to him with her thoughts, thinking perhaps they were in some sort of danger, only to find he'd blocked her completely. She couldn't get past his defenses, no matter how hard she tried. She kept her voice down. "Jesse?"

He stood and cocked his head to the side. "Is this a trick, Shea?" Cruthú let out a squawk from her cage, then flew across the room to land on his shoulder. She imitated his posture, staring at Shea with accusing black eyes.

Confused, Shea stood as well. "What? Is what a trick?"

Her eyes flew to the door just before a loud knock sounded, at the same time their visitor's scent permeated the room. Shea looked at Jesse, but he stared at the closed door. "You had me completely fooled, love. You're a much better actress than I ever could have guessed."

Her heart pounded. Not out of fear of him, but of fear *for* him. "Jesse, please. Don't answer it. I had no idea he was coming."

Another knock sounded on the door. Louder this time.

Ignoring her pleas for caution, Jesse strode to the door, unlocked it, and flung it open.

CHAPTER 26

Jesse stared at the male on the other side of the threshold, and it came to him that he had been a complete fool.

He felt Shea behind him, her warmth like that of the sun after a freezing winter, and he fought the urge to reach behind him and pull her up against him. She had fooled him utterly. With her body, her words, and even with her mind. She'd never planned to be with him. It had all been a trick to find out what he was about.

Her voice came from behind him, still playing the part. He had to admit, she was an *excellent* actress.

"What are you doing here? How did you find me?"

However, she was a fool if she thought this one could stop him. But no more a fool than he had been to believe her. "Come now, Shea. Let's invite our guest, or should I say 'guests', inside before we go throwing out questions that you already know the answer to." Stepping back out of the way, he threw one arm out in welcome, ignoring Shea's confused stare. "Please, come in."

Aiden stepped over the threshold, and went to go stand near Shea. Closing the door, Jesse observed the way he protected her with mild amusement. It was quite comical to him that the vampire believed he could keep him from her. Especially since there was no need. Not now. Not anymore.

"What can I do for you?" He didn't need to ask how they had been found. He assumed they'd been seen by one of Luukas's minions who were also tracking the demons. A touch inside of the vampire's head confirmed it. Mammot had given them away by coming here to the room.

"Hallo, mate. Fancy meeting you here." Aiden's tone was light, but his grey eyes were glinting with hatred. He gave Shea a tight smile. It fell from his face, and he placed a hand over his chest. When he lifted his head, Jesse detected shadows ghosting about in his bright gray eyes. Then they were gone.

"Excuse me, just a bit of indigestion there."

It wasn't a stomach ailment, unless you considered a demon that currently possessed you as such. Jesse wondered if the vampire really was as "off" as he seemed, or if it was all an act. Maybe the entire colony was all a group of actors who used their talents to obtain more and more power for their Master.

He couldn't say that he blamed them. He, himself, had done a lot worse, for nothing but his own personal amusement.

"What do you want?" Shea asked again. "What are you

doing here, Aiden? The last time I saw you, you told me not to come back. And now you're chasing me down? And where is Nikulas?"

Playing the game through to the end, I see. She really was good.

Linking his hands behind his back, the vampire strolled casually into their room. He appeared to be checking out the décor.

"He's off playing with demons. I told him I would stay in our room, as my inner demon tends to get his knickers in a twist when I'm around them." He stopped in the middle of the room, looking around. "This room is quite lovely. A bit Americanized, though, with the color scheme and all, don't you think?" He looked at Jesse. "No?" He began to walk around again.

Cruthú flew from Jesse's shoulder to land on the headboard nearest Aiden. She followed him around, jumping from object to object, watching him closely as he touched this and that, until he'd gone full circle. Finally, the vampire plopped down on the edge of Shea's bed and leaned back on his hands. "I've come to fetch you home. Luukas is in quite a state, to be honest, and we need you there. No matter my feelings about all of this."

She crossed her arms over her chest. With a quick glance at Jesse, she told him, "I can't. And I don't want to. I belong here. With Jesse."

Aiden gave her a blank expression, blinking hard. Eventually Jesse, who leaned casually against the door as he watched the exchange, drew his attention. Understanding dawned. "Ohh, yes. Because of your lusty attraction to our dark witch here." He shrugged. "I can see why you would fancy him, what with the whole sexy dark magic thing going on." Then he leaned forward, confusion creasing his brow. "But, Shea, wouldn't you be better suited to find a nice lady friend?" He held up his hand. "Now, we all know that you swing it both ways, and honestly, we couldn't care less. My point is: you can touch a female, whereas you can't have any physical contact with a male. And I don't know about you, but I'm all about the touching." He grinned, though it didn't quite reach his eyes.

"Does he ever shut up?" Jesse asked idly.

"Not really, no," Shea told him. Walking over to the bed, she sank down beside the other vampire.

Jesse felt his spine stiffening at the sight of her so close to another male, despite his intentions not to care.

"Aiden..." She paused, took a deep breath. "Aiden, Jesse is my mate."

He stared at her for a full minute. Finally, one eyebrow went up. "Ah, well. That's a right mess then, isn't it?"

Jesse was surprised when she adamantly shook her head. "No. It's not. It's good."

Though she was speaking to Aiden, her eyes found and fixed on Jesse. He felt her pushing against his mental shields, but he refused to let her in. She'd already done enough damage.

With a deep sigh, she continued. "I was with Jesse the entire time I was a prisoner at Leeha's fortress. I was forced to stay there, yes, but only because he was protecting me." She pleaded with Aiden to understand. "It was supposed to be me on that altar. Not you. Jesse refused to do it. He kept me in his room and magically sealed the door. No one could go in or out but him. I couldn't leave, but it also kept Leeha out. Until the day he finally let me go."

Aiden waved a hand. "Yes, Shea. I know all this." He rose from the bed and walked over to Jesse. "But you had no such qualms saddling me with the one demon who doesn't want to be here."

Jesse met Aiden eye for eye, but stayed as he was. "No. You weren't so lucky."

"No, I was not," Aiden agreed. "Maybe if I'd had flowing dark hair and sparkling green eyes?" He smirked, then turned and strolled away.

A smile threatened, but Jesse got it under control. The vampire had balls, he had to give him that.

Shea expelled a breath of relief when Aiden moved away from him. She was tense, waiting for him to lose patience with her friend, and rightly so. However, he was more interested in seeing how this would play out. Not because he harbored any ill feelings for what he had done, but because if he killed the host body, the demon inside would be free to possess another now that it was unchained from the altar. And the closest body, other than himself, was Shea. He might be angry with her, but he did not wish that upon her.

"Feel free to poke around in here if you wish," Aiden told him, pointing to his head. "I assure you I came here of my own free will. Shea knew nothing of my plans. Her reasons for gallivanting about with you are, apparently, true."

Jesse was tempted, but a part of him held back, unsure he really wanted to know what he would find in the crazy Brit's head. "Are you not afraid of me, vampire?"

"Terrified," Aiden said without humor. "But I think you've already done your worst with me as far as I'm concerned. Knowing what I know now, how you were only trying to protect our little Shea, I'm attempting to understand. You did what you felt you needed to do. There are worse things I would do for my Grace if she were threatened. Or even for Prickles."

Jesse frowned, glancing around Aiden to Shea, who remained sitting on the bed, watching them with her heart in her eyes. "Grace's hedgehog," she supplied.

"Ah." Somehow, that didn't surprise him with this one.

Aiden kicked his chin up a notch. "My Grace is arse over elbow for the silly thing. If anything happened to him, she'd be heartbroken."

"Of course."

"So, what do you say?" And this time Jesse found clear gray eyes glinting with intelligence staring back at him. "Truce? For Shea's sake?" Gritting his teeth, Aiden stuck out his hand.

Instead of shaking it, Jesse pushed himself away from the door and opened it wide. He paused. Looking at Shea, he said, "Don't forget your bag when you go."

She was beside him in an instant, grabbing his arm. "Jesse? What are you doing? Why are you leaving?"

He ignored Aiden's shocked exclamation, his eyes on her hand on his arm.

"I gave you what you came here for, Shea. But now, I'm doing what I need to do to correct the damage. Don't worry. I won't let you starve. I'll find you come feeding time." He sounded cold. He sounded like a complete ass. And he didn't give a fuck.

Her eyes filled with tears. "Jesse, I don't want to go. I want to stay with you."

"So they can track you, and therefore, me? How idiotic do you think I am?" Turning to Aiden, he said, "Take her. She's all yours." Then he walked out of the room, whistling for Cruthú. She swooped through the room, landing on his shoulder. With a quick look up and down the hall to make sure there were no humans about, he disappeared.

CHAPTER 27

Shea stared at the door, waiting for her heart to start beating again. "What just happened?" She looked back at the vampire who was again lounging on her bed. "Aiden? What the hell just happened?" Running out into the hall, she ran to the stairs, even though she'd seen Jesse disappear into thin air with her own eyes. Aiden appeared behind her with her bag in hand. Shea swatted at it. "Put that down! I'm not going anywhere without Jesse." Leaning over the railing, she stared down the center of the stairwell and listened. The only thing she heard was a couple of young girls giggling a few floors down.

"Okay," she said to no one in particular. Shea forced herself to calm. She'd had his blood. And he'd had hers. She could track him if he wasn't too far away. Closing her eyes, she took a deep breath and listened—not with her ears, but with her blood. She listened for the tiniest familiarity, the smallest pull.

There was nothing. Absolutely nothing. "Where the hell did he go?"

"Look, poppet. Why don't you just come back with me? The warlock said he would come to you when you needed to feed. He'll pop up when you least expect it, and then you two can hash things out if you still wish it. Right now, Luukas needs you back home."

She swung toward Aiden, unreasonably angry. None of this would have happened if he hadn't shown up there at that exact moment. "If he wants me back so badly, why doesn't he just call me back? His blood to mine. I would have to obey him."

"He wants you back, Shea. But he also wants it to be your choice. You're no good to him if you harbor a grudge."

Shea backed off. She could see Luukas doing that. He was an intimidating leader at times, but he was smart, and he was fair. "What about you and Nik? Do you want me back home?"

Aiden's mouth thinned, and he glanced away. But after a moment, he heaved a great sigh and turned back to her. "Of course, we do."

With a sound of disbelief, she shoved past him. The space was small, and her shoulder slammed into his chest as she passed. Pain shot up and down her arm, curling her hand into something resembling one of Cruthú's claws. Shea jumped away with a hiss of agony. "Dammit!" The curse wasn't gone.

The implications of that fact didn't escape her. However, it only solidified her decision to be with Jesse.

"Sorry, poppet. But you need to warn a bloke before

you up and switch directions like that." Aiden stuck to her like glue as she picked up her bag, careful to keep an eye on him this time, and marched back to the hotel room. "What are you doing? The exit is this way."

"I told you I'm not coming with you. I'm staying here." Dropping her bag on the floor, she sat down at the end of the bed so she faced the door, and prepared to wait as long as it took. She would wait there forever, if need be. "I'm not leaving, Aiden. So, though I appreciate what you're doing here, you can go ahead and go without me. Find Nik and go home. I'm sure Luukas will survive without me until I can straighten all this out."

He sat down beside her, but not too close. "Truly, then? You want to stay here and keep pissing around with *him*?"

Shea glared at him out of the corner of her eye. "Aiden..." she warned.

He leaned back against the headboard and swung his legs up onto the bed. "Before you make a decision you'll regret, don't you want to hear our plan?"

No. She didn't want to hear their plan. She didn't want to hear anything except the sound of Jesse's boots coming down the hall. "No. I really don't."

"But it's a good plan. I came up with it with a little help from my friend here." He waved his hand over his gut. "He pops his head up every now and again just to order me about. It's worse than living with my mum, and scares the knickers off Grace. I don't know why she stays with me. I truly don't." He perked up again. "Oh! But the plan. I was about to tell you."

Shea jumped up from the bed and began to pace. "Aiden! Please, just go." She couldn't take anymore of his blathering. She had other things to worry about. Like how she was going to fix what was going on with her and Jesse, and how she was going to talk him out of his foolish plan. There had to be another way to dethrone his father and take back control of the coven.

And how the hell she was going to find him so she could do all of that.

And as for the demons, they needed to be sent back to where they came from. But to do so would take the magic of the entire Moss coven, including Jesse, who would never agree to it. And if he wouldn't help them, the girls would take on the spell on their own—she didn't need Aiden to tell her that—whether they were ready or not. And Shea knew that as powerful as they would be someday, none of them were ready for something like this except for Keira. She was the only one who had been taught since childhood to control her magic.

Of course, there was one other way that she knew of to send the demons back to where they came from, without risking the lives of her friends. The only risk would be to herself.

Dammit.

"Shea? Do you want to hear the plan or not?"

She stopped pacing. She'd nearly forgotten Aiden was there. "I told you, no."

"Well, I'm telling you anyway." He grinned, and Shea felt sorry for women everywhere should they ever lay eyes on that stunning face. Especially Grace. She didn't stand a chance as his mate. "While you've been gallivanting about, Luukas has been following the demons. Well, not Luukas himself, of course, but some of the Council and others in the colony who volunteered to help. They are beginning to converge in groups, and it looks like they're getting ready to travel. And—" He paused for dramatic effect. "Guess where they're heading?"

Exasperated, but knowing she'd be allowed no peace until he finished, she asked, "Where?"

"Right back to us. Well, not to us. But to Canada. Which is near us—"

"Aiden!"

"Right. So, we can only assume that they need to be near the altar to do their hokey pokey and become themselves again." He rubbed his temple with his fingers. "Although why they would want to give up the bodies they have is beyond me. Why be demons when you could be vampires? It's rather bewildering. Of course, as old as they are, I wouldn't be at all surprised to find they were all a bit off their trolley. And there *is* the matter of the rot."

Shea didn't have the patience for this today. She opened her mouth to tell him so when there was another knock at the door. Aiden leapt from the bed, and both vampires went completely still as they stared at the closed door.

"It's the demon." Shea stated the obvious, as the stench of the thing foretold what they would find when they opened the door. "The one that took over Steven's body. He was here earlier, talking to Jesse."

Aiden bared his fangs, a low growl rising from his chest. "My demon doesn't play well with others, Shea. We need to go, before he decides to make an appearance."

She walked to the door, glancing back over her shoulder. "Go if you need to. I'm answering the door. He might know something." Though her every nerve ending was on fire to be this close to it, she whipped open the door and stood defiantly in its way. "What do you want?"

The thing raised its head, and Shea clamped her teeth together to hide her reaction. Under the oversized hood of its coat, gray skin barely clung to the muscle and bone beneath it. One eye was gone, and there was a hole in its cheek, showing a jawbone and a set of broken teeth. The pallid lips pulled up into some semblance of a smile. "Ms. Bennett," it drawled.

It knew her name. Shea's own skin felt like spiders were crawling all over her. But she knew better than to play its game. "What do you want?" she repeated, somehow managing to keep her tone bland.

"It's been a long time," it said. "How is your father?"

Icy fear stiffened her muscles and froze the blood in her veins. Shea found she couldn't move even if she wanted to. She stared at the thing in front of her in horror.

"Real shame, what happened to Elise." Its one good eye watched her closely, daring her to react.

The ice turned to fire as she realized why this thing had seemed so familiar to her. Rage filled her, consuming her so completely that she lunged for the thing before thinking it through. Her fingers curled into claws and swiped at its face as her fangs snapped an inch from its throat.

She was blocked by Aiden before she could make contact. Moving at vamp speed, he suddenly appeared between her the disgusting creature in front of her. Shea hissed in pain when they collided, her reflexes forcing her to jump back.

As the thing laughed at her over Aiden's shoulder, she bared her fangs and growled.

"Be careful, Shea," Aiden told her.

His voice sounded muffled. Shea watched as his bright gray eyes became muddled with shadows, and realized that he wasn't warning her to watch herself with the demon at the door, but the demon inside of him.

His mouth twisted into a grimace that was nothing like the Aiden she knew, and he turned around and put his back to her. "Get the fuck away from here, Mammot," Aiden told it. His British accent was gone. Even the way he held himself was different.

Though she'd been expecting it, the sound of its voice still surprised her. That wasn't Aiden speaking. It was the thing inside of him.

Instead of leaving as it was told, Mammot leaned forward. "Or you will do what, Waano? You have no power here."

"Do we really need to go through this again?" He didn't wait for an answer. "*Leave*, Mammot," the thing inside Aiden repeated. "Now."

Shea watched the transaction between the two with growing trepidation, despite the rage that still simmered in her blood. As a vampire, she was strong. And she could do a few mind tricks. But she was nothing compared to the ancient creatures facing off before her. If she got caught alone in a fight between them, she'd never survive it.

Shea mentally kicked herself in the ass. Her worry

over Jesse had gotten the better of her. She hadn't thought before she opened the door, she'd just reacted. Not that a locked door would've stopped the thing from coming in. But she should've listened to Aiden. They should've escaped out the emergency exit. Crawled out the window. Anything except confront it.

The demon, Mammot, lifted its chin. "I have something for the warlock."

She spoke over Aiden's shoulder. "He's not here, you sick son of a bitch."

"Tsk. Tsk. Still holding a grudge, I see." It shook its head, its voice dripping with remorse that she didn't buy for one second. "You know, it didn't have to end the way it did, Shea."

She bared her fangs at it. "You killed *my sister.*"

It held up one finger, a bloody bed where the nail should've been. "Ah! Ah! No. That's not exactly true now, is it?" Its one good eye stared straight through her. She felt it, crawling around in her head like maggots. "*You* killed your sister, Shea. Not me. For all you know, I was only borrowing her temporarily, and would've been on to another body long before the wedding. Although then I would've missed fucking that hot piece of meat she'd chosen to marry." He turned to Aiden. "I really like the way things are these days; much better than before. People don't wait for marriage to fuck anymore."

Rage and disgust shook Shea uncontrollably.

"Oh! I almost forgot." The thing in the hall stepped to the side and picked up a large briefcase from the floor. "The blood. I trust you will give this to the warlock when he returns?" Ignoring the low growl coming from Aiden, he held the case out to Shea.

After a moment's pause, she took it.

"Waano." It nodded at Aiden, pulled its hood down over its face, and wandered off down the hallway toward the elevator. She watched as it got inside. It waved to them as the doors slid closed.

Shea backed away from Aiden slowly. She had no idea what was going to happen now.

He closed the door and twisted the lock. Turning around, he tilted his head, spearing Shea with his haunted gaze. He didn't say anything, just ran his eyes up and down her body. Revulsion filled her, and made her want to scrub its gaze from her skin.

Aiden's eyes closed, and he cried out as his body suddenly bent in half right before he crashed to the floor.

"Aiden? Aiden!" Shea dropped the case and ran over to him, but he was out cold. Shea looked around, but no one else was in the room. There was nothing she could do but wait for him to wake.

She had no idea how long she sat on the rug beside him, watching for the slightest flutter of his eyelids. Minutes, hours, days. But when they finally opened again, the shadows had fled. He rose to his knees, holding his stomach while he gagged. "Ah, bloody *hell*. I wish he wouldn't do that." He retched again. "At the very least, he could give me a little warning."

Shea reached out to help her friend, but pulled back at the last moment. "Aiden? Are you all right?"

"Shower. I need a shower. And whiskey." And then he promptly vomited blood all over the carpet.

Shea jumped back out of the way. Running to the bathroom, she grabbed a towel and tossed it over the mess. "Well, Jesse's never gonna get his deposit back now."

Aiden let out a bark of laughter, and immediately groaned and threw up some more. "Shower," he mumbled when he was finished.

"It's over here," she told him. "You're going to have to get yourself there. I can't help you."

"Right, then." Leaving the towel, he proceeded to crawl the short distance to the bathroom.

Shea ran ahead and turned on the water for him, then got out of his way so he could get himself in there. "I'll call downstairs and see if they can send up some whiskey."

He nodded, concentrating on getting his clothes off. "I feel like I've been dunked in the sewer and left to prune."

"That's disgusting." Her stomach turned just thinking about it.

He yanked his soiled shirt off and started working on his pants between heaves, and Shea went over to the phone and convinced them to send up a bottle and charge it to the room. When that was done, she sat down to wait. It was a few seconds before she remembered the case.

Picking it up, she set it on the bed. It had two locks. They looked stronger than those found on a normal briefcase. With a quick tug, she broke them from their fastening and opened the case.

Vials of blood, each cushioned with cloth, filled the case. Hundreds of them.

The demon blood.

Her hands began to shake. Reaching out, she picked up a vial and stared at it. It wasn't glass, but some type of plastic or something. A loud knock on the door startled her so, she dropped it on the carpet. Swiping it up and setting it back in the case, she rushed to the door. But it was only Aiden's whiskey.

She shut the case again and took the entire bottle in to Aiden. The curtain was still open, and water was getting all over the floor. She found him sitting in the shower with his knees pulled up and his arms wrapped around his legs. Even as sick as he was, he was a beautiful male. Not as perfect as Jesse in her eyes, but damn close. Even she could appreciate that, though he was nothing but a brother to her. And a pain in the ass one, at that.

Clearing her throat, she made her presence known. "Here's your whiskey."

His head swung around toward her voice. "Would you open it, please? And hand it in here?"

"Sure." She opened the bottle and gave it to him. He gulped down half the bottle and lowered it with a hiss. "Ah, that bloody burns."

"Can I do anything to help?" Babysitting Aiden was the last thing she wanted to do. She needed to be searching for her missing warlock, but she couldn't just leave him like this.

"I'll sort it out in just a bit." He groaned and gagged, then drank some more. "What was in the case?"

Shea hesitated, but then berated herself for even thinking of not telling him. She needed to tell the others what Jesse's plan was, and Aiden would be a good start. Hopefully, it wouldn't bring out the demon in him again. As Jesse was blinded by his hatred for his father, she would have to make the right decision for him. He would see it was the correct decision once it was all over.

So, why did she feel so shitty about it?

She quickly told Aiden the gist of it before she could change her mind. While she talked, she grabbed a washcloth and the soap and got onto her knees beside him. Water soaked through her jeans, but it was the least of her worries right now. Careful to keep the cloth wadded up and not to touch his skin, she started to wash him.

She tried not to think of all the implications to Jesse. He had to understand why she couldn't allow him to carry through with his plan. There had to be another way to stop his father, and she would help him.

Aiden listened to the entire story, for once not interrupting her, until she was completely out of words. "You know we can't let him do this."

Shea nodded. "I know." She concentrated on not touching his skin while she scrubbed his back. "Stopping him was not the reason I came with him in the beginning." She peeked up at him to see how he was taking that news.

Tired gray eyes stared back at her impassively.

Her arm dropped onto her lap. The soapy water dripping from the washcloth. "I came with him because I...I just wanted to be with him. I can't really explain it."

"It's the mating instinct. We know who they are before any blood is exchanged." He lifted his face up to the water and ran a hand over his wet hair, slicking it back. "I doubt you would've been able to resist the bloke for long, even if you'd tried harder."

Adding more soap to the cloth, she began to wash his shoulders and arms.

"This is worse than having the werewolves help me," he grumbled.

She rolled her eyes. "I think you're exaggerating."

"But I'm not, though. You're like my sister, Shea. This is very strange."

"Well, you'll just have to deal with it."

"All right, then. But keep your hands away from my willy."

She laughed. She couldn't help it. Despite everything, it felt good to have Aiden being…well, Aiden.

After a few minutes of companionable silence passed, Aiden set his whiskey bottle down with a clank and grabbed the cloth from her. "Go. Go find him."

She sat back on her heels. "I wouldn't even know where to start."

"Well, you're not going to find him in the shower with me, that's for bloody sure."

"I thought you hated him?"

"I do. But I would rather know where he is and what he's doing."

So would she, but for entirely different reasons. She shook her head and took the cloth back. "I have a few minutes."

Aiden was quiet after that, except to ask her to scrub him harder now and again. When he felt sufficiently less disgusting and could stand up, she turned off the water and threw him a towel. With one hand holding his towel on, and the other on the wall, he stood with no help from Shea. "Thank you," he told her sincerely. "For holding steady through all of this."

"No problem." She went out to the dresser and found

one of Jesse's shirts for him to wear, as his was covered with blood. Holding it to her face, she inhaled the warlock's scent. Even that little bit had her fangs aching and her blood rushing. Removing the soft material from her face, she took a breath to clear her senses and threw it in to Aiden. "Here you go."

He eyed the offending item, his nose wrinkled in distaste. "Can't I borrow one of your shirts instead?"

"My shirts won't fit you."

"That's not my biggest concern right now."

For someone as fashion conscious as Aiden to want to wear something that didn't fit him like a second skin said a lot about what he thought about wearing Jesse's shirt. "Just put it on," she ordered.

He grumbled a bit about it, but finally did as he was told.

By the time he finished dressing and came out, Shea was waiting by the door with her bag, the case of blood, and Cruthú's cage wrapped up in her arms. It was a small thing, to bring the cage, but it made her feel closer to him, somehow. "Are you ready?"

Aiden checked his hair in the mirror. Shea could see he still wasn't feeling quite up to par, but he was trying to hide it.

"Where are we going? If it's to search for your arsehole of a mate, you can count me out. I would just be a third wheel. I'd rather go sit in the hotel room and wait for Nikulas. It will give me the chance to catch up on the last season of Vikings."

Shea opened the door and waited for Aiden to join her before admitting, "I don't know where he is, Aiden. I can't feel him. I wouldn't have the first clue where to look."

Pressing the button for the elevator, he took her bag from her and said, "You said he's bound and determined to get the demons out of their borrowed bodies and back into their own, yes?"

"Yes."

"Well, it would make sense to me that to do that, he would need to go where the demons are. Where else would a warlock who specializes in releasing demons be needed, but at the gates of hell themselves?"

A spark of hope ignited in her chest. "The altar," she said as the doors opened.

"The altar," Aiden agreed.

CHAPTER 28

By the time Shea, Nikulas, and Aiden landed in Seattle, the guys had nearly forgiven her for taking off with the "bloody bastard." Nearly, but not quite. Nikulas still gave her the occasional side-eye while shaking his head in disbelief. It didn't seem to matter to him that Jesse was her mate, something he should understand well, having been the first to find his own. In his opinion, if she hadn't run off with him in the first place, the mating would never have happened.

Though if what Aiden had said was true, who knows how long she would've been able to resist the urge to be near him? However, there was nothing to do for it now. What was done was done, and Shea was beginning to accept it. She had no other choice, really.

As they rode the elevator up to Luukas's apartment after dropping off her stuff at her own, Shea tried to calm her nerves. He would not be happy with her, and she had no idea how he was going to react, especially with everything that was going on.

She just wanted to get this meeting over with and head north. The closer they'd gotten to Seattle, the more certain she became that Aiden had been right. Jesse was near. She just knew it. She'd felt it as soon as they'd gotten off the plane—the call of his blood to hers. It was faint, but it was there. Which was to be expected if he was so far away. Being able to feel him at that distance at all surprised her. Perhaps it was the djinn sorcery in his blood, dark as it was, that made it that much stronger.

But before she ran off again, she needed to get a few things. And she owed it to Luukas to check in with him and try to explain. Maybe he would understand, his history with Keira being similar.

Keira opened the door before they had the chance to knock. Pushing the guys aside, she grabbed Shea in a bear hug. "I'm so glad you're back!"

Shea felt tears fill her eyes at the unexpected welcome. Wrapping her arms around the little witch, she hugged her back hard.

"We've been trying to call you!" Keira gave her one last squeeze and took her hand to drag her into the apartment. "I finally called Aiden, and told him to go find you." She prattled on as they walked, completely missing the look Shea gave Aiden.

"Did I not mention that part?" he said.

Shea turned back to Keira. "I lost my phone—"

"In the plane crash, we know." At Shea's surprised look, she explained. "We saw it. All of us witches. We get visions sometimes. It started with me and Emma, when we saw Grace and Aiden running from the demons in China. We never know when it's going to happen, but it seems to be when one of our family is in trouble." She stared steadily at Shea when she said this.

"So, you know."

Keira nodded.

"Does Luukas know?"

She nodded again. "I had to tell him."

"Of course," Shea said. "How did he take it?"

"About as well as you would expect."

Although she wasn't surprised, a tiny part of her had foolishly hoped he would be more open to it, now that they knew who Jesse was. Taking a deep breath, she looked around. They were all there: Nikulas and Emma, Aiden and Grace, Christian and Ryan, and even Dante and Laney—standing near the door, of course.

Being up here made Dante skittish. She met his eyes briefly before he looked away. His disapproval was easy to see. Her tentative smile fell. This, more than anything, hit Shea where it hurt.

Emma approached the two women. "Did he tell you how he's related to us?"

Shea shook her head. "No. Only that his name is Moss, and he's from your coven." She didn't mention what he'd told her about Ryan. She didn't feel it was her place to break that news. That was Jesse's story to tell.

"That explains the whole 'cousin' thing the last time I saw him." Even without the twist of her mouth and the fire in her eyes, Shea knew it hadn't been a pleasant reunion.

She looked at the two sisters who she had come to care

so much about in the short time she'd known them. "I'm so sorry." Looking up, she included Grace in that apology, who was standing back, wrapped in Aiden's arms. "I don't know why I went with him. I just...there's no excuse for it. But please believe me when I say, I had no idea this would happen." She shook her head. "No, if I'm going to be honest, I've always been attracted to him." She frowned. "No, that's not the word. Obsessed is more like it. But I had no idea what fate had in store for us. I had no idea he was my mate."

"And that's why you didn't tell Luukas that you were with Jesse the whole time you were held in Leeha's fortress," Keira said. "Nik told Em, and Em told me."

She nodded. "Yes. I felt the need to protect him. Even then."

Keira glanced at her sister before focusing on Shea again. "Well, who are we to argue with the gods? Whether we like it or not—and let's be clear, we don't—we need him to stay alive for you, so you can survive. And I very much want you to survive." As she said these last words, she looked over at the bedroom door with an almost defiant expression.

Shea swiped at the tears that had finally fallen. Luukas was standing in the doorway, leaning against the doorjamb, watching the exchange with a hard expression. He looked even worse than he had before she left.

Keira continued, her voice sharp with resolve. "But, for whatever reasons Jesse did what he did, we need to get the demons out of the vampires Luukas created. If we don't, I will lose him. And I'm sorry, Shea, as much as I love you, if it comes down to my mate or yours, I'm choosing mine."

Looking directly at her maker, Shea said, "It won't come to that, Keira."

"It might. And I just want you to know where I stand. Where we all stand." The other witches came to stand behind Keira in a show of solidarity.

Shea looked at them all in turn. "Jesse is your blood—"

"That warlock is a sadistic prick who doesn't give a shit about you or any of us," Luukas said from across the room. "Especially not his family."

He was right. Except for one thing. "But he does care about *me*," Shea insisted. Walking over to Luukas, she lifted her chin. She wouldn't try to defend Jesse, but she refused to be ashamed of him. "All I ask, Luukas, is that you give me the chance to find him and talk to him. He has his reasons for releasing the demons, and it's a…an understandable one."

"What reason is that?" Ryan spoke up for the first time. She hadn't stood with the other witches a few moments ago, but had stayed where she was. Rising from the chair near the window, she came to join the others now. "What possible reason does he have to release such a threat to us?" She seemed genuinely curious.

Shea repositioned herself so she could include them all in her response. "From what he told me, and from what I figured out myself, your families all ran to escape the new High Priest of your coven when you were young, correct?"

Those who knew their past nodded.

"That High Priest is Jesse's father, and he wants to take him out. He needs the demons to help him. He can't do it himself. So, he made a deal with them to help them find what they needed to attain their original forms, and their original power. In exchange for his help, they've agreed to help him get rid of his father, and will spare him and those he cares about. That includes myself, and my family. Which includes all of you."

With a quick glance at Luukas's set jaw, Keira spoke up. "Jesse is one of the most powerful witches I've ever seen. I don't believe he needs the demons. I think he has another reason for releasing them. One he doesn't want you to know about."

"And even if that's all true," Nik said. "Who the fuck wants to live in a world ruled by demons, Shea?"

Ryan frowned, tilting her head as though she was listening. She was communing with her spirits—the voices that used to drive her so mad, she would pump herself full of drugs just to drown them out before she met Christian.

It still creeped Shea out a little.

Understanding dawned on Ryan's face, and she gave her attention back to Shea. "Tell them what his father is," she told her. "You need to tell them."

All eyes turned to Shea. She had hoped to leave this part out, because by telling them what his father was, it also revealed why Jesse was so dangerous. But it looked like she wouldn't have a choice, and she didn't want to spend the entire night deflecting questions when what she needed to be doing was finding Jesse. "His father is pure djinn." The entire room went still, even the witches. "That's how he took over the coven, and why your families ran. He siphons magic from the coven. He's not a good leader."

"That's putting it fucking mildly," Keira burst out. "Sorry," she added to Shea. "My parents never told me why they'd run, just that they didn't agree with the new Priest's 'ways.'" She took on a thoughtful expression, and looked at Emma. "They must have kept that from us to protect us. If we didn't know about him, we couldn't think about him, and we wouldn't attract his attention. It's how the djinn work."

It's how the djinn work. Was that why Jesse was so interested in her? Because she attracted him with her obsession of him? As much as she would try not to think about him, she was never very successful at it.

Luukas strode out into the center of the room. "A djinn, Shea? We're dealing with a fucking djinn?" It was obvious he wasn't talking about the High Priest. "How the fuck do you expect me to welcome him into our group? How do you expect me to look at him every day? How, Shea?" His deep voice boomed throughout the room, the temperature dropping swiftly with his anger.

The tears threatened once more. "I'm so sorry, Luukas."

He appeared in front of her, his furious visage not three inches away. "Sorry?" he hissed. His fangs flashed when he spoke. "He fucked with my head. He made me believe I was being burned alive. He made me believe it was Keira doing it. He made me believe I had ripped her into pieces with my bare hands—the love of my life. I thought I had killed her! And you're *sorry?*"

Shea stood her ground, breathing hard. But kept her eyes averted, afraid that if she looked at him, she would be the one he tore apart. Keira had done many of those same things to him herself, and Shea wished she could point that out to him. But there was a major difference, and she knew it. Keira had done it against her will. Jesse had done it for amusement.

Keira's hand appeared on his arm. "It wasn't her fault, Luukas. She didn't set out to make him her mate. We both know fate doesn't always give us a choice."

His mate's touch calmed him, but not by much. He laid a gentle hand over Keira's, but his eyes glinted like steel as they narrowed on Shea. "Get out of my sight."

Holding back a sob, she gave him a brisk nod and turned on her heel. She kept her head high, not looking at any of them while she strode from the apartment. She made it all the way to her apartment, barely getting the door shut before she lost it. Falling to her knees on the hard tile, she burst into tears.

It occurred to her that she hadn't even had the chance to tell him she had the demon's blood. Or how she planned to stop Jesse.

A quick knock came from behind her. Shea wiped at her eyes and stumbled to her feet. She could tell by the scent it was Laney. Holding the door open, Shea invited her inside.

Dante's mate offered a sympathetic smile. "I know we don't know each other very well, yet. But from one girl to another who fell hard for the wrong guy, I get it. Luukas shouldn't be treating you like this."

Shea shook her head. "No, he should. He absolutely should. You don't know what he's been through, Laney. All of that stuff he said, Jesse did all that to him, and worse."

"Well, be that as it may, we're going to help you find him. Us girls."

She stilled. "Do you know where he is, Laney?"

Laney's brown eyes caught hers. "We do."

Shea swallowed hard. "I have to stop him."

Laney nodded. "We'll help you."

"Just let me get a few things."

Lines of concern creased the witch's brow. "I don't know much about weapons."

Shea was already heading to her bedroom. "Not weapons. They won't do us any good against demons. But I do have something that will. I'll explain it all to you on the drive up there."

A bright smile lit up Laney's face. "We'll meet you at the cars in thirty minutes. *All* of us. If we have to drag those guys kicking and screaming."

CHAPTER 29

Jesse left his hideout and continued through the woods on foot. He thought about the man who was partly responsible for his existence, and felt nothing at all, other than a keen urge to end his life.

His father was not an honorable male. Nor was he particularly fond of his one and only son. Daughters were rare and not worth the time to raise them according to djinn culture. Which is how his sister, Ryan, was lucky enough to get away from the bastard.

Jesse was not so fortuitous. But he carried only half of his genes. The other half had come from his mother, a Moss witch, whose beauty and magical allure had bewitched the djinn from the moment he'd seen her.

Much how Jesse felt about his traitorous vampire.

But all the things that had attracted his father to his mother had also made him grow to despise her, for she had been an extremely powerful witch. The most powerful the coven had ever known. And she had sent his father back to the djinn shortly after Jesse was born. Or so he'd been told. He didn't know the exact reasons why, though he could well imagine. His mother had made it a point never to speak of the male who had sired him.

When Jesse had matured into a young man, his father had returned, summoned by a young witch enthralled by the stories of him. His father killed his mother, taking over the position of High Priest of her coven and sucking the magic contained within it like an ominous leech. Over the years, it had made his father strong and the witches weak.

Except for those who'd managed to escape.

For many of the coven had run as soon as he'd arrived, rather than stay and fight, and Jesse had seen the wisdom in that. He had been nowhere near strong enough to take on his father at that time, and couldn't help the ones who'd decided to stay. So, he ran like the others, and promised himself that one day, he would return and send his father back from whence he came. And he would destroy the book that tied him to this world.

Over the years, Jesse had watched and waited as his own magical strength grew in leaps and bounds. He spent his time alone, with very little contact with others, for it took him awhile to learn to control the sorcery within him. It wasn't until he came out of hiding and re-entered the world that he discovered, quite by accident, that he was stronger than any other creature in existence.

When he felt he was ready, he began to ingratiate himself into the world of the supernatural, and eventually found himself working with Leeha. She was a foolish female, but his only focus was doing whatever he had to do to get what he needed to defeat his father. He had no sympathy for the creatures he hurt, or worse. He felt nothing at all.

Everything changed for him the night he had met Shea.

He'd found himself unable to concentrate, distracted by the seductive lure of his vampire. He couldn't stay away from her from the moment he'd first sensed her aura, and more than once he'd caught himself just before making a fatal mistake.

The fixation had only grown now that they shared a blood bond.

He heard a raven call high above, and glanced up through the trees to see Cruthú circling above. She refused to leave him, much as he'd begged her to stay near their home. He was on his way to meet with the demons. Not at the altar, as he knew everyone would assume the ritual would need to take place, but at a place much more suited for what he needed to do.

As he watched the raven's graceful flight, a light rain began to fall. Jesse picked up his pace while wiping the moisture from his eyes. The spot where he needed to be was about twenty miles or so from the mountain where he had brought forth the demons, and he was able to make the trip in just under a quarter of an hour. Jesse slowed down as he approached a large rock formation, circling around until it was on his left and a steep drop-off was on his right. During the day, he knew the view would be beautiful. Miles and miles of unspoiled forest as far as the eye could see. He'd come here quite often when he'd needed a little time away from Leeha and her insanity.

Cedar, cottonwood, and pine trees towered above him, blocking out the stars except for the circle of sky directly above the clearing where he now stood. It was necessary to be in that particular spot to do what he was about to do, for a series of the earth's ley lines connected directly in the center. The perfect spot for a spell this intense to work.

A deep croak sounded above him, and Cruthú disappeared, only to reappear a few moments later flying in what Jesse termed her "panic mode." Someone was coming, and it wasn't someone the raven considered a friend.

Jesse breathed in the scent of rain and trees and crisp, chill air. However, it didn't work as it always did, calming him and focusing his thoughts. A feeling of unease trickled down his spine.

Something was wrong.

A few seconds later, he heard them: twigs snapped and pine needles crackled as a large group made its way through the trees. From what Jesse could tell, it appeared to be at least thirty demon-possessed vampires heading his way. And from the stench that drifted toward him on the slight breeze, it was none too soon. With a flick of his will, he lit the small fires interspersed throughout the clearing. The strong scent of burning firewood chased away the smell of rotting bodies and cleared the air.

As he waited for them to arrive, Jesse walked the area, finding and marking the exact spot the ley lines connected by listening to the vibrations in the earth. There he kicked away the weeds and debris that had fallen from the trees, and drew a large circle in the dirt. He connected the ends, sealing himself within the protection of the circle with a few spoken words. He didn't fear the demons; the chances of them being able to overtake him were practically non-existent.

But he trusted his instincts, and he wasn't taking any chances.

The first row of the demons strode into the clearing—the leader, Mammot, front and center. He stopped when he saw Jesse standing within the circle and held up one rotting hand to halt the others behind him. Eyeing the warlock, he did a sweep of the area. Searching for what, Jesse couldn't be sure. A trap, perhaps?

Cruthú swooped in, loudly voicing her displeasure, and the demon leader gave her a scathing look. "What are you doing here?"

Jesse raised one eyebrow. "As I am the only one who knows the ritual, I would think you would want me here. Where is the blood?"

Mammot, or Steven, laughed without humor. "So, the son is more honorable than the father."

It took Jesse no time at all to figure out he had accused the wrong vampire of betraying him. Thinking it over, he wasn't surprised. As a matter of fact, he'd been expecting some ruse or other. Demons could not be trusted.

But Jesse could play this game, too. As a matter of fact, he excelled at this game. "And you're surprised?"

Mammot came closer. "Your father told us you were lying. He told us he was the only one who knew the spell to reunite us with our original blood."

"My father is a djinn. It is common knowledge they will say or do anything to get whatever it is they crave. If you haven't figured it out by now, he had an ulterior motive, other than saving his own skin."

"Perhaps that he'd misjudged the threat you pose."

Jesse shrugged. "Perhaps he shouldn't underestimate me." He paused. "And perhaps neither should you."

The demons caught the veiled threat, and moving forward as a group, they surrounded their leader. Thirty demons. In such close proximity to each other, they fed from each other's energy until the air began to hum with their combined energy.

Jesse waited to see what they would do.

"We have the blood," Mammot finally told him. "The real blood. Not the fake shit we gave your vampire whore. Let's get on with the spell."

The mention of Shea gave him pause for a moment, but Jesse quickly recovered. "You betrayed me to my father, and yet you assume I will still do this spell." All eyes turned to him. "What if I've changed my mind?"

Mammot marched up to the edge of the circle. Sticking one bony finger at Jesse, he growled, "You will do it, warlock. We had a deal."

"A deal you broke by involving my father in all of this." He didn't bother to state the obvious, that his father should not have known about them at all. "If you let my father in on this, he won't rest until he destroys me. You see, I am the only true threat to him that exists. And once I am gone, he will suck the energy from you until you are weak, at which time he will enslave you. You will be his own personal hosts for his parasitic ways."

"He came to us—" Mammot began.

"And told you I was just like him, too caught up in my

lust for power. He told you I didn't mean anything I promised, and that once I had what I wanted from you, I would break our deal and send you back to where I found you. Or something similar?" They didn't deny it, and Jesse threw back his head and laughed. "You, Mammot, of all creatures should know when you're being fucked around. It is a specialty of yours. Is it not?"

One of the others glanced nervously at his leader. "How do you know this?" he asked Jesse.

Mammot growled at the one who had spoken. "Do not respond to this one's ramblings. He's only trying to save his own ass."

Ignoring him, Jesse responded to the question. "Because he is djinn. It is what we do."

"If that is what you do," Mammot reasoned. "Then who's to say you wouldn't do the same thing to us? The way I see it, is we need to get rid of both of you as soon as possible."

Jesse wasn't so easily fooled. He'd known all along these things couldn't be trusted, and had been expecting some such twist in the game. "Was this not your plan to begin with?"

Mammot made a sound that resembled a snort, but didn't come out quite right. "If you're so smart, warlock, then why did you bring us here?"

Jesse told him the truth. "Because between thirty demons and my father, you are the lesser of the two evils to release upon this world."

"Ah. The sentiment warms my heart." Mammot put his hands on his hips and scowled up to the sky, where Cruthú continued to keep a watchful eye on things.

"Unfortunately, you were correct in your assumption that we planned to get rid of you. We did. We also planned to get rid of your father. By betraying you and bringing him into the deal, we were hoping to have you both right where we wanted you. We won't share this world with a djinn, or even a half-blood. However, it seems your father is the more intelligent of the two of you." He looked around dramatically. "He was smart enough not to show up."

Jesse cocked his head to the side, trying to understand the logic of the demon by confessing his treachery, rather than just playing along with the original plan upon seeing Jesse was the only one there. Perhaps he thought they were safe, now that things had progressed this far. Perhaps he thought Jesse would have no qualms about going back to the original deal since he was the one who appeared to be holding to his end of the bargain. He was genuinely curious now, and couldn't resist asking, "You admit all of this straight to my face, while you stand here waiting for me to perform the ritual that will allow you to become yourselves again. Are you not concerned at all that I will refuse to do it and chain your souls back to the altar instead?"

One side of Mammot's mouth turned up in a morbid semblance of a smile. That feeling of unease again rippled down Jesse's spine. "Maybe it is *you* who should not underestimate *us*, warlock."

Jesse should have known by the gloating look that came over the demons' rotten faces. He should have suspected by the way the rest of the group snickered like schoolgirls.

Raising his hand, Mammot quieted the others. "I don't think you'll be giving us any problems, warlock. Your vampire whore is on her way to upset your plans as we speak, and I would think you would like her to arrive in one piece. Am I correct? I left a few friends behind to escort her here. You know, so she doesn't get lost."

Jesse became perfectly still. He felt strangely calm, even as his gut churned with the urge to let loose his sorcery and take the entire group out where they stood. "You lay one rotting finger on her, and I will send you all back to the altar and bury it under hundreds of miles of earth. You won't be able to stop me."

That gruesome smile returned. "It's a good thing there is another who knows the spell then. If you don't want to do it, I can guarantee that she will."

CHAPTER 30

Shea pulled the SUV around the mountain and parked beside Jesse's vehicle. Telling the witches to stay where they were, she got out and rushed inside, calling for Jesse.

She returned a few minutes later. "He's not here," she told them. "I would know if he was here."

"He was here. We saw it," Laney told her.

"Where else would he be? Any idea?" Emma asked.

Another SUV pulled up, full of pissed off vampires. It stopped with its headlights pointed at the side of their vehicle, but no one got out. True to Laney's prediction, the girls didn't even make it out of the parking garage before their males were loading up into the other vehicle and following them north.

"See? I told you they'd follow us," Laney said.

"Of course they did," Keira agreed. "Gods forbid us poor helpless females go out into the world to take on evil by ourselves. We might break a nail or some other such horrifying thing."

Even Ryan laughed at that. An uncomfortable truce had been made between her and Shea, but even so, she'd been quiet for much of the drive. When everyone had calmed down, she spoke up from the back seat. "I can see if I can find out where Jesse is."

But Shea was looking up at the sky, listening. "No need," she told her. "I think I hear Cruthú."

"Cru-who?" Grace asked.

"Cruthú. His raven. She never leaves him." Running out to a break in the trees, she searched the dark sky, but she saw nothing but clouds. A light drizzle began to fall as she stood there. Heading back to the vehicle, she told the other females, "I can't see her, but she sounds upset. Which means Jesse is in trouble. I'm going."

"I don't hear anything," Laney said.

"Because you don't have super crazy vampire hearing," Emma told her.

"We're coming with you," Keira said.

Their eyes met—Shea's grateful; Keira's chilly but determined.

"I'm doing this for you," she told Shea. "Not him."

Shea nodded. "I know. But thank you anyway."

"Should we let the guys know what we're doing?" Laney asked.

Shea didn't even spare the other vehicle a glance. "Nope. They'll follow us, or not."

"Oh, they'll follow us," Emma said as she looked around Shea from the passenger seat. "I can feel Nik's fury from here." She smiled and waved into the bright headlights.

"I wonder why they're not trying to stop us?" Ryan asked.

"Pfft." Grace waved also. "Because they know they only get away with being so overbearing because we let them. This is serious shit, dude. If they tried to stop us, Em would just freeze their asses and then they couldn't help us if we actually needed it."

Emma laughed. "I so would, though. It would teach them right."

Shea got back in and shut the door. "All right. I'm going to drive in Cruthú's direction, getting us as close as I can. Then I'll stop and check out the situation before you all come anywhere near there. If anything happened to any of you, it would be the end of me. And I really don't want to go through all this for nothing."

None of the others bothered disagreeing. They all knew it was true. Vampires were extremely attached to their mates. And not just for the amazing sex.

She turned around and looked at each of them in turn. "Are you sure you're ready for this?"

"No," Ryan answered. "But I'm doing it, anyway."

Shea locked eyes with her. Out of all the witches, she hadn't taken to Ryan like she did the others. She hadn't known why at the time. But now, she did. Maybe it was time to make more of an effort. "Thank you," Shea told her earnestly. "And I'm sorry I called you a slutty hooker when I first met you."

Ryan grinned. "I *was* a slutty hooker when you first met me."

Shea smiled back, then looked around the car again. "So, we're good?"

"Oh, for gods' sake, Shea." Keira rolled her eyes. "Just go. We have demons to send back to hell."

Shea backed out and took off in the direction she'd heard the raven. She had filled the girls in on her history on the drive north, and even told them about her sister. When she finished with her story, they were all quiet for a while as they took it all in. A few questions had been asked and answered, and Keira had even wondered aloud if Shea and Laney came from the same ancestors somewhere down the line, both being "Protectors."

Shea had never thought about it, but now she wondered if the "holy" bloodline was really a magical one. She would have to research that once things settled down again.

They'd gone over and over different ways to attack what they had to do, and finally came to the conclusion that the witches would stick to their original plan. Only, instead of sending the demon's souls back to being chained to the altar, Shea and her holy blood would send them back to hell. Blood and all.

They were about seventeen miles away from Jesse's home when Shea leaned forward over the steering wheel and pointed toward the sky. "There! There she is!"

Emma looked in the direction she was pointing. "How are we going to get over there?"

"We'll have to go on foot." Shea pulled off the road and threw the vehicle into park. "Stay here for a minute while I check things out."

But Ryan spoke up before she jumped out. "Wait." She

stared at Shea, but she knew she wasn't really seeing her. "There are guards. They'll see you." Then she shrugged. "At least, that's what they're telling me."

No one had to ask who "they" were. It was hard for Shea to trust the word of spirits, but decided it was better to be safe than sorry. "I'll be careful." Closing the door, she glanced over at the guys, who had pulled up right behind her, and gave the hand signal telling them she was checking things out and would be right back.

A minute later, she discovered Ryan had been right. There were three possessed vampires guarding the path off the road. Retreating quickly but silently, she hurried back to the cars.

She opened the door, but didn't get in. "The spirits speak the truth. There are three of them blocking the path. So, here's what we're going to do." Leaning back so they would see her, she waved at the guys to come and join them.

Five large vampires got out and surrounded her. They didn't say anything, but Shea could feel their displeasure, and downright fury from Luukas and Dante. She didn't bother speaking to them. They didn't have time to argue right now.

"Okay, I'm going to distract the three that are guarding the path. Once I lead them away, you all circle around and find Jesse and the demons. But don't let him know you're there until I get there. Got it?" She turned to Keira. "Can you fill the guys in on the plan? Oh! And can you cloak everyone?"

She nodded. "Piece of cake."

"No." The word was growled out between clenched teeth. "I will go."

Everyone turned to look at Dante. It was the first time he had spoken to Shea since she'd returned. She blinked hard, pushing down the emotions that were threatening to rise and distract her from her goal. She shook her head at him. "No, Dante. I will go. This is my fight. You need to let me do it my way."

He stared at her a moment, then crossed his arms over his wide chest. "Don't be stupid. You're the only one I like out of this entire crew."

Shea didn't know what to say, but finally managed to nod.

"I resent that, commander," Aiden told him.

Dante just gave her a look that clearly said: *and this is why.*

Luukas spoke from behind her. His voice was low and controlled, but she could hear the underlying anger. "What do you plan to do, Shea?"

She turned to look at her maker, the only one who knew who she really was. "With the girls' help, I'm going to send them back to hell permanently—Keira will fill you in—and perhaps we can save who we can once they are out of the bodies." She gave him a small smile. "Saving you in the process."

"I'm not the one who will need saving when all of this is over." His eyes flicked over to Keira, who gave him her most innocent expression.

"I'm glad you guys came," Shea told them. "It will help to have you there."

"You didn't give us a choice." Nik glared at Emma as he said this.

She smiled sweetly back at him.

"We will discuss all of this later," Luukas told her. "Right now, let's concentrate on what needs to be done. But know this, Shea"—he paused until he had her full attention—"I am only here to protect my very stubborn witch, and to help send these fucking things back to where they belong."

He didn't need to say he wasn't there for her, or for Jesse. The implications were more than clear. "I understand," she said. "And I appreciate it anyway."

The witches got out of the SUV, and gave Shea encouraging smiles and words. Keira gave her a quick hug. "We'll see you in a minute."

Shea hugged her back. "Be safe." With a quick nod at the guys, she jogged around the vehicle and entered the trees.

It didn't take her long to find the possessed vampires. As she crouched behind the underbrush watching them, she let the call of Jesse's blood calm her. It was much stronger here, even though his thoughts were still blocking her.

He was still alive, and that was all she could ask for.

Keeping one eye on the demons, she let her instincts take over. Her mate was in trouble, and nothing would keep her from him. Especially not a few half-rotten demons. Her tongue ran over her fangs, long and sharp and ready to rip apart any who dared try to keep her from Jesse.

When she had ascertained there were only three

guards, she stepped out from the shelter of the underbrush. Not bothering to conceal her footsteps, she ran past them, smiling to herself as the alarm was raised.

And the chase was on.

She glanced back once to make sure all three were following her. After she confirmed that none had stayed behind to catch her friends, Shea dug in and kicked it into high speed. Dodging trees and leaping over fallen branches, she cut a direct path to her male, following the call of his blood, knowing the witches would follow her with the guys' help as they followed her scent.

Soon she smelled the strong scent of burning wood and knew she was getting close. Baring her fangs on a hiss, she jumped a fallen tree and kept going. Something touched the back of her neck, and she was glad she'd braided her hair and tucked it up before they'd left her apartment. A second later she felt a rush of warm air on her skin and smelled acrid breath. Her entire body shuttered in disgust, and Shea pumped her arms harder and dug in her toes, pushing herself as hard as she could go.

She led them in a circle around the spot where she knew Jesse to be, giving the witches time to get in place without being sensed. Cruthú called from high above her, and she sounded happy and worried at the same time. Shea didn't spare her a glance, concentrating on outrunning the vampires who used to be her friends and a part of Luukas's colony, but were now controlled by the demons inside of them.

Hopefully, there was enough of them left in there to be saved.

When she thought enough time had passed, Shea cut

sharply to the left and headed straight toward Jesse. She leaped a small creek, and nearly stumbled as she landed on the other side when Jesse's voice suddenly appeared in her head.

Shea, get the FUCK out of here.

CHAPTER 31

Jesse quickly shut down his rising emotions. He'd felt her shortly after Steven had told him she would be coming, and he bit back a curse. Taking a deep breath, he remained calm, knowing the slightest change in his pulse would alert them. They possessed vampire bodies for a reason.

Though he kept his emotions at bay, his mind raced. He needed to warn her. Or better yet, keep her away entirely. But there was only way to do it: he would have to lower his shields and speak directly to her thoughts. And once one defense was down, others would soon follow if he wasn't very careful.

Ever since he'd left the hotel room, he'd refused to let her into his head, knowing it would distract him from what he had to do. He couldn't be worried about her, or listening to her try to argue her way out of what she'd done. But he also didn't want her in danger.

So, he waited. Waited until the demons were speaking

amongst themselves. As soon as it was as safe as it was going to get, he lowered his shields and told her to get away, then raised them again before she could respond. He had a feeling it would do no good. She was stubborn, and her vampire instincts would tell her to protect him. But he had to try.

As he sensed her coming closer and closer, he pushed down his fear for her. Damn hardheaded female. She was going to get herself killed. He could handle this on his own.

Cruthú reappeared, circling the clearing, her feathers nearly invisible against the dark sky. She called to Jesse, swooping happily in and out of the trees.

His hands shook, the force of emotion he buried within coming through physically, and he clasped them behind his back so they wouldn't give him away.

His ears perked up when he heard footsteps crashing through the underbrush straight ahead. The others heard it a few seconds later, and all heads turned to their left.

Shea appeared, running so fast human eyes wouldn't be able to track her. Three rotting vampire bodies chased her. She ran straight for Jesse, not sparing so much as a glance at the others standing there.

With a wave of his hand, Jesse sent the three chasing her flying through the air to land at Steven's feet. Shea came to a stop in front of him, just outside of the circle. She was barely even breathing hard. Tucking away a few stray hairs, she smiled at him, flashing her fangs. When he didn't return the greeting, it fell from her face as she speared him with green eyes aglow with hunger and the need to fight. "I didn't call Aiden. I didn't ask him to come and get me. I want you to know that right off. Just in case this all goes awry."

He found it quite amusing that she had no regard whatsoever for the immediate danger she was in, mostly because of the looks on the others' faces, though he appreciated Mammot's shocked expression the most. Turning his attention back to the stunning vision of his vampire in full hunting mode, he only said, "I told you to stay the fuck away." But his tone lacked the bite he was hoping for.

The corners of her mouth turned up just slightly. "But then how would I save you?"

Mammot suddenly appeared behind her. One arm shot out, placing a knife at her throat. He didn't grab her. There was no need. Before she could move, the blade was partially embedded in her throat. Blood tricked down her pale skin to soak her shirt. If she tried to get away in any direction, it would slice through her windpipe and she would be out of commission until she healed herself.

Alarm flashed in her green eyes and her lips peeled back into a snarl. She was about to try it anyway. He could sense her movements before she made them.

"Enough!" Jesse roared.

Shea stilled, though a deep growl rumbled within her. Despite the danger they were in, his body reacted to the sound, becoming uncomfortably hard. He shook his head, clearing his thoughts.

"Your timing is perfect, vampire," Mammot murmured in her ear. "I was just trying to convince this one that it would be in his best interest to do the spell as planned. Your being here will certainly improve his attitude."

Shea's eyes locked onto his. He wanted to open his

mind to her, to reassure her, but it was too dangerous. He couldn't be distracted. Movement to the left caught his attention.

The demons were shifting about restlessly and talking amongst themselves. A number of anxious sounds rose in the air.

"She brought others," one of them said.

Eyes skittering about, Mammot asked, "Where?"

The demons shuffled around, lining up shoulder to shoulder until they formed a protective circle around Mammot, Jesse, and the spell circle. "I don't fucking know," it said. "But I smell them."

When Jesse looked back at Shea, she was smiling. Her green eyes were aglow and her fangs were fully extended.

He gave her a small shake of his head, trying to warn her, but she paid him no heed. Wrapping her small hands around the arm that held the knife to her throat, she braced her booted feet and threw her hips back, sending the demon off balance even as she screamed in pain. She stepped back with one foot, bent forward and pulled him with her, throwing him over her hip. Then she stomped on his wrist with her booted foot until he dropped the knife.

At the same time, five females and five males suddenly became visible outside the circle of demons.

Jesse broke the circle and yanked Shea away from the demon. He pushed her behind him just in time.

Mammot bounded to his feet. Jesse faced off against him, teeth bared much like his vampire would do.

"I will kill that little whore," Mammot told him.

Jesse kept one hand behind him, wrapped around

Shea's wrist. He fought to remain calm and keep his shields up. "As I told you before…" Magic brewed within him, mixing with the sorcery of the djinn. "Shea is not to be harmed. Allow her and the others to leave, and we can continue."

As they stared each other down, Shea spoke up from behind him. "I'm sorry, Jesse. I can't let you do this. I can't let you free them."

He had to. He had no choice. "You cannot stop me, Shea."

CHAPTER 32

Shea's heart reached out for him, but the male she knew was gone. Replaced by the calculating monster who had tortured her maker and his mate without remorse. All she felt from him was...nothing. No emotion. No regrets. Nothing.

Except cold resolve.

"Jesse—"

"If you try to stop me, I will do whatever I have to do. Do you understand?"

Shea felt tears threatening, but she would do what was right, even if he hated her for it. "Then so will I."

He partially turned, enough to look at her and still keep one eye on Mammot. His eyes glowed a bright yellow. "Don't do this, Shea. Do not fight me on this."

The tears that threatened overflowed and slid down her cheeks, but her resolve was as firm as his. "We will find another way to deal with your father."

"There *is* no other way," he told her through clenched teeth.

Mammot hocked up a wad of phlegm and spit it at her feet. "Glad you're seeing our way of it, warlock. Get your whore the fuck out of here, and let's get this party started, shall we?"

Shea rolled her eyes, but apparently Jesse had had enough. With the slightest movement of his arm, he sent the entire group of demons flying past the ring of vampires to land in a pile in the dirt.

Mammot sprung up from the center, his grotesque face twisted in rage. But he had no time to do anything else before he was met with another threat.

Aiden stood before him…no, not Aiden. Waano. "You really should learn to mind your manners, Mammot."

Mammot didn't back down, and Shea felt a shot of fear for her friend at the same time she heard Grace's intake of breath. But she needn't have worried.

Aiden's hand shot out and wrapped around the other demon's neck, lifting him off the ground with barely any effort at all. "I don't like them," he growled into Mammot's face, indicating Luukas and his vampires with a toss of his head, in position to protect their friend's body. "But I fucking hate you more."

The others had untangled themselves by now, and were rallying behind their leader. Hisses rent the air as they prepared to go after Aiden.

"Emma," Keira said quietly.

"I'm trying," she answered.

Shea turned back to Jesse, letting the witches handle it

while she tried to talk to him. "Please, Jesse. It doesn't have to be like this."

"And how will it be, Shea?"

She swallowed hard, unsure of how to deal with this stranger before her. "We can send them back where they belong, and we'll figure out another way to stop your father."

He looked around, making a point to bring the vampires to her attention, who were keeping tabs on the demons when they weren't practically spitting their hatred at him. "And then what shall we do, love? Go back to your place and live happily ever after? Have Saturday movie nights with all our close friends? They will never accept me, Shea. I don't belong there. And you will never choose me over them."

"I don't have to! They *will* accept you as mine, Jesse. But you have to give them a chance and a reason to do so."

He threw his head back and laughed. It wasn't the same sound that had once warmed her all the way to her toes. No, this laugh was cold—mocking.

Shea looked around at the others, not knowing what else to say to convince him. She saw that Emma finally managed to get the vampires who were possessed under control, and the witches were making their way toward her and Jesse. They entered the circle with a few wary looks at him, as Luukas and the others came up behind him. All except Aiden, who was frozen with the other demons.

When Shea gave Emma a questioning look, she shrugged. "We can't trust him. He's one of them right now."

Shea turned back to Jesse. "Please," she begged him one last time.

For a moment, she saw him, the male who protected and cared about her. But he was gone as quickly as he'd appeared.

"I've been a complete fool. I won't make that mistake again," he told her, right before Luukas and Nikulas grabbed him from behind. As he struggled, Keira stepped in front of him, chanting a spell to weaken his power as they pulled him from within the circle. It wouldn't stop him completely. He was too powerful. But it would hopefully give them enough time to lock him out of the circle until they could evict the demons.

"Shea!" Luukas shouted.

She had to make a choice. With tears streaming down her face and her heart ripping in two, Shea removed the knife she had strapped onto her thigh back at her apartment. It wasn't just any knife, but one that was blessed with the holy blood of her entire family. She took it to her wrist, speaking words she hadn't spoken since the death of her sister. Words she'd known since before she could talk.

They felt foreign on her tongue.

She repeated the invocation for each wrist. Blood dripped onto the earth.

As soon as she was done, Keira rushed back to her, calling the others inside as she closed the circle again and spoke the words to seal it. Grace handed a container to Ryan, and they reinforced it with salt. The witches and Shea were now protected inside.

Shea cried out as Luukas and Nik were thrown aside

by nothing but the force of Jesse's rage, and she lost her place for a moment. When they both got up and came running back for more, fangs bared, she breathed a sigh of relief. She didn't fear for Jesse. She could feel his power, and it was like nothing she'd ever seen or felt before.

Christian and Dante jumped in to help them, a spine-tingling roar coming from the latter.

"Keep going!" Keira told her.

But Emma, seeing Nik get a backhand to the jaw by Jesse that looked as though it was hard enough to separate his head from his neck, faltered in her magic. It was only for a second, but it was all the demons needed.

They rushed the vampires, and in the commotion, Jesse walked calmly up to the outside of the circle to stand in front of Shea. She stared at him, trying so hard to get through to him how sorry she was as she continued the verse that would send the demons to hell.

Jesse stood absolutely still as complete chaos broke out behind him. Luukas, Nik, Christian, and Dante were too busy fighting off the demons to try to stop him now. Shea could only hope the circle would hold.

Bright yellow eyes turned to Keira, and she immediately cried out in pain, her hands clapping down on either side of her head.

Luukas, sensing his mate's distress, flung two demons away and rushed Jesse, fury igniting his power and making him a terrifying sight to behold. But without looking away from Keira, Jesse stopped Luukas's charge and sent him back into the melee with only a wave of his hand.

Shea looked to Laney. The witch had her eyes on

Dante, and by the sweat beading down her face, she was concentrating hard.

But it wasn't enough. With a spoken command, Jesse broke the seal and stepped into the circle.

A shout of alarm was heard, and Nikulas kicked off a demon and came running toward Emma. The others, seeing the witches were no longer protected, let out roars of fear and rage, and made their way to their mates. All except Aiden, who wasn't fighting on either side, but watching it all with a blank face.

"Grace! Get in here!" Emma grabbed her arm and put her in the center of them. Now that the circle was broken and their plan was going to hell, quite literally, the witches did what they could to help their males. "Shea!" Grace shouted. "Forget it! Emma lost it. We can't hold them!"

"We can hold them," Ryan shouted.

"Not everyone has spirits protecting them, Ryan!" one of the witches yelled.

"You do now," she answered.

But Shea couldn't take her eyes from Jesse. They stood in the middle of all the craziness, like the eye of the storm, staring at each other until Jesse finally said, "I'm sorry, Shea. But this is the only way. I must do this."

Her arms fell to the sides, her holy blood running into the ground at her feet. "I will never forgive you if you go through with this. I don't want to live in a world ruled by the children of hell."

His eyes darkened in pain, and a spark of hope lit her from within, but he only nodded. He would accept her hatred to do what he felt he needed to do. With another wave of his arm, he sent the others from the circle, leaving only him and Shea. In the next second, he held out his hand, and a large backpack came flying from the woods where the demons had hidden it. It busted through any bodies in its way and landed in his palm. As soon as he had it, he began to close the circle again.

She heard the demon leader tell him to hurry, and Shea knew immediately what it was: the demon blood. The *real* blood.

Furious that he would give up on them so easily, Shea bared her fangs and lunged at him, knife raised above her head. She wasn't thinking, just reacting. After all they had been through to be together, after all *she* had been through to accept him as hers, the fact that he was willing to throw it all away, throw her very life away, was more than she could take.

Jesse sidestepped the knife, grabbing her arm to keep her from falling from the circle. But she hadn't quite gotten her footing, and someone else yanked her off balance by the back of her shirt. She fell from the circle just as the seal went up, and was instantly pulled up from the ground and wrapped up in a chokehold. Shea screamed, her body jerking from the shocks of pain shooting through her, the knife falling from her hand.

Mammot yelled next to her ear, "Do it, warlock. Or I will tear her fucking head off."

Shea could do nothing to stop him, her body a prisoner of the pain ripping through her.

A wave of fury struck her from the front, pushing her into her attacker. The demon tightened its hold on her, and she felt fangs sink into the side of her neck.

Shea screamed again.

"Release her!" Jesse's roar was heard above everything else. With a growled command, he left the circle and was immediately attacked by demons from either side and thrown back in. He was on his feet in a flash, throwing bodies in every direction without touching them.

Gritting her teeth against the pain, Shea began to chant, igniting the holy flame in her blood. The demon holding her tore his fangs from her throat, screaming in pain as her blood burned through him. And suddenly, she was free.

Jesse caught her as she fell, lifting her up into his strong arms. "Are you all right? Shea!" He fell to his knees, still holding her, and cradled her against his chest. "Please tell me you're all right."

She tried to answer him, but could only nod. He lifted his head, and she reached up, touching his face, and tried again to speak. This time she managed to get the words out. "Please, don't do this." Her bloody fingers left red streaks down his cheek.

The muscles in his jaw jumped. He looked around, taking in the fighting around him, then back down to her.

He was faltering. She could feel it. "Jesse, please. Don't do this. Let us send them back, and I swear to you we will help you deal with your father. Jesse"—she touched his face again—"you can still change things."

"And if I do, Shea, what will that accomplish?"

"You will have me," she told him simply. She wanted to tell him more. Wanted to tell him that in spite of it all, she cared about him. That she knew now she'd fallen for him during those weeks he'd protected her in his room, right after he'd saved her from becoming one of the monsters around them. She wanted to tell him so much. But they had no time.

I feel the same about you.

His voice came to her, and Shea couldn't hold back a sob. He hugged her to him again, and she wrapped her arms around him as he pressed a kiss to her wounded throat.

I'll fucking kill him.

She pulled away. "Jesse?" She didn't need to say anymore. He knew what she was asking him.

CHAPTER 33

He had to make a choice. Jesse searched Shea's face. She was barely hanging on to consciousness. With a deep inhale, he made a decision, and felt the tension leaving his body. It was the only choice he'd ever had, really. "Only for you, Shea."

"Thank you," she whispered, and her eyes rolled back in her head, her body going limp in his arms.

Rage lit his blood. Carefully laying her down on the ground, Jesse rose and surveyed the chaos around him. Bodies lay strewn about the clearing, mostly demons, and one of the vampires. Cruthú dove in and out, plucking at demon heads and faces. Waano had finally joined in the fight, and was currently in a battle of wills with Mammot. Luukas, despite his weakened appearance, was still going strong, ripping apart anything that came anywhere near his witch, as was Nikulas. The rest was a confusing swarm of flying fists and fangs.

He looked around and caught Keira's eye as she sent a

demon flying right before he jumped on Luukas's back, mentally telling her what to do. Her hazel eyes widened, and she quickly nodded. Calling to the others, they congregated together and joined hands within the circle.

The witches began to chant the words to the spell, led by Ryan. He watched as the scary one's mate, Laney, caught each demon in turn with her dark eyes. The air shimmered around her as one by one, they screamed in fury and they fell to their knees. Jesse watched as the entities were thrust from the host bodies to hover in the air above them.

Other spirits appeared, corralling the demons and herding them into the circle. Jesse added his own influence, helping Ryan control her spirits. He would need to speak with her when all of this was over. It was time she knew her true history.

Jesse didn't bother closing the circle this time. Holding out his wrists, he opened his veins, directing the blood to flow over Shea's. It would work, he was certain, for it was Shea's blood that mixed with his own in his veins. He repeated the words he had heard her say, the same words the witches chanted behind him. The wind whipped around them, and the ground began to boil at his feet, their mixed blood bubbling as steam rose from the wet dirt. A small chasm opened in the middle of the circle, and his eyes met with Ryan's. The air vibrated with sorcery, voices rose in strength, and the terrifying sound of demons screaming in rage withered away and died as their souls were shoved into the boiling ground, and back to hell, where they belonged.

The chasm closed. The dirt tumbling in on itself,

taking the bag of demon blood with it. The wind calmed, and the rain cleared the air.

When it was over, Jesse picked Shea up from the ground and walked away, intending to take her back to his mountain until she woke up. Cruthú landed on his shoulder, chattering happily. She was obviously pleased that he had made the right choice and decided to keep her pretty human pet.

"WARLOCK!"

Looking down at the beautiful female in his arms, he sighed, stopped, and turned around.

Luukas stood at the front of his group, one arm holding his witch tightly to his side. Blood trickled down the side of his face and from his fangs. There was a challenge in his eyes, and Jesse briefly closed his eyes. He didn't want to deal with this right now. "Shea is mine," he told the vampire. "She comes with me."

"We could use your help," Keira said.

They stood there, watching him, waiting to see what he would do. He looked down at his Shea, and his concern must have shown on his face.

"She will be fine," Luukas said. "She just needs to rest."

Jesse adjusted his hold on her. It would make her happy if he stayed and helped. And maybe, just maybe, it would begin to close another gap. He raised his chin. "What do you need?"

CHAPTER 34

Shea came awake, slowly at first, like she was drifting up through a cloud, and then all at once. Her eyes snapped open and she sat up in a panic. Wings flapped in her face, and she had to apologize to Cruthú for startling her. The silly bird must have been sleeping beside her.

She was in Jesse's bed, and wearing one of his T-shirts…and nothing else. Swinging her legs off the side, she stood too fast. Her head swam and she immediately sat down again. "Jesse?" She was impatient to find out what had happened, and what she was doing here. The last she had seen, it had been complete mayhem. She tried to stand again as Cruthú squawked her disapproval.

"Whoa, whoa, whoa. What are you doing? You need to sit, Shea." Jesse appeared in the doorway, wearing only a loose pair of lounge pants with a towel thrown over his shoulder. His hair was wet. He must have been bathing.

Shea looked him over, allowing herself the pleasure of

seeing him unharmed before it was ruined by the knowledge of what happened.

He dropped the towel over the back of a chair and came over to her, hooking a finger under her chin and lifting her face. His eyes darkened with concern. "You don't look good."

"I feel fine," she lied. "What happened, Jesse?" She braced herself for the answer. It never came.

"You need to feed," he said. "Everything is okay, Shea."

"Luukas and Nik and—"

"They are all still alive."

"Keira? Emma?"

"All fine. You'll be seeing them tonight if you feel up to it."

She nodded. She wanted to ask if he had carried through with his plan. She wanted to ask if Aiden had survived. But she was afraid she already knew the answers to those questions, and found she wasn't ready to speak of it aloud. "Did you do this?" With a wave of her hand, she indicated her clean, barely-dressed self.

He gave her a strange look. "Yes."

"Thank you," she told him.

"You're welcome." He paused. "You need to feed," he repeated.

But she shook her head. "I'm fine." She said it without really thinking about it. Right now, she was more concerned with her friends than with herself.

She was afraid to ask what else had happened. Afraid to know if Jesse had finished what he'd set out to do.

Shea suddenly noticed that he had fallen silent. She

looked up, and found him standing with his arms crossed over his chest. He wouldn't look at her.

"What?"

He finally looked at her then, and she almost wished he hadn't. "Are you ever going to admit that I am yours, Shea? And you are mine?"

"What?" She tried to think of what she'd said. "Jesse, I—"

"Still haven't accepted me. No matter what the gods have decreed. Yes, I see that."

She shook her head. "No, no. That's not it. Not it at all."

He turned away, and sat down at the small table. Leaning back, one hand played with her hair bands lying on the tabletop while the other rested on his strong thigh. "You must choose, Shea."

Forcing her eyes away from his body, she frowned. "What do you mean?"

He looked at her then, and her body immediately responded to the heat in his gaze. "I mean, after all that has happened, do you still want to be with me?"

"Can't you hear that for yourself?" She didn't understand why he was asking. The guy could read her thoughts. "Feel free to barge on in there."

"I want to hear you say it. Out loud."

Though he put on a tough persona, Shea saw it now, the vulnerability that lay beneath the power and the icy exterior. It wasn't that he didn't feel anything; it was that he wouldn't allow himself to. Behind the set jaw and the twisted smile, he needed reassurance.

But she wanted to do more than reassure him. She

wanted to bring out the parts of him he kept hidden. Wanted him raw and exposed and vulnerable. Perhaps it was the hunter in her. Perhaps it was her own twisted needs and desires. But she never again wanted to encounter the iciness he had shown her earlier.

Pushing everything else to the side, she focused on the male in front of her. *Her* male. Shea rose from the bed, and walked over to stand in front of him, enjoying the way he couldn't seem to keep his eyes from roaming over her from head to toe and back again. His pulse kicked up, just barely, and not enough that anyone else would notice.

But she did.

Grabbing the hem of his T-shirt, which fell to mid-thigh on her, she lifted it up and off and tossed it to the side.

"Shea, this isn't what I—"

His words cut off when she came closer and knelt between his legs. She ran her hands up his lean thighs, enjoying the way the muscles went rigid beneath her touch.

Her words didn't seem to do the job of convincing him how she felt, so she would have to show him.

He gripped the arms of the chair, and she ran her hands over the hard muscles in his arms. She loved the feel of him, something she'd imagined so many times while he'd kept her here. This time, she was determined to enjoy the fact that she could touch him. And she was going to touch him everywhere.

Cupping his face in her hands, she felt the roughness of stubble. She let it scrape her palms as she slowly lowered her hands down his throat to the soft hair in the middle of his chest. She followed it down over hard muscle, the ridges of his ribs and stomach.

By the time she reached the waistband of his pants, the air was heavy with lust and emotion. Shea lifted her upper lip off her fangs, fighting the need to pierce his skin. Jesse's moan turned to a sharp intake of breath when she gripped the material of his pants and tore them in two, exposing his cock to her hungry gaze. He was hard and long and thick, and Shea leaned in, inhaling his masculine scent before tasting him with her tongue.

"Ah!" His hips jerked, thrusting toward her mouth.

But she pulled back, and held him still with a hand at the top of each thigh. When he stilled, she again ran her tongue over the tip, before taking him into her mouth and grazing him with her fangs.

His head fell back, but he lifted it again almost immediately to watch her. "I'm going to come if you do that again, vampire."

He was breathing hard, and Shea enjoyed the sight of his stomach muscles tensing. But she wasn't going to give him his pleasure so soon. No. She wanted more.

She leaned away, and he reached out to touch her breasts. Shea let him, loving the feel of his rough palms against her tender skin. Her nipples stiffened and he teased them harder still as they stared at each other.

Let me in, Jesse.

Whether he heard her or not, she didn't know. Taking him in her mouth again, she teased him with her tongue, licking his length and even his balls. Drops appeared at the tip, and she tasted his essence, her moan of pleasure mingling with his.

But she wanted more.

Backing off again, she kissed his inner thigh, licking the pulse there, before—with a hiss of need and warning—she reared back and struck. Jesse cried out in pain and pleasure as she sank her fangs into his inner thigh. His legs fell open wider, and his dark, wicked blood flowed into her mouth. Shea drank eagerly.

"Ah, gods! Yes, love. Drink." His hands tangled in her long hair, holding her head to his thigh. When she removed her fangs, he pulled her up to kiss her.

Shea moaned when his lips took hers. The kiss was not gentle, but a claiming, much as she had just done to him.

Breaking it off, she pushed him back against the chair and struck his throat. As his blood flowed into her, her body lit up with a fire only he could handle. His hands caressed her back, then moved down to massage her ass. He tried to pull her up into his lap, but Shea released him from her bite and again went to her knees.

"Shea, I want to be inside of you." His voice was rough with longing and his eyes burned with need, and she knew the fire was inside him, too.

But she shook her head and took him into her mouth. Only this time, she was done teasing. Running her tongue around the wide head, she sucked him in as far as she could, over and over, until he was calling her name and his hips moved with her rhythm as his hands again wrapped themselves in her hair.

Shea lifted her head and licked his length. He was hard as a rock, the blood pulsing though the veins. A low growl started deep in her core, rumbling to the surface as she flashed her fangs at him. She looked up to find him watching her with eyes gone bright as the sun.

"Yes," he gritted out.

She hissed her pleasure, and took him in her hand, holding him steady.

"Do it, Shea."

Fast as a snake, she took him in her mouth and sank her fangs deep into his engorged shaft. Jesse cried out, pulsing hard in her hand as he came. She drank it all, and when he finished, she licked him clean and lifted her head.

He stared down at her with his soul in his eyes. Raw. Exposed. Vulnerable.

Shea let her own emotions show. "I choose you," she told him. "I choose you, Jesse. Just as you are."

Reaching down, he tilted her face to his and kissed her like a man starved. She returned the kiss, letting everything he felt wash over her. Her fang pierced her bottom lip, and he groaned when he tasted it. She let him drink, strengthening the bond between them.

Jesse was the one to break off the kiss this time. Holding her face in his hands, he just looked at her for a long, long time. "I choose you, too."

And then he kissed her again, and took her down to the floor.

CHAPTER 35

"So, where are we going?" Shea asked for the fifth time. Jesse smiled, enjoying her light mood. "You'll see." He had an easy kind of peace inside of him. Something he hadn't felt in...well, never. Not since he could remember.

They had spent the entire day and night in his bed—enjoying each other and talking about little things. They took Cruthú out to fly when the sun went down, then came back inside, neither of them anxious to face the real world again.

But it was time for her to know. Much as he would like to, he couldn't keep her all to himself forever.

Her cat eyes flicked over to him when they entered the city, but she said nothing, just stroked the raven's feathers and waited with a patience she only now decided to display.

However, the quiet was short-lived when he pulled into her apartment building and parked the SUV.

"Jesse, what are we doing here?" She kept her voice low, as though she were afraid the others would hear her.

He turned to her, taking her hand in his. "We can't hide in my mountain forever, love."

She searched his face, tightening her hold on his hand. "Are you sure?"

He nodded.

"Okay. But I want you to know, I am with you. No matter what. I choose you."

Her words filled him with warmth, and he had the overwhelming urge to drag her across the seat and take her right there in the parking garage. "Thank you, Shea."

She touched his face with her free hand, and he turned his head and kissed her fingers. "Come on." He opened his car door. "And bring that spoiled bird."

Cruthú clicked her beak at him.

Shea was nervous on the ride up in the elevator, though she tried to hide it. He took the raven from her arm and put the bird on his shoulder, then took her hand. "It will be okay, Shea."

"Just please don't kill Luukas," she said. "Or any of them, really."

He bit back his smile. "I promise. I won't kill anyone today."

Though he wouldn't exactly call them friends, he and the other vampires had come to an understanding in the clearing. While Grace used her powers to heal those who were hurt, and Luukas fed those vampires who weren't too far gone to rejuvenate from his blood, Jesse had helped the others clean up the bodies who were beyond saving. He would never be completely forgiven for what he'd done to Luukas and Keira, but they had formed a sort of uncomfortable tolerance for each other's presence that day.

For Shea.

They arrived at Luukas's floor, and Shea walked slowly down the hall to his door. She took a moment to get herself together, and when she was ready, Jesse knocked on the door.

Keira opened it, smiling brightly at Shea. "You're here!" She grabbed her hand. "Come on in." Glancing up at Jesse, she said, "You, too."

Shea looked over her shoulder, and he could feel her questions poking around in his head, but he shut her out, not wanting to ruin the fun.

Everyone was there, for Jesse had called while Shea was sleeping and told them they were coming. The witches hugged her and the males welcomed her from a safer distance. Jesse received a few uneasy looks, and even a couple of nods hello, which he returned.

One witch in particular—Ryan—stared at him a bit longer than the others. He played with the idea of telling her why she felt the connection to him that caused her to look at him with such confusion, but decided against it.

I think that will wait for another time.

He smiled at her, and after a few seconds, she smiled back. Jesse had to hold back a laugh when Christian noticed the exchange and bared his fangs at Jesse while pulling his mate into his arms.

Shea suddenly stopped talking and looked around. "Wait, where's Grace? Where's *Aiden?*" Her features were filled with alarm as the rest of the room went quiet.

* * *

Shea felt like the floor had just dropped out from beneath her feet. "Where is Aiden?" she repeated. "And Grace?"

Luukas came out from the office when he saw they had arrived. Shea swung toward him, barely taking in his much-improved appearance. "Luukas? Where is Aiden?"

Everyone looked at each other, anywhere but at Shea.

Her heart stopped as horror filled her.

Oh my gods, the demon took him. He's gone.

There was no other explanation for the strange way everyone was acting. He hadn't survived when Jesse fulfilled his deal with the demons.

She felt a scream welling up, when the front door suddenly swung open, slamming into the opposite wall, and Aiden came strolling in.

Shea stared at him in shock.

"All right, Shea?" he asked her. "You look like you've seen a ghost." He waved a finger at Jesse. "Pat her on the back or something, mate. I think she's choking on something."

"You're here," Shea whispered in awe.

Aiden frowned. Reaching over his head, he pulled Mojo from his hood. "Of course, I'm here. Where else would I be?"

Grace came in and closed the door behind her. Her face was flushed and she was smoothing down her hair. Coming to stand beside Aiden, they exchanged a heated look between them. Grace cleared her throat and looked around. "What's up? Why's everyone so quiet?"

Because she couldn't hug Aiden, Shea hugged Grace instead. "I got here and you guys weren't here. I thought... I thought...when the demon...." She couldn't even say it out loud.

Grace hugged her back, saying over her shoulder to Jesse, "Didn't you tell her? You asshole."

"Tell me what?" Shea sniffed and let go of Grace. The others were all staring at Jesse.

"You didn't tell her?" Nikulas asked from the couch where he was lounging with Emma. "What the hell, man?"

It was Dante who finally approached her. "I think what these morons are trying to say is that Aiden is fine. Waano is gone. Back to hell with the rest of the them."

Shea couldn't believe what she was hearing. "Tell me that again?"

Dante sighed with impatience, but did as she asked. "The demons are gone. The warlock sent them back to hell. With your blood and his."

Dante wouldn't lie to her. Out of all of them, he was the one she trusted most to tell her the truth. Overcome with emotion, all she could do was turn and stare at the male beside her.

He cocked an eyebrow. "I'll expect a full apology when we get home. But first, you promised me that if I sent them back to hell, you would help me remove my father from the throne. We're here because the others have offered to help."

Shea stared at the male she had fought so hard to accept, feeling a bit overwhelmed.

And when he stared back, he didn't hold back his feelings for her. "I don't give a fuck what other people think, love. Except you. Haven't you figured that out by now?"

Throwing herself in his arms, Shea whispered. "I think I owe you that apology."

"I would be more than happy to accept it, in your apartment when we're finished here."

She leaned back and touched his beloved face while the others sighed and wandered off to amuse themselves for a while. "I think I need to apologize right now."

He smiled, and Shea had never seen anything more beautiful. "Your choice, love."

"I choose you," she told him, her voice thick with tears. "I always choose you."

THANK you SO much for reading Jesse and Shea's story! I really hoped you enjoyed it! If you'd like to read more of the vampires from Deathless Night, Sign up for L.E. Wilson's Newsletter to read an EXCLUSIVE bonus scene!

And if you're ready to back into the world of Deathless Night, CLICK HERE to read Night of the Vampire, book 1 of the Deathless Night-Into the Dark series where you'll meet Killian Rice, a vampire who runs (and performs!) in a male strip club in New Orleans. And Lizzy, a witch running from her past in New York City. As soon as he tastes her, Killian knows she is his. But taking her as his mate will be the end of his coven's uneasy truce with the Moss witches...

ABOUT THE AUTHOR

L.E. Wilson writes Paranormal Romance starring intense alpha males and the women who are fearless enough to tame them — for the most part anyway. ;) In her novels you'll find smoking hot scenes, a touch of suspense, some humor, a bit of gore, and multifaceted characters, all working together to combine her lifelong obsession with the paranormal and her love of romance.

Her writing career came about the usual way: on a dare from her loving husband. Little did she know just one casual suggestion would open a box of worms (or words as the case may be) that would forever change her life.

Coffee and music are a necessary part of her writing process, though sometimes you'll find her typing away at her favorite Starbucks. She walks two miles to get there, to make up for all of those coffees. On the weekends she likes to have date nights with her favorite guy.

On a Personal Note:
"I love to hear from my readers! Contact me anytime at le@lewilsonauthor.com."

Keep In Touch With L.E.
lewilsonauthor.com
le@lewilsonauthor.com

CPSIA information can be obtained
at www.ICGtesting.com
Printed in the USA
LVHW102218220622
721923LV00022B/441